ORDEAL THERAPY

R. JULIAN HAFNER

A catalogue record for this book is available from the National Library of Australia

Publisher:
ASPG (Australian Self Publishing Group)
P.O. Box 159, Calwell, ACT Australia 2905
Email: publishaspg@gmail.com
http://www.inspiringpublishers.com

National Library of Australia Cataloguing-in-Publication entry

Author: Hafner, R. Julian

Title: **Ordeal Therapy**/R. Julian Hafner.

ISBN (print):   978-1-922618-73-3
ISBN (eBook):   978-1-922618-74-0

She slid gracefully into an armchair, and I sat down in a matching one that faced hers at an angle. I never sat behind my desk when working with patients. Most of my therapy was face to face, although there was a comfortable examination couch against the wall opposite the desk. I used it for occasional physical examinations, and very rarely for therapy that was best done with the patient lying down.

She then handed me an envelope. Inside was a brief referral note from a general practitioner whose name I didn't recognise. 'Thank you for seeing Ms Julia Richmond who has been distressed by flashbacks suggesting child sexual abuse.' The heading stated that she was age thirty-two and single.

'Have you read it?' I asked casually. She nodded. A negative reply would have surprised me. Most of my patients read their referral letters, admitting it with little embarrassment. Referring doctors generally knew this, and were cautious about what they wrote. Rarely was one thoughtless enough to write an insensitive or inaccurate account of matters that were painful or embarrassing.

'It doesn't say much,' I added.

'I don't have a regular GP. I approached Dr Fry just to get a referral. He doesn't know anything about me, really. You were recommended by an acquaintance of mine.'

'May I ask who?'

'I'd rather not say …. at least, not now.'

'That's OK' I said, concealing my irritation. It was useful to know the source of a recommendation. It revealed something about the new patient, and it was handy to know which of my colleagues or patients trusted me enough to risk recommending me to their friends and acquaintances.

'I was wondering who had suggested me, because I don't have any kind of reputation in the area of CSA.'

'You're assuming I know what CSA means.'

'I'm sorry. Child sexual abuse.'

'At least that sounds less like a label,' said Ms Richmond.

'I don't want to label you. It's just a name for a problem you may or may not—'

Ms Richmond interrupted me angrily. 'I know bloody well it happened.'

Her face had flushed. It highlighted her beauty. A high forehead and strong, wide jaw-line softened by generous lips. Pale, almost flawless skin with a hint of translucence. Auburn hair loosely curled and cut fairly short. Apart form a touch of eyeliner, she wore no make-up.

'I think there are two issues here,' I said, struggling to keep my anxiety from showing and at the same time trying not to sound pompous, which tends to happen when I feel threatened. 'First, there is the question of the nature and extent of the sexual abuse that you believe you suffered. Then there's the question of whether I'm the best person to try and help you.'

Ms Richmond relaxed. 'My acquaintance was very positive about you. She said you were caring and sensitive, but firm. That you weren't a rigid Freudian or behaviourist, but used whatever was likely to work best. That you didn't just push drugs. I know we haven't got off to a very good start, but I'd really like to try and work with you.'

Then a warm, charming smile.

'OK. Let's start over. Maybe I should explain my fee structure. Then you'll know what you're up for if we do decide to go ahead.'

'Money's not a problem,' said Ms Richmond. 'I have private health cover that allows up to twenty-four psychotherapy sessions a year. If we need more, I can afford to pay. I'm a solicitor, a junior partner with Buckram and Mintner.'

I knew the firm, which had a good reputation, and referred me occasional clients for medico-legal reports. Ms Richmond had to be a very smart lawyer to have junior partner status at her age.

'What I suggest,' I said carefully, 'is that you tell me a little more about the flashbacks you've been having.'

'They started about three months ago. I remember that first one clearly. I was lying on the sofa in my living room trying to relax after a tough day in court. My speciality is family law, and I'd been involved in a particularly messy custody case that included allegations of child molestation. Completely out of the blue, an image of a huge black bear rearing up on its hind legs flashed into my mind. It was so vivid I reacted as if it was real, but it vanished before I went into a full-blown panic.'

'Go on.'

'Once I got over the shock, I put it down to stress and ... well, I'd been drinking a lot more than was good for me. So I assumed it was just a one-off thing, and I cut back on the booze a bit. Then it happened again about a week later, around the same time, between nine and ten in the evening. But this time I felt I was choking and that my chest was being crushed. I thought

I was going to have a heart attack.' Ms Richmond paused. She had described a classical panic attack, but I was beginning to wonder what these frightening experiences had to do with sexual abuse.

'As I was struggling to make sense of what had happened, I suddenly realised where the image of the bear must have come from. I remembered I stuck a big poster of a grizzly bear on the wall of my bedroom. I would have been eleven or twelve. It wasn't horses with me' – she smiled wanly – 'for some reason it was bears.'

Ms Richmond paused again, unexpectedly coming to the brink of tears.

'There's no hurry,' I said. 'We've still got half an hour.' I'd scheduled fifty minutes, the usual time for new cases.

'This is so difficult.'

I was moved by her distress. 'I know,' I said. 'I'm listening carefully to everything you tell me.' I hadn't written any notes because I wanted her to see that she had my full attention.

'When I remembered the bear poster I began to remember other things. Horrible, disgusting things. While they were happening, I'd stared at the poster. Looking back, I think I must have dissociated, gone elsewhere. The poster helped me, somehow, to do that.'

So far, Ms Richmond was making sense. It wasn't uncommon for children to cope with sexual abuse by dissociating. This created a kind of psychic numbness that took away some of the pain. And dissociation was linked with repression, a mechanism that allowed memories of the abuse to be buried deep in the unconscious mind. But I knew that complete repression of such memories was rare.

'If it's too painful to tell me exactly what you remember ...'

Another wan smile. 'Actually, I'm surprised we've got as far as we have. My natural father left when I was seven, and my mother married Paul about four years later. He was the one. It happened while my mother was away. She was in a private clinic for about three months. Depressed, suicidal, although I only found this out later. Soon after she came back, he left the marriage, which had lasted less than a year, anyway. As far as I know, my stepfather never sought joint custody or even access, either to me or my younger sister. Perhaps not seeing him made it easier for me to bury the whole hideous thing.'

Ms Richmond took a deep breath, looking directly at me. 'OK. Here it is. Christ, the bastard! He didn't waste any time. He came into my room one night. I hadn't fallen asleep. I thought he'd come to comfort me about my mother, she'd gone away "for a rest" the day before. He sat on the bed and told me that I might not enjoy what was going to happen now, but it was going to happen anyway. He said that if I ever told anyone, he'd find ways of making me suffer that I couldn't even dream of, and that he'd make it even worse for my little sister. And that no-one would believe me anyway.'

Almost paralysed by anguish and tension, Ms Richmond forced herself to keep talking. She described a brutal rape that included both vaginal and anal penetration. It had been so painful that she screamed uncontrollably until her stepfather put his hands round her neck and threatened to strangle her.

My reaction was the same as it always was when patients told me of sexual abuse. A mixture of impotent rage, sickening disgust and despair. Sometimes, when the abuse was prolonged or unusually sadistic, I was unable to hold back tears. I knew this was judged unprofessional, but my patients didn't seem to mind. Right now, I was dry-eyed.

'And was the same pattern repeated?'

'About three nights a week, mostly the same, although sometimes he'd force me to suck and rub his penis until he'd come.'

'Did you fear the same thing was happening to your sister?'

'Yes. But I couldn't ask her. Not without revealing what was happening to me. I was very protective of her, and of course my stepfather knew this. I couldn't protect her from him except by praying that he'd keep choosing me as a victim instead of her. And by not telling anyone, including my mother.'

There was a silent clock on the wall behind Ms Richmond. It was positioned so that I could glance at it with a slight shift of my eyes. When I needed to check the passage of time, I didn't want to be obvious about it. The clock told me it was nearly 50 minutes since Ms Richmond had entered my consulting room.

'We've covered a lot of ground today. You needed a lot of courage to tell me what happened, and that's made me feel I want to work with you. But we need to finish now. I suggest we meet again in two days. I've got a vacancy on Thursday, mid-morning. Is that OK?' Ms Richmond nodded, and I went on. 'I'll need to hear more about your background, understand more about you as a person. After that, we should be able to work out the beginnings of a therapy programme. I'll try and arrange times that fit around your work commitments, but that won't always be possible. Then it's a matter of your deciding what your priorities are.'

'That sounds OK to me.'

I escorted her out of my consulting room and through to the alcove occupied by Janet, the secretary-receptionist whom I shared with Michael, another psychiatrist.

'Janet, is that Thursday morning slot still free?' Checking the computer, Janet said it was. Ms Richmond was duly booked in.

It was now five minutes past four, but there was no sign of the patient scheduled for four o'clock.

'Mr Robard just cancelled,' said Janet. 'He has flu, apparently, so I don't think we can charge a cancellation fee.' I agreed, relieved that I had some time to think before my 4:45 pm patient arrived.

Back in the consulting room, I sank into my armchair. I felt uneasy and tried to work out why. Then it dawned on me: I'd just made an error so basic that a second year psychiatry trainee would have avoided it with ease. I should never have agreed to accept Ms Richmond as a patient. As I'd implied to her, I had no expertise in treating victims of child sexual abuse. Earlier in my career I'd successfully treated several cases, but for the past few years I'd always referred them on to therapists who specialised in the area, and who often got good results. All were women.

Personally, I didn't believe in choosing therapists on the basis of gender. But with child sexual abuse, it had become customary for therapists to be women. I had yielded to fashion and political correctness. Until now.

Ms Richmond had played me like a violin. First, she had created tension between us, got angry with me. Then she'd told me I was 'Doctor Wonderful' and that I just had to be her therapist. Then she'd melted the tension with her smile. But why me?

My thoughts were interrupted by a phone call from Janet, letting me know that my fifteen minutes before five appointment had arrived. Luckily, the session proved undemanding. If I seemed unusually distracted at times, my patient gave no sign of noticing. We finished just after a quarter past five. Janet worked from nine to five and either my partner Michael or I closed up if we left after she did. I very rarely worked after half past five, but Michael sometimes stayed later. I knew he'd already gone so locked up the rooms and left.

It was unusually mild for October. An Indian summer was bringing cloudless skies, and even in central London, the air was clear and still.

My rooms were on Harley Street, long the required London address for ambitious private medical practitioners like myself. Now, after six years of a ten-year lease, held jointly with Michael, my practice flourished. At forty-one, I was one of the most successful private psychiatrists in London, with several celebrities among my clients. I'd taken a huge risk going into full-time private practice straight from a senior registrar post in the National Health Service. This was still unusual in Britain, where medical practice was dominated by the NHS, for which nearly all psychiatrists worked. Most of them spent only a small proportion of their time in private practice.

The risk had paid off, professionally and financially. Five years ago I'd taken out a huge mortgage on a spacious flat on Baker Street, only about a mile from my rooms. I'd already paid off a third of it. Today, as usual, I was walking home.

My thoughts turned to my failed marriage. Celia had blamed me, saying I'd become remote, unavailable, preoccupied with work, and increasingly unpleasant to be around. I had blamed Celia, and my rage towards her had only recently begun to fade, over a year after the divorce became absolute. Instead had come guilt. At least, I kept telling myself, we had no children to screw up.

By now, I'd reached the end of Weymouth Street and entered the small public gardens that lead through into Paddington Street. They were directly on my way, but if they hadn't been,

I would have made a detour. I missed a garden of my own, and they took its place.

It was autumn and I never tired of the colours of the leaves. Today, set against the clear blue sky, their beauty moved me close to tears.

Once out of the gardens, it was only five minutes to my flat. I let myself into the wide, high-ceilinged entrance-hall and walked up four flights of stairs to the top floor. There was a lift, which I rarely used. Walking up the stairs was part of my exercise programme, along with my daily walks to and from my rooms. I used to jog and work out regularly, but had lapsed when my marriage broke up. Even so, I had a strong attachment to the idea of fitness. Five feet eleven tall and quite strongly built, I'd managed to stay slim at about seventy kilos. But I was puffing as usual when I opened the door to my flat.

I walked down the corridor and turned left into the large, comfortable sitting room looking out over Baker Street, now full of rush hour traffic. Triple glazing and massive early Victoria walls kept the noise to a faint background hum.

Pouring myself a gin and tonic, I sat down on a soft leather armchair and tried to relax. But I couldn't stop worrying about Ms Richmond. I reviewed what I knew about child sexual abuse and the return of repressed memories.

I was sure that Ms Richmond didn't suffer from false memory syndrome. She'd mentioned no previous therapy, which ruled out the possibility that her memories had been created by hypnosis or suggestion. All the evidence so far suggested she'd truly suffered horribly at the hands of her stepfather. But there were still some problems. First, it was very rare for memories of sexual abuse in preadolescence to be totally buried and then suddenly recalled well into adulthood. This rarity invited suspicion. Second, why had Ms Richmond come to me? As a solicitor specialising in family law, she must have known of several therapists who were recognised as experts in the field of child sexual abuse. Perhaps, I speculated, she knew them personally and wanted to avoid the embarrassment of approaching one of them with problems of her own. But this was London, not some country town. She could easily have found an expert therapist who existed outside her social and professional network.

Then there was a third reason I tried not to think about. On ethical grounds, I shouldn't have accepted Ms Richmond as a patient. I should have referred her on to a recognised specialist in the field. I knew if I mentioned it to Michael, with whom I regularly discussed clinical problems, he would urge me to do just that. But I refused to contemplate breaking my agreement with her, deciding to keep Michael ignorant of the problem.

After a second gin and tonic, I lifted myself from the sofa and went into the kitchen to microwave a frozen dinner. By the time I'd eaten this, helped down by a glass of sauvignon blanc, it was time to watch the ten o'clock news. Then I showered and went to bed.

I was carrying out a prefrontal leucotomy on Ms Richmond. She was on the couch in my consulting room, her limbs twitching from the effects of a seizure. I'd induced this with an electroconvulsive therapy machine. It served as an anaesthetic. Her head was shaved, ready for me to drill into her right temple. I turned the drill on. Ms Richmond opened her eyes. The sound of the drill became the ringing of the phone beside my bed. I woke up and put the receiver to my ear. 'George Milton here.' Silence. 'Hello. Who's there?'

'Dr Milton. It's me, Sarah. I'm so sorry to ring you in the middle of the night, but I'm really desperate and there's no one else.'

The clock radio on my bedside cabinet said 1:40 am.

'How can I help you?'

'You can stop me jumping in the fucking river.'

'Where are you ringing from?'

'A phone box. I left my mobile at home. I'm in Wandsworth. Near the river.'

'Tell me what's happened.'

'It's Sid. He went berserk and threw me out, said he'd kill me if I came back.'

'Had he been drinking?'

'We'd both had quite a few.'

'Did you take anything else?'

'Nothing, honest. Well we smoked a joint earlier. Just one.'

I felt a tightening and throbbing in my left temple which often developed into a headache. 'So what do you want me to do?' I asked, noting an edge to my voice.

'I want you to come and take me somewhere safe. I'm cold. I've only got a dress on. I'm frightened. I'm panicking, and my agoraphobia is coming on really badly. I'm closer to the river than to my flat. The river would solve all my problems.'

'It'll take me at least twenty minutes to reach you. What about Life Line?'

'It's just phone advice late at night. They tell you to go to the nearest emergency clinic. Last time I did that, I ended up in the local loonie bin. I'd rather jump in the river. Anyway, it's too far to walk to the nearest hospital and what cabbie would come to this part of town in the middle of the night?'

I realised there was no point in further debate. I was stuck. I had to go and rescue Sarah. She sounded a bit drunk and this made an impulsive suicide attempt more likely. If she did end up in the Thames, I didn't fancy her chances.

'All right, I'll come. Tell me exactly where you are.'

Sarah pin-pointed her location with surprising clarity.

'I should make it in about twenty minutes. Just hang on.'

I put the phone down. Now that a decision had been made, the throbbing in my temple lessened. Perhaps I wouldn't get a headache after all. I put on a track suit and pocketed my phone, wallet, and keys, stopping at the hall mirror to check my appearance. I smoothed down my dark brown hair, inspecting the face that stared back at me. It's regular, clear-cut features were still pleasing enough, in spite of the dark shadows under my eyes.

I took the lift down to the basement which had been cleverly converted into a garage with single parking spaces for each flat. A few minutes later I was well on the way to Hyde Park Corner, planning to go over Vauxhall Bridge. At this time of the morning, with little traffic about, it was the quickest route.

My mid-sized BMW was seven years old and didn't stand out. I considered this a virtue in Wandsworth at two o'clock in the morning. The area wasn't as dangerous as some other parts of southeast London, but there was still an element of risk from marauders.

I caught sight of a waving figure standing next to a telephone box. I did a u-turn and pulled up beside an agitated Sarah.

'Thank God you're here. I was worried you wouldn't come. It seemed ages. Did you get lost or something?'

'No' I replied. ' Your directions were spot on. It's barely twenty minutes since we spoke.'

Sarah looked up at me from her five foot three inches. Her thick eye make-up streaked her cheeks, making it obvious she'd been weeping heavily. The dishevelled state of her shoulder-length blonde hair emphasised her waif-like good looks. She started to weep again. 'I'm so grateful you came. I really was desperate. What I told you about the river was true.'

'I believe you. Now that I'm here, what do you want to do?'

Sarah hesitated. 'This might sound crazy, but I want you to take me home and calm Sid down.'

Sid's name triggered vivid memories of a previous meeting with him. Tall and broad-shouldered, he towered above Sarah. I was intimidated by his obvious physical strength and aggressive manner. The idea was to try couples therapy, and I cautiously explained what might be involved. 'There's nothing wrong with our bleeding marriage,' he said loudly. 'The problem is Sarah's agoraphobia. If you did your bleeding job and fixed that, every-thing would be fine.'

I didn't dare argue with him, even though I knew he was wrong. I changed tack and suggested the three of us work together at trying to improve Sarah's agoraphobia. This took the focus off the marriage and Sid relaxed a bit. He seemed at the point of agreeing when Sarah, with perfect timing, mentioned their sexual problems. Things rapidly got out of control, and Sid stormed out.

I didn't give up. I wrote Sid a polite note, asking him to come and see me on his own. Of course, I'd got Sarah's agreement, although she seemed a bit hesitant. When she handed Sid the envelope, he tore it to pieces, yelling that he knew more about agoraphobia than that 'half-witted quack.' At least, that's what Sarah told me.

With this guerrilla warfare in the background, I wasn't keen on meeting Sid again, especially in the early hours of the morning, uninvited, and at his flat. So I suggested to Sarah that it might be better if she spent the night at a hotel and phoned Sid in the morning. She could go home if it seemed safe. But even though I offered to pay for the hotel, this didn't appeal to her.

'I'm too upset and frightened to be on my own. I have to be with someone. Perhaps I could come and stay the night with you?'

I gently pointed out that professional ethics made this impossible, however honourable the motive.

'Well, that only leaves Sid. And it's not just me I'm worried about. He was in such a state when he threw me out, he could do anything. Smash the place up. Roam the streets. Beat someone up. He might even be in the lock-up.'

The thought of Sid spending the night in a police cell cheered me up a little. But the chances were he was still at the flat, and still very angry.

'If we do go back to the flat,' I said, 'we must have a plan.'

'That's easy,' countered Sarah. 'You knock on the door and when he answers tell him I'm in your car. Ask him if he'll have me back.'

I pointed out some flaws in her plan. At the top of my list was the likelihood of Sid knocking me to the ground. I suggested we telephone first.

'I suppose we could,' acknowledged Sarah. 'But what if he doesn't answer?'

'Let's just try,' I said firmly. 'We can use my mobile. You speak to him first.'

Sarah dialled the number.

'Sid, is that you? It's Sarah.'

To my relief, what followed sounded like a fairly rational conversation. Sid had obviously calmed down, although I noticed that his voice got sharply louder when Sarah mentioned my name.

'It's all sorted out,' said Sarah, returning my phone. 'He wants me back. And he wants you to come in, too. He says now's a good time to sort a few things out.' She paused. 'He promised not to hit you.'

We arrived at the flat a few minutes later. It was on the third floor of a small block owned by the council. I was still worried about being king-hit by Sid, but he smiled in welcome, ushered me through to the small, cosy lounge, and made sure we were seated comfortably. He'd already made a pot of tea.

'When I threw Sarah out,' he said, 'I was so angry that if one of us hadn't left, I would have hit her. And I've never done that.'

Sarah confirmed this.

'After I calmed down a bit' continued Sid, 'I started to worry about her. I went out to see if she was hanging about near the flat. When I couldn't find her, I began to get this strange feeling. I can't describe it … it was like … well, as if my mind was breaking up, splitting into pieces, escaping out into space. I don't think I've ever had such a bad feeling. It was so awful I wanted to die rather than go on feeling like that.'

'What did you do next?' I asked.

'I went back inside and called the police. I told the police officer I spoke to I was reporting a missing person. When he found out she'd been gone less than an hour, he got stroppy and told me not to waste his time. I said to myself I'd wait half an hour and then call them again. I was just going to when Sarah rang. You don't know how happy I was to hear the sound of her voice.'

And then, incredibly, Sid began to sob.

A look of utter astonishment appeared on Sarah's face, and she moved over to Sid, putting her arm around him. While Sarah and I waited silently for Sid's sobbing to subside, I reviewed what I knew about the couple.

Sarah was working class and proud of her East End origins. She had first come to see me nearly a year earlier. Her main complaint was severe agoraphobia. She had devastating panic attacks whenever she went out alone. This kept her virtually housebound. It was only because her mother had agreed to accompany her that Sarah was able to consult me in my rooms.

I quickly discovered that Sarah had become agoraphobic soon after she started living with Sid. It took longer to discover that Sid suffered from morbid jealousy. He worked as a foreman in a local factory, and his status freed him to make phone calls. He rang Sarah as least four or five times a day to see how she was, he claimed. His real agenda was to check up on her. If she didn't answer, he would cross-examine her when he got home for lunch or after work. If she wasn't in, he'd fly into a rage when she got back, accusing her of infidelity. He would go on and on, forcing her to repeat in precise detail everything she'd done since he'd last seen her. He would find inconsistencies in her account, and insist she repeat it, sometimes over and over. His was a classic case of morbid jealousy, or Othello Syndrome. A colleague had told me about a patient of his, a husband who chained his wife to his leg in bed at night. At least Sid wasn't that bad!

It had been in the hope of sorting some of this out that I'd suggested couples therapy, but Sid's dramatic reaction had scuppered that. Then it was a stalemate. Although both Sarah and I knew what the real issues were, Sarah struggled to avoid facing up to them. She had come to feel totally dependent on Sid, and couldn't risk alienating him. Sarah had many other psychological symptoms in addition to her agoraphobia, and I resigned myself to helping her with those. Although this was unrewarding and often frustrating, I couldn't bring myself to discharge Sarah from care. I clung to the hope that a chance to confront the real issues would eventually come up. And now, perhaps it had.

'What is it that's upset you so much?' I asked Sid cautiously.

'I don't know,' replied Sid. 'But I feel just like I did when my mother walked out on us.'

Then Sid described a tumultuous early childhood dominated by his mother's threats to leave, which she'd acted upon several times, vanishing for a few days and then reappearing as if nothing had happened. Until Sid was ten years old, when she hadn't come back.

The links between these painful events and Sid's behaviour towards Sarah were obvious to me, but had been totally invisible to Sid. As gently as I could, I pointed them out. I encouraged Sid to access more childhood memories. He remembered being convinced that his mother was leaving him for someone else, whom she loved better. I suggested that his extreme possessiveness and jealousy of Sarah, and his constant fear that he would lose her, mirrored these feelings towards his mother. When Sarah became agoraphobic and housebound, Sid's anxieties about her were reduced. There was more sobbing from Sid, and more sympathy from Sarah. After some further discussion, Sid claimed to have seen the light, and promised to change. He was almost pathetically grateful to me as I left, saying that he'd come with Sarah on her next appointment.

I was relieved to find my car where I left it, and still with four wheels. As I drove home, I felt a mixture of elation and depression.

Elation because I'd had one of the most challenging and rewarding clinical experiences that I could recall; depression because it was now twenty past four in the morning and I had a full day's work ahead. I was not one of those people who could manage easily with a few hours' sleep. Tomorrow I would feel woolly-headed and be prone to silly errors. I cursed myself for taking Sarah on in the first place.

Although I saw her privately, she paid nothing, because of an arrangement I had negotiated with the local NHS trust, which paid me the equivalent of one NHS session a week to see health service patients privately. I had sought the arrangement because I hated the idea of restricting my practice to the well off. As a bonus, patients referred from the NHS tended to suffer from unusually complex and interesting problems. Sarah was no exception.

I was back in bed by a quarter to five, but I couldn't sleep. I was too wound up by the night's events. I started to think about the day ahead, and especially about getting up on time for my first patient, scheduled for half past seven. This meant I could see patients working inflexible hours. Some of my colleagues started even earlier, and some worked into the evening as well. I'd never understood how they managed this, but I suspected that they took a passive approach to therapy, requiring little energy. This I could never do.

On weekends, I generally did a lot of writing. Letters to referring GPs or other doctors, medico-legal reports, and sometimes work on an article for a professional journal. Earning a living had always taken priority, so my academic output was small. I'd written a few good papers based on case studies, and I sometimes got referrals from other psychiatrists who had read them. Two of these papers were about sexual perversions, or paraphilias as they're currently called. This meant that I had fairly regular referrals of this kind, and I was viewed as an expert in the field. I had mixed feelings about this, because treating paraphilias was extraordinarily difficult. But I'd felt unable to turn away legitimate referrals, especially when I was trying to make a name for myself.

Apart from work, my life was a void. My mother had died a few months before Celia and I had split up. She'd been seriously ill for nearly a year, and so I'd done some grieving before her death. Even so, I'd found losing her very hard to deal with and I knew I hadn't got over it yet. Looking back, I could see that I'd displaced some of my grief onto Celia. This probably helped trigger our final breakup.

I saw little of my father. Never close, our relationship had become increasingly stiff and uncomfortable. He'd coped very badly with my mother's death. Rather than grieve, he'd plunged into a new relationship, which was becoming turbulent. His energy was spent on managing this, and he had even less interest in me than usual.

I had plenty of professional colleagues, but no close friends. After the marriage break-up, hostility or embarrassment had cut my ties with the few couples Celia and I had been close to. I suddenly had a bleak thought that almost all my human contact came from my patients. They had taken the place of family and friends. I had no life of my own. I lived by proxy, through my patients and the dramas they played out daily in my consulting room.

Feeling as depressed as I had at any time since Celia and I parted, I thought of ringing Janet at home, asking her to cancel all my appointments, and going back to bed. Instead, I showered, dressed, made more coffee and some toast, and forced myself out into rush hour Baker Street. The weather was still fine, and walking through the public gardens worked as an antidepressant.

Paying full attention to my patients was a struggle. Bleak thoughts, having finally surfaced, kept pushing into my mind. I prayed for cancellations, but everyone turned up and I saw patients solidly until half past five. I had a professional meeting at half past seven, and I stayed on afterwards for drinks, alcohol postponing my self-torment until I woke up next morning, hung over. My first thought was of seeing Ms Richmond at eleven o'clock. A surge of excitement tinged with anxiety worsened my headache but got me out of bed and into the shower. I walked to work quicker than usual, and the exercise eased my headache.

'I spoke to my acquaintance again and she assured me that I'd made the right decision, that you were my best hope for a cure.' Ms Richmond uttered this with total conviction.

'Well, I've had no second thoughts about our agreement,' I lied. 'Let's stick to the plan. Tell me more about yourself, starting with your family of origin. Oh ... there's the matter of what we should call each other. I prefer Christian names, but I can live with Dr Milton if you're uncomfortable with George. Can I call you Julia?'

'That's fine by me, George.'

We covered a lot of ground. I formed a picture of a happy, affectionate young girl devastated when the father she adored left the family and went to live with another woman. Then, three years later, came her mother's depression and departure for a clinic, and her stepfather's vicious, cold-blooded sexual abuse. As a result, Julia lost her trust in adults, and became convinced that any close relationships were doomed to end prematurely and in pain. So she had avoided them, putting all her energies into study.

These efforts and a brilliant mind had brought her professional success, but she had no close friends or interests outside her work.

At the end of our allotted time, I asked Janet to arrange eight further sessions twice weekly. We assumed that more would be needed later, but these could be arranged in light of progress.

During the next two sessions, I became uneasy about the rules I was breaking. I'd allowed Julia to avoid telling me much more about herself, settling for a mixture of personal snippets and chat about issues irrelevant to the tasks we'd agreed on. And when she had asked me personal questions, I'd talked about myself, trying to make it sound better than it really was. Normally, I deflected personal questions, especially when they side-tracked from the work at hand.

But the mistakes I made inside my head were the worst. I lusted after Julia. Her image pushed my bleak thoughts aside and transformed my depression into painful longing. My fantasies about her, often arousingly sexual, had an intrusive, almost compulsive quality. I'd had many young, attractive women as patients, but I'd never felt such an intense physical attraction to any of them. I'd allowed myself sexual fantasies, but my personal and professional standards had always stopped me from going any further. I utterly despised psychiatrists who broke the rules and had sex with their patients. I wasn't sure if my lust for Julia was unethical: it seemed beyond my control. Of course, I knew I'd never act upon my feelings.

We started our fifth session at half past four on a Monday evening. I was hung over after drinking myself to sleep the night before. Janet and Michael both left soon after five. Just as I was wondering if Julia sensed how much I was affected by her presence, she got up and sat on the arm of my chair, gazing at me steadily.

'I've been wanting to do this ever since our first session,' she said, leaning forward and putting her lips on mine. She probed gently with her tongue, and this aroused me so strongly that my mind threatened to detach itself from my body. Rational thought deserted me. Julia stood up, gently tugged me to my feet, and then pressed the full length of her body against mine. She kissed me again, and I responded, my loins the centre of an arousal almost painful in its intensity.

'Let's make love,' murmured Julia.

These words made me so anxious that for a few moments my desire vanished. I thought of Janet, puzzled by unfamiliar sounds, coming in to see if I was all right. Then I remembered that Janet had gone. My desire returned.

Julia removed her blouse and skirt, then her bra and panties. Her body was as beautiful as I had imagined it. I couldn't help noticing that the triangle of her pubic hair, neat and dark, had a reddish tinge. Embracing again, we lowered ourselves to the floor, making love without inhibition until quite suddenly, Julia stopped. She detached herself and dressed quickly, saying nothing. My senses floating, I didn't react until she turned to leave.

'Julia, please don't go.' She ignored me and walked out.

TWO

As I opened the door to my flat, I realised I had no recollection of the walk home from my rooms. I'd focussed so hard on making sense of what happened between Julia and me that my progress had been automatic. Fixing myself a large gin and tonic, I sank into an armchair and gazed out of the window. Out there on Baker street, everything seemed normal.

I couldn't believe how stupid I'd been. One lapse had destroyed both my sense of personal ethics and my professional integrity. I had joined the ranks of those I most despised: psychiatrists who had sex with their patients. Those found out were struck from the medical register, unable to practice and headed for financial and social oblivion. I was sure that Julia wouldn't complain to the authorities about me. But I had to live with what I'd done.

I'd just fixed my fourth gin and tonic when the intercom buzzed. It was Julia. 'George, I have to see you. Please let me in.'

The desperation in her voice overcame my doubts. I pressed the button that opened the street level door and spoke into the intercom. 'Flat eight's on the top floor.'

'Would you like a drink?' I asked her as she sat down on the sofa in my sitting room.

'Thanks. Whisky and soda. Easy on the whisky.'

As she took her first sip, Julia gazed directly at me. 'I haven't been completely honest with you, George.' She was silent for a few moments. 'It's a sin of omission, really. You see... my stepfather is one of your patients. Paul Kirk, the cabinet minister.'

Julia's revelation stunned me.

'Why on earth didn't you tell me before?'

'I assumed you wouldn't take me on.'

'I suppose... in theory... it shouldn't matter that much. But along with the problems we discussed at our first meeting... you're probably right.'

'But that's just part of it,' said Julia. 'I have this problem I haven't mentioned before. I need you to help me with it.' Another silence. 'I want to punish my stepfather for what he did to me. I can't do it on my own. I need you to help me.'

'In what way?'

'I want you to help me arrange his death.'

By now I'd run out of emotional responses. I felt numb, hoping that Julia was playing some kind of harmless game with me, a game I hadn't yet understood.

'Are you serious?' I asked.

'Absolutely.'

Her cold, unblinking stare and flat tone told me she meant it.

'I'm having a lot of difficulty with this,' I said. 'But for the moment, carry on.'

'I know a little about my stepfather's psychiatric problems. Let me explain how. He married again about three years after leaving my mother. This was his third wife, and I've cultivated a relationship with her. Not just to keep tabs on my stepfather; I genuinely like her. The marriage is a disaster, she tells me, but she stays with him... for various reasons. Telling me what he's really like – as opposed to his public image – is one of her ways of coping.'

I knew I had to be very careful. How much did Julia really know? What if she was bluffing, hoping to trick me into revealing personal details about her stepfather that she could use to harm him? Keeping patients' personal details strictly confidential was one of my profession's top commandments. Otherwise, patients would never reveal their secrets.

'Tell me what you know about his psychiatric problem.' Asking Julia this seemed the only safe choice.

'I knew he was sick even before the sexual abuse. He had a study, a fair-sized room that he always kept locked. Even the daily help was allowed to clean it only in his presence. Late one summer night I'd gone downstairs to get a cool drink from the fridge. I heard these strange grunting, gasping noises coming from his study. I thought of knocking to see if he was alright, but the noises stopped. Then they started again. For some reason, I went out of the back door to try and look in from the outside. The curtains were drawn, but by standing on tip-toe I was able to see about half the office through a chink. The light was dim, but I could make out the figure of my stepfather. He had his back to me. He was naked except for what looked like a pair of women's panties. He was wearing some kind of harness made of rope and straps, and this hung from the ceiling, although I couldn't see how, exactly. His body was jerking and he was still making these strange noises. I didn't understand what he was doing, but I knew instinctively it was sick, dirty. Ugh!'

'Have you always remembered that scene, or was it buried until you recalled the sexual abuse?'

'I've always remembered it. Of course, it was years before I understood what he was doing, that it's a well recognised sexual perversion with its own scientific name. I assume he still does it, although his wife's never mentioned it. This is where you come in. I need to know exactly what he does, where, and how often.'

'Julia, you know I can't possibly tell you that. It would be a disgraceful, unforgivable breach of ethics. I could get struck off. Anyway, why do you want to know?'

'I've read a lot about autoerotic asphyxia. I know that fatal accidents are quite common, nearly always caused by the failure of safety devices. If I find out enough details, I think perhaps I can modify his apparatus, or get someone else to. Maybe his wife hates him enough. It would be the perfect murder.'

'Don't you realise how dangerous it is to tell me this? You're asking me to help you murder someone. This is about the only time I'm allowed to breach confidentiality. You must know about the recent changes in the law obliging me to try and warn your stepfather if I think you're serious. And you certainly seem to be. Julia, it's my duty to warn your stepfather, directly or through the police.'

'I've thought of that, you idiot. That's why I seduced you.' Julia's gaze was malignant. The only response I had left was nausea. I felt its sickening progress up from the pit of my stomach. It stopped at the base of my throat.

'Seduce me? You mean it was all planned?'

'Not in detail. I had a broad strategy, but mostly I played it by ear. Things fell into place.'

A rush of anger sluiced away my nausea. 'You're crazy. If any of this comes out, it'll be your word against mine. If you put in a complaint about me, I'll just deny what happened. If you persist, I'll reveal your plans to kill your stepfather. Which you'll deny, of course. It would be an exercise in futility, a stalemate. Damaging to both of us.'

'There's one more thing I haven't told you,' gloated Julia. 'I went to the police straight after we had sex. I said I'd been raped, but wasn't sure about laying charges. I withheld your identity. Of course, I had a physical examination, and they took vaginal swabs. There was plenty of semen for DNA testing – if it comes to that. I'd thought of adding a few scratches and bruises myself, but realised that would be overkill. I know all about these things, of course. Personally. And as a lawyer. Which meant I was able to make sure they did exactly what I wanted. Now do I have to spell it out? If you don't deliver, I can ruin you.'

The nausea came back. I was too shocked to feel anything else. 'Julia, let's slow down a bit. Suppose I agree to help you. I'd need to know exactly what your plans were. Right now, I can see lots of problems with them. For a start, you're assuming your stepfather still practices autoerotic asphyxia. What if I told you he was cured?'

'I want you to show me his case notes,' countered Julia. 'I'd like to see them now, as a token of your... good faith.'

A sense of unreality took hold of me. This was the turning point. Showing her the files might lead anywhere. Even if I managed to save my career, my self-respect would be destroyed. If I refused, I might feel better about myself, but my career was finished. I had to choose between self-loathing and professional self-destruction. I chose the former.

'OK. But the files are in my office. You're not suggesting we go there now?'

'Why not?' responded Julia. 'Parking's easy this time of night. We can go in my car.' I capitulated. Ten minutes later we were sitting in my consulting room and Julia was opening her stepfather's file. She read silently for a while and then exclaimed, 'Here it is! "Paul shows a worrying trend, taking greater risks during his paraphilic activities. It seems the more successful he becomes professionally, the more he courts self-destruction." Dated only last month. Well, that sorts out the first problem. He's still doing it. Where's your photocopier, by the way?'

'Why do you need a copy? You've found out what you wanted.'

'Phase two,' replied Julie. 'Gathering all the details I can. I'm going to study the notes tonight. Tomorrow I'll ask you to fill in the gaps. I'll ring you. I expect you to be available any time.'

'But I can't just drop everything.'

'Listen,' Julie said softly but with emphasis. 'You're mine. I can identify you as a rapist any time I want to. Just in case you're in doubt about that, here's a copy of the police report. No-one reading this will believe a word you say against me. Especially after DNA testing. From now on, you'll do exactly what I want.'

Julia photocopied the notes herself. 'I'll let myself out. Oh… I'll need keys to both your flat and your rooms. Tomorrow. And there's one more thing. I enjoyed having sex with you. You're a very attractive man.' She left before I could think of anything to say.

I replaced Paul Kirk's case file, then pulled it out again. I'd been seeing him for about eighteen months, averaging once a week. My notes occupied many pages. If I studied them, I'd know what Julia might learn. Suddenly, I felt claustrophobic, trapped in the scene of what was now a double crime. The two rules I'd just broken – in the space of a few hours – were crucial to both my professional and personal ethics. As I locked up the rooms, a blend of self-disgust and nausea accompanied me into Harley Street.

Walking on automatic pilot, I tried to think of a way out of the mess I was in. I considered going to the police and telling them the whole story. With my lawyer, of course. I had a contact in Scotland Yard whom I'd advised on a forensic case. He owed me one. But Julia had set me up so neatly that I knew she'd win any legal battle. Even if I was able to have the rape charges dismissed, I'd still have to front the General Medical Council for having sex with a patient. I'd be struck off. With no career, no income, and hefty legal fees, my flat would have to be sold. Professional indemnity didn't cover what I'd done. I'd be left with nothing. Except perhaps a few fragments of self-respect.

I didn't really believe that Julia would murder her stepfather. I understood her feelings towards him: she had reacted to her recently recovered memories as if the events themselves had just happened. Homicidal rage was a natural response. I assumed it would wane before she got anywhere near trying to modify the apparatus her stepfather used for his sexual deviations.

This meant I had to play along with her. If I was right, she'd soon lose her murderous feelings and realise her plan was not only impractical, but totally crazy. Reading the case notes might speed this process up by confronting Julia with an image of her stepfather as he now was, and not as the evil, sadistic man she remembered. These thoughts reassured me so much that my mood lifted. By the time I'd showered and got into bed, I was relaxed enough to fall asleep almost at once.

The ringing of the phone woke me. It was Julia. 'I've read the case notes. There are some things I don't understand. And you haven't written much about the apparatus he uses. We need to meet. I'll see you at ten o'clock in your flat. That'll give you time to get my keys cut.'

I hung up without protesting. The bedside clock said it was twenty past seven. When, I wondered, did Julia sleep? It would have taken her several hours to do justice to my case notes. But she sounded fresh and full of energy. So much for my theory that she'd soon lose her passion for murder.

At seven forty, I phoned Janet. 'Sorry to ring you at home. Something's come up. Don't worry. I'll explain later. Can you cancel all my appointments today? Say I'm sick.'

I was rarely ill, and even then I preferred to work rather than stay at home feeling sorry for myself. In the eight years that Janet has worked for me, I'd had to ring her like this only twice before: once when a severe bout of flu incapacitated me for forty-eight hours, and once when my mother's health had suddenly deteriorated and her death seemed imminent. But on that occasion she had rallied.

There was a small shop near Baker Street where I could get the keys cut. There were five: three Yales and two Chubbs. I hoped I wouldn't have any trouble with the Chubbs. Luckily, the key cutter had the necessary blanks and didn't ask any questions. My next stop was a shop that sold electronic equipment. I knew that Julia would ensure that my mobile was switched off when we talked so I bought the most sensitive recorder I could find, one that was small, completely silent, and could be easily hidden. If Julia discovered I was recording her, I was finished. But with our conversation digitally saved, perhaps I had a chance of protecting myself.

The entrance buzzer rang soon after I got back. It was Julia, ten minutes early. In the middle of setting up the electronic recorder, I knew I didn't have time to do it properly, so I abandoned my attempts and bundled it into a drawer. As soon as she came in I handed her the keys, identifying them. She led the way into the sitting room.

'Let's get right down to it,' Julia began. 'How much do you actually know about the apparatus he uses?'

My best approach, I thought, would be honesty. Julia was smart enough to pick up any lies or inconsistencies, and I didn't want to risk alienating her. Not if I wanted to make sure she didn't try to kill Paul Kirk.

'Well, I've never seen it. And he's never described it to me in any detail. But from all that he's said, I can probably put together a reasonable descript--'

'We'll come back to that,' interrupted Julia. 'According to your notes, he experiences huge relief after each use of the apparatus. Then tension gradually builds up again until after three or four days he feels compelled to use it again. Is that right?'

'Pretty well,' I replied. 'But if he's overseas on government business, he won't risk taking the apparatus with him. Unless he can rig something up locally, he has to wait until he gets back. Then he might have as many as three or four sessions within a week.'

'How typical is he of autoerotic asphyxiators in general? Tell me more about the syndrome.'

'How much do you want to know?'

'As much as I need to work out a way of killing the bastard.'

I took a deep breath. 'OK. Just interrupt me if I get off the track. First, it's quite rare for anyone to seek treatment for autoerotic asphyxia. Most cases come to light at the scene of death or at post-mortem. Coroners tend to report them as accidental hanging or suffocation. American research suggests about nine hundred such deaths in the United States each year. That's something over three deaths per million population. The figures are probably similar here, but I've not seen any recently published research. Obviously, these deaths represent only a small fraction of those who practise autoerotic asphyxiation. So we have to assume it's not that rare. I'm guessing, but there are probably over six thousand regular self-asphyxiators in greater London alone.'

'Why do people do it? Is it only men?'

Julia's interest had rekindled her natural warmth. In spite of the impossible circumstances, I felt renewed stirrings of sexual attraction.

'Early theories assumed only men did it. They relied on the Freudian idea of castration anxiety. By masturbating under threat of death, and surviving, the basic oedipal dilemma was both created and resolved.'

'I'm actually quite psychologically minded,' said Julia, 'but I'm afraid you've lost me.'

I tried again. 'The oedipal situation is basic to Freudian, psychoanalytic thinking. Age between two and three, the male child begins to see the father as a rival for the mother's affection. He fears punishment – castration – by the father for desiring the mother. If this oedipal dilemma isn't resolved, it always resurfaces in adult life. One way of managing it is autoerotic asphyxia. The threat of death while masturbating represents an unconscious fear of castration by the father. Survival equals successful defiance.'

'Do you really believe all that bullshit?'

'Well, psychoanalytical explanations aren't very fashionable at the moment. But I think they perfectly fit some people. Others are best understood differently.'

'According to your theory, my stepfather wanted to fuck his mother,' Julia said crudely. 'And he's still trying to, but it's got him all tied up in knots.'

I grimaced at Julia's vulgar pun. 'Nearly everyone first reacts to psychoanalytic notions with disgust, scorn or laughter. I was the same. But over the years I've been forced to recognise their power to explain things that are otherwise mystifying.'

'You're beginning to sound patronising, George. What about a simple, common sense explanation?'

'I don't think there is one. Mainly because autoerotic asphyxiators usually have other sexual deviations, especially bondage, fetishism, and masochism. This means the asphyxiation is just one aspect of various elaborate rituals. Self-bondage with ropes, straps and chains not only constricts and immobilises, but can be very painful. Most of the men found dead are naked or wearing items of female underclothing, and pornographic material is often present.' I paused, waiting for Julia to comment, but she said nothing.

'For your stepfather, the excitement centres around the process of asphyxiation, and the sensation it causes. He uses a rope round his neck, carefully padded so as not to leave any marks, to constrict his carotid arteries and reduce the blood supply to his brain. This increases the intensity and duration of his orgasms, probably the main motive of anyone who uses self-asphyxiation more or less on its own.' I hadn't mentioned women, I realised. 'It's interesting that women who practice autoerotic asphyxia rarely seem to have other sexual deviations. For them, the main object appears to be achieving a spectacular orgasm. Women are much less likely than men to have fatal accidents.'

'I told you I remember seeing my stepfather wearing women's panties. Did he mention that?'

'Not that I recall. But many self-asphyxiators find wearing women's underclothes exciting. But cutting off the blood supply to the brain is usually the crucial element, as it was for your step-father. Having a mind-blowing orgasm at this point may cause loss of control, and that's when accidents happen. Ropes get jammed or tangled, even caught up in long hair. Safety devices either fail, or can't be used because loss of consciousness has occurred.'

'If you wanted to murder Paul Kirk,' asked Julia, 'how would you modify his apparatus to make sure his death seemed accidental?'

'I'd have to see the apparatus, ideally in use.'

'But you must have some idea.'

Julia was right. I probably knew enough to arrange a fatal accident, assuming I could access both the apparatus and where it was used. But I couldn't tell her that, just in case she defied my predictions and went ahead with her plans. I decided to stall.

'As I said before, it's rare for self-asphyxiators to seek treatment. Your stepfather came to see me after a near-fatal accident. He didn't want to die, but he didn't want to give up his perversion either. It was too exciting, too central to his life. So we talked to begin with about making his apparatus safer. That worked, but only for a while. Then he got back to gradually increasing the level of risk, although he didn't admit this until recently. I suggested he try safer ways of achieving the same effect, such as inhaling amyl nitrite, but for him the use of ropes and straps is too big a part of the thrill.'

'Suppose,' said Julia, 'I'm able to get his wife to find the apparatus. It's bound to be in his study – uh, pun not intended!'

I wondered how Julia could make such flippant remarks while discussing plans for a murder.

'Then,' continued Julia, 'I could get a detailed description. Or she might be able to observe him secretly while he was doing it.'

This sounded encouraging. Even if it was possible, it might take weeks to arrange. By then, I was convinced, Julia would be willing to abandon her lethal intentions.

'I think that's a brilliant idea,' I said enthusiastically. 'When are you next seeing Paul's wife?'

'Tomorrow, as it happens. For lunch. Although in her case it will be nibbling on a piece of lettuce. She's a hair's breadth away from anorexia.'

'Please don't suggest she comes to see me.'

It was a feeble joke, but Julia laughed.

'Your case notes fascinated me. Not just the perversion stuff. I realised that I didn't know my stepfather at all. What he told you about his childhood, that was awful. I'm not surprised he turned into a complete monster.'

My pulse quickened. Was this a chance to try and change Julia's feelings?

'Yes, he was horribly abused by his father, physically and emotionally. Perhaps his father was the real monster. A true sadist. Some of the things he did to Paul...'

'But are they all true? Could he have made them up... to try and justify his bizarre behaviour? I'm assuming, by the way, that he never told you about raping and abusing me.'

'There was no mention of that. I accepted him as he was, without making any judgements. He knew this. No, I'm sure what he told me was the truth. He did say there were a few things he felt so bad about that he wasn't ready to bring them up. Perhaps you're one of them. He left a few gaps when he talked about his wives. I accepted that. He'd shown so much courage in telling me about his hideous childhood.'

'I don't think for a moment it justifies what he did to me,' said Julia. 'I still hate him and want to see him dead. But I can't help feeling a little sympathy for him. Reading about what his father did to him made my flesh crawl. The beatings were bad enough. But locking him up for hours in that tiny cupboard under the stairs. Starving him. Lifting him up by his ears. Making him hold a brick above his head and belting him if he lowered it. Threatening to put his eyes out. Choking him until he ... oh!'

'Yes,' I said. 'Choking him until he passed out. This seems to have been one of his father's favourite "punishments." Add savage beatings with straps... perhaps we can begin to understand.'

Julia looked puzzled. 'Surely, the last thing he'd want to do as an adult was repeat the things that destroyed him as a child?'

'You'd think so. But there's this thing called repetition compulsion. It's a drive to repeat early traumas. There are many explanations for it, none of them totally convincing. With very abused, neglected children, almost the only physical contact they get is during abuse. In a perverse way, the physical abuse becomes reassuring. Their existence is confirmed by someone touching them, if only to cause them pain. As adults they repeat the trauma on their victims, with whom they identify.'

Julia looked at her watch. 'I have to go shortly. We've covered a lot, and I think I've understood the main points. Today's Tuesday. I may not need to see you again this week, as long as we can talk on the phone.'

'Does this mean I can resume my normal practice schedule? Not that I'm functioning very well at the moment. Perhaps I should take the rest of the week off.'

'Aren't you seeing my stepfather this week?'

'Yes, of course, it slipped my mind.'

'I think you should carry on as normal. It's vital you have the session with Paul. I want you to find out as much as you can about --'

'Julia,' I interrupted. 'If I suddenly start probing, take a new tack, he'll get suspicious, defensive. You'll have to trust my judgement on this.'

'Remember,' said Julia. 'I just have to make one phone call and you're history. If you say one word about any of this to my stepfather... Now, I really must go.'

After Julia left, I rang Janet to tell her I'd be in as usual tomorrow and probably for the rest of the week as well. I'd explain things when I saw her. It was close to lunch time, but I had no appetite. I resisted the temptation of alcohol. I needed a clear head.

I was seeing Paul Kirk tomorrow. How should I handle it? Either I told him about Julia or I didn't. If I did, he'd alert his security staff, Julia would be questioned, and she would identify me as the man who raped her, saying I'd invented the whole story to discredit her. If I didn't tell him, I might be risking his life. Professional ethics apart, it all hinged on that. I had to judge the chances of Julia attempting to kill Paul, either in the way she'd revealed to me, or, if that proved unworkable, in some other way. The chances, I thought, were very low. I made my decision. I wouldn't tell Paul Kirk anything about Julia.

Once the decision was made, I relaxed a little, but I was still preoccupied with Julia and too wound up to stay in the flat. I spent the afternoon in a cinema, then walked a little, planning to eat in a small French restaurant I'd recently discovered. The food was so good that even on a Tuesday it might be booked out. I rang to check. They had a table, and I spent nearly two hours enjoying their food and wine. Back in my flat, I watched some TV. After the ten o'clock news, I went to bed.

Next morning, as usual, I saw my first patient at seven-thirty. When I came out of the consulting rooms at twenty past eight, Janet had just arrived, earlier than usual. I'd worked out an explanation for yesterday that was as honest as I could make it.

'Morning, Janet. Thanks for fixing things yesterday, I really appreciate it.'

'All part of a day's work, George,' smiled Janet.

'Were there any unexpected problems?'

'None.'

I hated the idea of deceiving Janet. She was reliable and trustworthy. Michael and I depended on her, probably far too much, for the smooth running of our practice. When Michael and I interviewed Janet for the job of secretary-receptionist, she was in her early forties, recently divorced, and with two teenage children. Her employment record was patchy. She was plump and rather plain. Her wispy brown hair had sprung free at the back from her attempts to constrain it. But she interviewed very well, and I found myself liking her immediately. I'd never regretted offering her the job.

'About yesterday, Janet,' I began. 'It was to do with Julia Richmond. She has this major crisis and I couldn't avoid getting involved.'

Janet looked at me quizzically, but said nothing.

'The problem was, I didn't know when I'd be able to get away. So it made sense to cancel the whole day. As it happened, I was free by lunch time, but I decided not to come in. Anyway, it's most unlikely to happen again.'

I could see that Janet wasn't convinced. She knew me too well. In most psychiatric practices, a trusted secretary had full access to case notes. But my practice included an unusual number of celebrities and others in the public eye. Often, they were obsessed with secrecy, and expected that their case notes were seen by me alone. When not in use, they had to be locked away with unusual security. This meant that Janet's knowledge of patients generally relied on what I was free to tell her, and the letters I wrote, which were often exercises in tact rather than clinical analysis. Because I trusted her totally, I sometimes told her things that, if leaked, would have made headlines in the tabloids. I'd said nothing about Julia.

'Paul Kirk rang to say he was running about fifteen minutes late. He should be here by ten fifteen. Oh – here's your half past eight patient now.'

I didn't recognise celebrity status as an excuse for being late. But I had to accept that a cabinet minister might sometimes be held up. Paul's attendance at my clinic was surprisingly free of fuss. At work, only his closest colleagues knew about it, including his personal security staff. One of these always came with him, sitting in the consulting room throughout the session. His regular minder had a glazed look, which I assumed was an attempt to blend into the background, but it made him look more like a Berserker about to go off than one of our patients.

Paul and his minder arrived at ten-twenty. I'd ended my eight-thirty session at twenty past nine, leaving me some time to make some final choices about what I'd say to Paul.

'How've things been?' I asked as soon as Paul had settled into his armchair.

His distinguished face was more drawn than I had ever seen it. In worrying contrast to his usual impeccable grooming, his hair was untidy. I knew he was fifty-six. For the first time, he looked it.

'Not too good. I had another near-miss on Monday. It's got back close to what it was when, you know, just before I started seeing you.'

Paul had told me last time that his risk-taking had increased but not to the extent that he was now revealing.

'Is there anything else happening, Paul, anything that might be causing you to take more risks?'

Paul dropped his gaze. He was silent for so long that I was about to repeat the question. Then he looked at me intently. 'George, I've told you things I've never told anyone else. In the time we've worked together, I've come to trust and respect you. In spite of your youth.' A hint of a smile, to which I responded with a broad grin, adding a touch of self-depreciation to let Paul know I was on his wave-length.

'Of course,' Paul went on, 'I've never discussed matters of government with you. But today I want to tell you something concerning my work as a minister. I'd prefer you didn't make notes. I know you lock your files away safely, but since Watergate...' Another thin smile. This time I didn't smile back. Instead I nodded and put down my ball-point.

'I suppose there's an element of confession in this. I'm not a religious man – far from it – but I feel the need to .... confess. That's the best word for it. Like a priest, I know you'll accept what I say without judging me. I've done bad things, unforgivable things, in my work, in my personal life, towards women... But I don't want to talk about that now. You've helped me understand a lot, how I never forgave my mother for letting my father treat me worse than an animal. I know he dominated her totally, that she felt powerless. But she just stood by. I even saw a hint of satisfaction, almost enjoyment, in her eyes, as she watched me being tortured, humiliated. I can see that treating the women in my life so badly is a symbolic act of revenge on my mother. Which doesn't make me feel much better about it. But, as I said, I don't want to talk about that now. I want to tell you about betraying my country.'

I tried to disguise my shock by keeping an even tone. 'Whatever you tell me, it will remain between us, you can be certain.'

'I'm not worried about that. But I am worried about your safety. If I'm exposed, our security services will wonder how much I've told you. They've never been comfortable about me seeing you, even though I've assured them we never discuss anything remotely concerned with national security. As you know, I've always refused to tell them exactly why I see you. Although with your reputation, they doubtless think it's something to do with kinky sex.'

I didn't think that was quite fair, but I let it pass. I was getting anxious. 'Why should my safety be an issue?'

'It's not just our own security services. Since perestroika and the break-up of the Soviet Union, it's all been rather free-enterprise. Gathering secrets, swapping them, selling them, it's no longer the monopoly of governments. These days, there's a huge overlap between industrial espionage and national security issues. Spying has become big business, carried out as much by private organisations as by governments. It can be enormously profitable. If anyone in the business thinks you have secrets, secrets that have real cash value, well, they'd approach you. This could involve threats, blackmail.'

I suddenly felt empty. Julia. She was blackmailing me. But to get at state secrets? Not unless she'd invented the whole sexual abuse story, and gained her knowledge of Paul's sexual deviations quite differently than she'd claimed. I realised Paul was talking again, and forced myself to attend.

'I regret deeply having put you in this position. When I came to see you, I was so desperate for help that I didn't think through all the implications... and I hadn't committed my act of betrayal. What makes it even worse, 'I've come to like you. But now, telling you about it is safer than not telling you. It'll give you a chance to protect yourself. And I ... I really do need to confess.'

I no longer had any problem attending to what Paul said.

'In essence,' he continued, 'I've grossly abused my position as a cabinet minister. I deputised briefly for the defence secretary and during that time I became aware of highly sensitive negotiations about the transfer of nuclear technology. When cabinet refused such a transfer, I was approached privately by a representative of the country which sought the technology. I was offered a truly obscene amount of money to get cabinet to change its mind or to find some other way of delivering the goods. I knew I couldn't influence cabinet, it was united in opposition to the deal. As it happened, I had exactly the right contacts in the Ministry of Defence and the Home Office. I was able to arrange for the technology transfer to proceed in secret. Other than me, only three people were involved, two at the highest level. It was a miraculously smooth and clever operation, although it cost me over half the total pay-off. Not that I'm complaining. I still have millions – I won't say how many – in a Swiss bank account.'

'You've been taking more risks with self-asphyxiation since the deal went through?'

'I hadn't made the link. But you're right. No, you don't have to explain. It's to do with my increased guilt and shame.'

It was a bit more complicated than that, but I nodded agreement.

'Getting back to my confession. You need to know the name of the country involved. It's Iran. Now when I made the deal, I wasn't aware of any close links with nuclear weapons. I've since found out that what we sold them means they'll probably be able to build explosive nuclear devices within two to three years. If that had been known, I wouldn't have been able to broker the deal. I wouldn't have tried. I've been outmanoeuvred, badly, by the Iranians. None of us involved in this can tell anyone without revealing our complicity.'

'Now that you've told me, Paul, do you feel any better?'

'Funnily enough, I do. But I can see that you don't.'

'You've just told me I may be in some kind of danger. Of course I don't feel better. I'm upset. Bloody upset.'

'And angry. I've never seen you look angry before.'

Paul was spot on. But I was still a psychiatrist, supposed to analyse my feelings before expressing them, or deciding not to. I could tell Paul that I was furious with him. Supposing, though, he had invented all this as part of an incipient psychosis I hadn't detected? I knew I was clutching at straws. This wasn't just psychiatry any more.

'George, we have to make a decision about whether or not I continue as your patient. It's up to you, mainly. I'd like to carry on with therapy, but it may be safer for you if I stop. I just don't know.'

'Let me think about that. I suggest we keep next week's appointment. We can discuss it then. I'd hoped that today we'd talk about ways of reducing risk during your rituals. But my mind's all over the place. I'd prefer we ended the session now.'

'I'm disappointed. But I understand. Before we finish – do you think "confessing" will restore some balance, reduce my self-destructive urges?'

'I hope so.' I got up and moved towards the door. Paul followed, and we shook hands in the waiting area.

'There's one last thing,' said Paul, moving close and speaking softly in my ear. 'If anything happens to me, I've instructed my solicitor to personally hand you a letter. It contains information that should give you any protection you might need. But it won't come to that, I'm sure. Try not to worry. I'll see you next week.' His minder, as usual, preceded him out.

It wasn't quite eleven o'clock. Getting through the rest of the day was going to be a struggle. At least I had a thirty-minute break before the next patient was due. Glancing at Janet's list, I saw I had no new patients scheduled. None of those on the list were likely to be very demanding. I'd be better off talking to them than cancelling, which would leave me alone to think catastrophic thoughts. I decided to carry on.

Somehow I got through the day. By the time I got back to my flat at six I was utterly exhausted. The first thing I did was reach for the gin bottle. I was adding tonic when, with a start, I saw Julia sitting in my armchair.

'I didn't see you,' I said. 'I'm totally knackered.'

'You can fix me a drink while you're at it. The usual. Light on the whisky, remember. I've got lots to tell you.'

And I've got lots to tell you, I thought. But I'll save it.

'As planned, I met my stepfather's third wife for lunch. She surprised me and had a huge piece of chocolate cake. After her lettuce.'

'Then she's not anorexic,' I said. 'More like bulimic. I bet she vomited afterwards.'

'Ugh. I've never been able to do that.'

'Nor me. We'd never make good bulimics.' I was wondering how long we could keep up this fatuous conversation when Julia came to the point.

'She denied any knowledge of Paul's... unusual sexual activities. But I don't know if she was lying or hadn't caught on to what I meant. Obviously I had to approach things cautiously, very indirectly. I couldn't just ask "does your husband wank himself off while dangling from a rope?"'

I couldn't help laughing. 'So what did you conclude, Julia?'

'Even if she does know, I can't ask her to help. It's clear the marriage isn't working, and that's probably because of Paul's treatment of her. But she has no money of her own, and Paul lets her spend as much as she likes of his. That's a powerful motive to hang in there. Oh, God! Another pun.' A brief pause. 'Excuse me. I need to use your loo.'

Julia's exit gave me a chance to see if she'd found the digital recorder. I was sure that searching my flat was one of her motives for coming round while I was at work. It was still where I'd hidden it, ready for use. I turned it on.

'Do you still want to kill him, Julia?' I asked as soon as she sat down on the sofa. I had reclaimed my armchair.

'Yes. My stepfather deserves to die for what he did to me.'

'The rape was twenty years ago. Paul Kirk is a different man now. He's a cabinet minister. Perhaps he's done enough good to balance the evil he did to you.'

'It doesn't matter. I'll never be happy, never feel clean, until he's dead.'

'Are you still planning a fatal accident for him?'

'Yes. But it depends on getting into his study, finding the apparatus, and removing or modifying any safety mechanisms. I've thought of a way. You and me going round to his house while his wife's there alone. Getting her to invite us in. Me faking a gastric upset, you distracting her, so I can get into his study. It's always locked – I was able to confirm that – so we'll have to get hold of the keys somehow. Perhaps you could steal them during one of his therapy sessions.'

I encouraged Julia to continue, even though her plans were totally unrealistic, at times verging on the psychotic. She finally settled on following the daily help as she left the Kirk residence and stealing her handbag, making it look like a mugging. I had to point out that this innocent woman probably didn't have a key to Paul's office, reminding Julia that, at least in the past, he allowed his study to be cleaned only in his presence.

'George, you don't sound at all keen. You're supposed to be helping me, remember.'

'I'll be honest with you, Julia. I'm still hoping you'll change your mind, decide not to try and kill Paul. I thought going into details might help you see how many problems there are with your plans. I hoped talking it all through would --'

'Shut up!' Julia yelled. 'You're a devious, hypocritical bastard. I'm not going to change my mind. And you're still going to help me. You know what'll happen if you don't.' She stood up and left.

After Julia's huffy departure I sat drinking steadily, trying to digest all that had happened, to work out a strategy. I felt dazed, and the more I drank, the more incoherent my thoughts became. Finally I gave up, and walked unsteadily to bed.

THREE

I woke up on Thursday morning with a serious hangover. Before getting up I tried to piece together exactly what Julia and I had talked about before she left in a huff. Then I remembered it was all on record. Julia spelling out her plans to kill Paul Kirk. I probably had enough to stop her accusing me of rape, but she could still complain to the General Medical Council. She couldn't prove we'd had sex without DNA testing. In the absence of criminal charges against me she'd have to arrange this herself, but I'd have to agree to it. If I refused, suspicions would be aroused, but if Julia's credibility was sufficiently undermined by my lawyers, I'd probably get away with it. Although even unproven allegations of such grave misconduct might wreck my career.

Because the recording was so important, I downloaded a duplicate on my computer and saved it on a USB. I'd keep the USB locked up with my files, and the recorder at home.

Making this decision freed me up to worry about the other big problem in my life, which forced me to confront yet another ethical dilemma. Paul Kirk had revealed information to me that might have a crucial bearing on world affairs. Should I alert the authorities – although I had no idea which ones – or should I keep quiet? There was nothing about this in the Royal College of Psychiatrist's ethical guidelines! Finally I decided to keep silent, at least until I'd spoken to Paul again next week. Perhaps he'd say it was no longer a problem, or show clear signs of some psychotic or delusional disorder. And I'd told him his secret was safe with me. This might have been unwise, but I wasn't ready to break a personal oath. Once I'd decided this, I felt less anxious. It may be denial, I thought. But it allowed me to focus my thoughts on the day ahead. I got ready to leave for work.

Thursday's list of patients had Sarah's name against the eleven-thirty slot. I hadn't seen her since the night she dragged me out of bed to stop her jumping in the Thames. She looked the most interesting of that morning's patients, the only one I had any enthusiasm for seeing. She arrived a little early, and Janet asked her to wait. Just after eleven-thirty, I peered out of my consulting room door and asked her to come in.

'Morning, Doctor Milton,' Sarah said cheerfully as she sat down.

'Morning, Sarah. Nice to see you. Things settled down OK?'

'Well, I'm a lot better. Sid wanted to come with me today, he said so he could thank you for what you did that night, though there's other things I'm sure. But I said I had a lot to discuss with you and I'd prefer he came next time. He wasn't too pleased.'

'As I said, he's welcome any time, it's up to you, mostly.'

'I know, Doctor. Anyway, I've been really good, better than for a long time. And Sid's really trying, but it's a struggle for him. Like, he knows he shouldn't act so jealous of me, but he can't help it.'

'Does this stop you doing what you really want to do?'

'That's just it. I've gone and got a job, you know that's what I've been wanting to do, but Sid, he used to make such a fuss, it was easier to give in. Especially when the agoraphobia was bad, which it was whenever Sid and I argued. This time I didn't let him stop me. The job's not much. I work in this office, three days a week, a bit of a dogsbody really. But they're training me. My keyboard skills are pretty good, and I'm learning to use Microsoft 365 on the computer. There's the chance of going full time. My agoraphobia, I can hardly believe it, hasn't been a huge problem. It would be if I had to travel far, but the office is only five or six stops on the bus. The first trip was sheer hell, I almost jumped off at the traffic lights. But I forced myself to stay aboard, and the panic started to settle. By the time I reached my stop, I wasn't feeling too bad.'

I'd worked with enough agoraphobics to know what an ordeal Sarah had described and how much courage she'd needed to go through with it. 'Well done, Sarah, that's fantastic, I know what it took. But Sid, how did he cope? Is he giving you a hard time?'

'Like I said, Doctor. He's really trying. He doesn't accuse me of things, but he's still thinking them, I'm sure. He has this tortured look when I talk about work, and I know he's imagining me having sex with the entire office, doing things I'd never dream of. Although there is this rather dishy bloke in accounts...'

This was typical Sarah. Swearing she'd never been unfaithful to Sid while fantasising about having an affair. She'd probably fall for the office Romeo. I carefully edited my thoughts. 'Sometimes, when a woman's no longer trapped by agoraphobia in what's become a "compulsory marriage," she begins to imagine leaving her husband. These thoughts are scary, because for the first time it's possible to act on them. Some women actually do it, and often it turns out for the best. But before you do anything like that... why not give Sid a chance to prove he can change?'

'Oh, it hasn't got to that. I still love him. With a bit more help from you, we'll get through this.'

'Maybe Sid should have a therapist of his own,' I suggested. 'I'll bring this up next time. Please make sure he comes. Look – why don't we bring our next appointment forward? What if we meet next week? Let's try and make it late afternoon on one of your days off. Sid should be able to leave work a bit early.'

We spent the rest of the session discussing Sarah's tendency to flirt, of which she had little conscious awareness. It was one of the things that fuelled Sid's jealousy. I'd noticed it when I'd first met Sarah, but knew I had to wait for the right moment before discussing it in detail. She coped well with the confrontation, and left with a thoughtful look on her face.

I managed the rest of the day surprisingly well. Thoughts about Julia and Paul kept surfacing, along with surges of anxiety, but I was able to push them back when I needed to. My clinical work was a little erratic, but no-one complained.

There's a professional meeting that was scheduled that evening, and I decided to go straight from work. The buffet would be enough to keep me going. Although the talk was interesting, I didn't take much of it in. I stayed on afterwards, drinking too much. Some of my colleagues seemed distant, disapproving. Oh God, I thought, I'm getting a reputation as a drunk. But that seemed the least of my problems.

I was getting used to waking up with a hangover. Friday morning was no worse than yesterday. I'd cut back when all this was over, I told myself.

'Are you feeling OK George?' asked Janet when I approached her alcove at the end of my first morning session.

'To be honest, I'm not. I'm really worried about two of my patients. Julia Richmond, that trouble I had, well it's still brewing.

And Paul Kirk, I haven't mentioned, but he's causing me a lot of … I just can't tell you about it, I'm afraid.'

'I can see you're worried, George, you look terrible this morning. Almost as bad as yesterday.'

Janet's occasional bluntness had its place. Today I didn't need it.

'Have any of my patients said anything?'

'Not directly. But one or two have asked me if you're all right.'

Somehow I got through the next two sessions. Michael knew I tried to have a thirty-minute break at eleven, and another at three. He tried to do the same so we could meet and talk at least twice a week. Less driven than I, Michael took an hour off for lunch as well.

These meetings were important for both of us. Even if we had no clinical matters to discuss, we enjoyed chatting and weren't averse to gossip, Michael's knowledge of which never ceased to amaze me.

He put his head round my door just after eleven o'clock. 'Morning, George. You free?'

'Sure. Come and sit down. Coffee?' I returned shortly with two cups.

Good coffee was an indulgence we shared with Janet, who had an expensive machine in her alcove. The brew was kept hot in a glass jug. Patients were offered some if they had to wait more than a few minutes, and Janet claimed that its therapeutic powers greatly exceeded both Michael's and my own.

'You look serious, Michael. What's up?'

'Actually, George, it's you. I can see things aren't right, and Janet… well, she's worried about you. I was hoping you'd talk to me, we've shared problems before.'

Although we rarely socialised outside work, Michael and I had become close. I'd talked about my marriage problems, and now Celia had left me, he'd replaced her as a confidant.

He was right to expect that I'd talk to him about personal problems, especially if they were affecting my work. 'Michael, I wish I could talk to you, I really do. You have good judgement, I always listen carefully to what you say. But this time I can't. Not yet. I promise I'll tell you everything as soon as it's safe.'

'Safe? Are you in some kind of danger? From a patient?'

'Please don't push it, Michael. It is about a patient, two actually, but neither are threatening me physically.'

Michael looked relieved. He'd brought in a newspaper, and he started reading it, I guessed as a circuit-breaker. This gave me a chance to reflect. Neither of us had been seriously threatened by a patient, although it was an occupational hazard, especially for those working in the NHS. There was a sizeable group of people with paranoid psychosis. Such people create a system of delusions, often a complex conspiracy in which they live as the object of persecution. Anyone in this delusional system could be in danger, usually because they're seen as a threat. Sometimes 'innocent' people become targets because they refuse the paranoid person's irrational requests for help in destroying the conspiracy. Psychiatrists are most at risk when they order compulsory treatment for such a person. If the patient fails to respond to treatment, and this isn't uncommon, the psychiatrist usually becomes part of the delusional system, sometimes as the chief conspirator. Death threats often result, and occasionally, attempted murder. Mercifully, very few psychiatrists have been killed. I'd wondered if Paul Kirk had developed a paranoid psychosis, but in reality he met none of the diagnostic criteria. Julia certainly didn't.

'Michael, was there anything else?' I asked, coming out of my reverie.

'Well, I've got no clinical stuff to discuss. What about you?'

'A purely clinical problem would be light relief at the moment.' I immediately regretted saying this, thinking it would stir up Michael's worries about me.

'For me, light relief would be seeing a patient who isn't depressed. Today's menu is a long list of depressives. What have I done to deserve it?'

'Be thankful you don't have a long list of paranoid psychotics.'

When we resorted to this kind of banter, we broke the rules. Calling someone a paranoid psychotic, a depressive, or a schizophrenic, was to label and dehumanise. In public we always said 'patients with...,' adding the diagnosis. In private we sometimes lapsed.

Michael realised he'd get nothing more out of me, and went back to his consulting room. I waited for my eleven-thirty patient, one of the most challenging on my books.

Sylvia Hill was thirty-three, and she'd been seeing me about once a week for nearly five years. She was a diagnostic and therapeutic nightmare. In fact, she made the psychiatrist's bible, the *Diagnostic and Statistical Manual*, look like a collection of fairy tales. The *Manual* now, in its fifth edition, divides mental illness into hundreds of distinct categories, all based on psychological symptoms. I thought of the many problems with this approach, which I saw as an attempt to enhance the status psychiatry has as a branch of medicine. Without their status as doctors, psychiatrists would be on a par with social workers, clinical psychologists, and other university trained mental health workers. But unlike medicine, I reflected, psychiatry has no bodily symptoms or reference points. An underlying physical basis has never been discovered for any of the most common or severe mental illnesses. The same psychological symptoms are found in many disorders, and the more symptoms a patient complained of, the more psychiatric diagnoses could be made. In Sylvia's case, I could apply over a dozen.

This absurd situation had led many mental health workers to reject the *Diagnostic and Statistical Manual*. But this didn't solve the problem. I knew from experience that patients sometimes read the *Manual* themselves, usually to dispute a diagnosis that I or someone else had given them. Many patients valued a psychiatric diagnosis, which they saw as something solid in a quicksand of uncertainty. Mental health workers still needed the shorthand of diagnosis to communicate effectively. For example, a properly made diagnosis of major depression immediately put antidepressant drugs foremost in the mind of an experienced clinician.

Although I didn't rely on it, I took pains to use the *Manual's* official jargon when writing to colleagues, and especially in medico-legal reports. Otherwise, I strove to understand my patients as human beings, seeing their symptoms as part of their own struggle with life. Often, adding a psychiatric diagnosis was helpful; the danger, I thought, lay in paying too much attention to it, which often obscured the real problems and how to fix them.

The phone on my desk rang. It was Janet letting me know that Sylvia had arrived. I braced myself and said I was ready to see her.

She sat down and looked at me blankly. As usual, she wore thick make-up including large false eye-lashes, the left one insecurely attached and threatening, each time she batted her eyelids, to come adrift. I felt sad as I looked at her face. Without the layers of make-up she would have been attractive. She had a strong, well formed face with high cheek bones and a broad, straight nose. It suddenly occurred to me that she used the make-up to hide the strength in her face, turning it into a caricature of the feminine.

Over the past few months, Sylvia had been fairly predictable. She'd start off by listing the complaints that had been distressing her the most, and then she'd weep. Next she'd get angry with me for not helping her. I waited for this sequence to unfold.

'It's been the OCD, George. It was so bad I nearly cancelled today, I thought I wouldn't be able to get ready on time.'

Sylvia, like Sarah, was one of the patients I saw through the scheme I'd organised with the NHS. She was the only one of these patients who called me George. She'd used the initials OCD as shorthand for obsessive compulsive disorder.

'Tell me exactly what symptoms you've been having.'

'Mainly the checking and tidying, but the washing's a problem, too. I'm back to counting fifty while I wash my hands, and I have to start again if I'm interrupted or lose count. And I had to check that I'd locked the front door six times when I left this morning. After the fifth, I'd managed to get to the bus stop, but I had to go all the way back and check again. Then I was lucky, I just caught a bus, otherwise I would've been late.'

If obsessive compulsive disorder had been Sylvia's only prob-lem, treatment would have been fairly straightforward. But she had numerous other syndromes.

'What about the panics and the social phobias?' I asked.

'Well, the OCD's been so bad I haven't left the house hardly. So the social fears weren't a problem. But I've had some whopping panic attacks, some real doozies.'

'And your mood?'

'Really depressed.'

Then the tears came. Sylvia's mascara ran down her cheeks. She took a tissue from the box I offered and dabbed carefully at her eyes. Miraculously, her false eye-lashes stayed in place. 'I'm more depressed since I've been seeing you, George, I'm sure I am. Before, I was so caught up with the OCD, panic and all that other stuff, I didn't realise how depressed I was. You've made me worse.'

In spite of all the practice I'd had, I still found it difficult to cope when patients attacked me. I was realist enough to accept that failures were inevitable. But they still hurt.

'I'm sorry, Sylvia. I do seem to have made you worse in some respects. But in other ways I think you've improved a lot.'

'Such as?' demanded Sylvia, a defiant look appearing on her tear-streaked face.

'Well...' I came to a stop, panicking a little when I couldn't think of any. Then I recalled how bad she'd been. 'Do you remember nearly five years ago, when you first started seeing me, you were convinced you had this bad smell coming out of you?'

Sylvia looked wary. The flow of tears eased. 'Yes, I do remember about that.'

'We did a lot of work on it, and it's no longer a problem. Isn't that true?'

'I suppose so,' said Sylvia begrudgingly.

Fixing her delusions about smelling had been a major therapeutic coup. She'd believed that her vagina gave off a rotten, disgusting smell that everyone noticed, even if they were the other side of the street. In reality, there was no smell. But the delusion kept her virtually housebound, horrified of going out because of the effect she had on people. Her mother, with whom she lived at the time, did all her shopping. Antipsychotic drugs hadn't helped. With great difficulty, I'd persuaded Sylvia to join a small therapeutic group that I ran. The other patients had repeatedly told her that she didn't smell. After many months, she finally believed them.

'Sometimes,' I said, 'when a symptom is cured, other ones take its place. That's happened to you. The social fears have taken over from the delusions of smell. But we've actually made a lot of progress with them.'

'Perhaps you're right, George. Perhaps it's not as bad as--'

Sylvia was cut off by the ringing of the phone on my desk. I picked it up, apologising. When I had a patient with me, Janet rang through only if there was no alternative. 'Yes, Janet?'

'George, there are two police officers here to see you. They say it's a matter of the utmost urgency. They insist on seeing you at once.'

'Tell them I'll be out as soon as I've explained the situation to my patient.' I put the phone down and took a deep breath. 'Sylvia, I'm really sorry, something's come up, it's never happened before. The police are outside, they say it's an emergency. We have to stop now.'

'It's nothing you've done, is it?' Sylvia's alarm and concern touched me in spite of mounting panic.

'Please don't worry, Sylvia, I'll be here in two weeks, I'm sure. See you then.'

We left the room together. In the waiting area stood a man and a woman, neither in uniform. The woman spoke first. 'Doctor Milton. I'm Inspector Naomi Douglas, Police Special Branch. This is Detective Sergeant Wills.' There was no offer of a handshake. 'We'd like to talk to you in private.'

'Come through to my consulting room.' They followed me through and accepted chairs. 'I'm afraid I've got no idea what this is about.'

'I'll come straight to the point,' said Inspector Douglas. 'We're investigating the death of Paul Kirk, the cabinet minister. We know he's a patient of yours.'

I was getting used to unpleasant surprises, but this one froze me.

'I have a search warrant.' She handed me some papers. 'Please read it. You'll see it gives us the power to search the premises and to remove any material we think might help with our enquiries.'

My eyes focussed on the first page, but its meaning wouldn't register. I put the papers aside. 'Please tell me what's going on.'

'Just before nine this morning,' replied Inspector Douglas, 'Mr Kirk's wife rang her husband's office and asked to speak to the head of security. She told him her husband was locked in his study, and had failed to respond to her repeated knocks. She had no key, apparently for security reasons. A private ambulance was called, and then I was contacted. Sergeant Wills is one of my assistants.'

Wills said nothing, staring at me impassively. In his mid-thirties and strongly built, his thick black hair was cut with surprising style.

'By the time Wills and I arrived,' continued Inspector Douglas, 'the two ambulance officers and Kirk's security chief had forced open his study door. I won't tell you what they found because I'm hoping you'll see it for yourself shortly. The ambulance officers wanted to try resuscitation, but fortunately the security chief was able to stop them. It was obvious that Kirk was dead, and he knew how important it was to touch nothing until we arrived.'

'Why do you want me to visit the scene?'

'Before I say any more, you must understand that all this is covered by the Official Secrets Act. The papers I gave you include a form stating you'll abide by its requirements. Please sign it.'

'Before I sign anything, I want to know a bit more about what's happening. Why the search warrant, and how on earth did you get it so quickly?'

'We're dealing with the suspicious death of a cabinet minister, a matter of national security. The British Security Service – better known as MI5 – is already involved. That's where I come in. The main function of Police Special Branch is to work with MI5 and serve as its public face. As soon as I learned from his security chief that Paul Kirk was a patient of yours, I applied for a search warrant. It was approved within two hours. As soon as I got it, I came round. You see, we weren't sure if you'd cooperate, as it's vital we have his case notes. Frankly, I've no intention of searching your rooms, but I've got the power to do so – and to remove all your files. It might be months before you got them back. I don't have to spell out what that would do to your practice.'

My feeling of paralysis was beginning to wear off. I had to find some kind of card to play. 'That sounds a bit like blackmail.'

'Doctor Milton. Just give me the case notes and come back and look at Paul Kirk's body. That's all I'm asking. Do that and I'll leave you alone. Refuse, and within five minutes I'll have this place so full of police officers you won't have room to move. You decide. But now. We can't waste any more time.'

I had no choice. 'OK. I'll sign. And I'll go with you to Paul's home. But only if you stop treating me like a suspect.'

Inspector Douglas smiled. 'I'm sorry. Force of habit. You're not on our wanted list. And there's no crime, is there?'

Perhaps she's human after all, I thought. Not unattractive. Early forties, trim, fit-looking, fashionable business suit. I'd never pick her as a police officer. After completing the paperwork I stood up and led the way through to the filing area. Janet was hovering nervously nearby.

'Please give me the keys,' said Inspector Douglas. 'I want to get the file out myself.'

I showed her which key it was and pointed to the correct drawer. As she pulled it out, I remembered the USB. Thinking it was the safest place, I'd attached it to Paul's case folder. Inspector Douglas noticed it at once.

'I see there's a USB in here. Do you usually record your therapy sessions?'

I was beyond panic. A sense of hopelessness engulfed me. 'I almost never do. That's the only one.' Now wasn't the time to explain. Instead I reminded inspector Douglas that I had patients booked solid until five thirty, and wanted to make the visit to Kirk's as brief as possible.

'Allow two hours,' she suggested.

'That means you should be back by two thirty,' said Janet. 'I'll do my best to smooth things out. Don't worry, George, I won't leave the office, I'll send out for some sandwiches. And I'll let Michael know what's happening.'

We arrived at the Kirk residence about fifteen minutes later. The private ambulance was parked outside. There were no patrol cars, but I assumed our unmarked police vehicle wasn't the only one close by. On the way, Inspector Douglas revealed an assumption that I was an expert in autoerotic asphyxia. But, although I'd studied it intensively, I had little first-hand knowledge.

The house was three storeys and end of terrace. We went straight to Paul's study, which was on the ground floor. The door was guarded by a stocky young man who I assumed was another of Inspector Douglas' assistants. There was no sign of Paul's wife, and I didn't ask about her.

The body was still hanging from a hook in the ceiling, feet on the floor, knees bent at an angle of about thirty degrees.

'Of course we had to leave the body suspended,' said Inspector Douglas, grimacing slightly. 'One of our forensic pathologists has already examined the scene. He took some blood for toxicology and measured the body temperature – obviously that couldn't wait – but otherwise the body hasn't been disturbed. As soon as you've completed your inspection, we'll take it down.'

I studied the room from the door. Paul's large mahogany desk faced me. There were two windows, one on the right, facing an alleyway, and the other opposite me in what was the rear wall of the house. Neither was barred, and the one on the right was open about six inches. A large antique cabinet, a small conference table, and several chairs made up the rest of the furniture. A built-in book case took up the entire length of the left hand wall.

I walked over to Paul's suspended body. A leather harness was fitted tightly under both arms and round the upper part of his chest. It was attached to a rope which passed through a metal ring hanging from the ceiling hook. The other end of the rope formed a slip knot round Paul's neck, which was protected by a padded circular collar.

In my reading I'd come across similar devices. Asphyxiation relied on bending the knees, which tightened the noose round the neck. Straightening the knees immediately loosened it again. A harness like Paul's was unusual. It meant that both his chest and neck were constricted at the same time.

Without a safety mechanism, Paul's apparatus was very dangerous. If he lost consciousness during self-asphyxiation, the full weight of his body would be suspended. Even though the load was shared with the harness, the pressure round his neck would be more than enough to cause death by strangulation.

Then I noticed a length of thin nylon cord hanging from the harness. The free end was tied in a loop. 'Is it OK if I pick up this length of nylon cord?' I asked Inspector Douglas.

'If you're going to touch anything, put these on.' She gestured to Wills, who handed me a pair of surgical gloves.

I moved a chair over to the body and picked up the length of cord. Then I stood on the chair and looked closely at the hook and metal ring. The hook was painted the same colour as the ceiling, which made it almost invisible to the casual observer. The ring was hinged and designed to split open if a small lever on its outer side was pulled out. The metal ring would have fitted over the hook perfectly. So this is the safety mechanism, I thought. If Paul lost consciousness and his body sagged, the nylon cord would tighten. This pulled on the lever and opened the metal ring, releasing the rope. Although he might be injured when he fell to the floor, he certainly wouldn't die of strangulation. But why wasn't the safety device connected up?

'Well, any conclusions?' asked inspector Douglas. 'How does what you've seen fit in with Kirk's case history?'

I wondered how much I should reveal. The only card I held was my special knowledge of Paul's psyche, so I decided to play it carefully.

'He's rigged up an extraordinarily sophisticated piece of apparatus,' I replied.

'Obviously he's fine-tuned it over the years. It includes a virtually foolproof safety mechanism, but for some reason it wasn't connected up. That's why he died.'

I didn't mention my concerns about his clothing. He was almost fully dressed, but he had told me that he removed all his clothes before starting his ritual, and usually put on a pair of woman's knickers.

'Surely that means suicide,' said Inspector Douglas. 'No safety mechanism and almost fully clothed.'

'I agree. Perhaps only an autopsy will clarify things further. And a thorough search of his study. If you haven't done that already.'

'His keys were on his desk and we were able to open all the locked drawers. I've got security clearance for that. In one drawer we found a collection of straps, some lengths of rope, and a metal ring, obviously a spare. Also two pairs of women's panties. We couldn't tell whether he wore them, sniffed them, or what. We found nothing else unusual. Oh, I didn't tell you about the safe. It's concealed in the bottom of the cabinet, bolted securely to the floor and we think to the wall as well. There's a key, which we have, and a combination lock. We've no idea of the access code, so it'll take a while to open.'

The autopsy was scheduled for nine-thirty tomorrow morning. Since tomorrow was Saturday, and I had nothing else on, I asked to be there. Inspector Douglas agreed, subject to the chief forensic pathologist's approval. This was a formality, but she'd ring me if there were any problems. Once this had been agreed on, there was no reason for me to stay.

'Any chance of a lift back to Harley Street?'

'Wills and I are staying on until the body's safely in the ambulance,' said Inspector Douglas. 'But there's no reason why Barry'– she pointed to the man who'd guarded the door - 'shouldn't run you back.'

I was in my rooms again by two-twenty. Knowing I could rely on Janet's discretion, I outlined what had happened at the Kirk residence.

'I hope this is the end of your traumas, George. I'd like to see you back to your old self.'

'I hope so too, Janet. But even if this sorts itself out, there's still Julia Richmond.'

Just then my two-thirty patient came in, and I went through to my consulting room, armed with the case notes Janet handed me.

I barely coped with the afternoon's work. I couldn't stop thinking about what might happen when Inspector Douglas accessed the USB she'd found in Paul's case file. And I wondered why I hadn't heard anything from Julia. At five-thirty I ushered out my last patient and walked home to Baker Street in a daze.

Back in my sitting room I resisted a gin and tonic, surprised at my will power. There's not much I can do, I thought, except wait. Should I try and contact Julia to warn her she'd be getting a visit from Inspector Douglas as soon as she'd heard the recording? If I warned Julia, she'd be very angry that I'd taped our last conversation, but might have time to come up with a convincing explanation. If I didn't, she'd be even more angry with me. At the thought of Julia's rage, I picked up the phone and dialled.

'Julia, it's George Milton.'

'I was going to contact you when I was ready. What do you want, George?'

'It's complicated. I can't explain over the phone. You've heard about your stepfather, of course.'

'My stepfather?'

'You mean you don't know? Haven't you been contacted or heard anything on the news?'

'George, I don't know what you're talking about.'

'Oh, God! Julia, he's dead. Paul Kirk's dead.' I waited for Julia's response. It came after a brief silence.

'If this is a joke, it's in very poor taste.'

'It's no joke. The police were at my rooms this morning, wanting me to "help with their enquiries." They've taken Paul's case notes, but they didn't ask about yours. Unfortunately, there's another way they might connect you with Paul's death. That's why I need to see you. As soon as possible.'

'Christ, George, now you've really got me worried. Can't you tell me on the phone?'

'Like I said, it's complicated, but there's another reason. You'll think I'm paranoid, but my phone could be tapped.'

'And I suppose your flat's bugged, too.' More than a hint of sarcasm. 'So you'll want to meet me in a crowded public place. It's a good thing I haven't got agoraphobia. What about Waterloo Station, under the clock?'

There was a hysteria in her voice. I tried to sound reassuring. 'Julia, my place will be fine. How soon can you get here?'

'Fifteen minutes. I'll let myself in.'

Waiting for Julia to arrive, my willpower ebbed, and I poured a gin and tonic. But I was light on the gin. I tried not to feel bad about the recording. There was no other way I could protect myself. It wasn't my fault that Inspector Douglas had got hold of it. Julia would want to listen to the recording I'd kept at the flat. If she knew exactly what was on it, she might be able to come up with an explanation that satisfied Special Branch. Or whoever else was now involved.

Julia let herself in. As she came through into the sitting room, I could see I'd been right about her near-hysteria. Her eyes were unfocussed and her face flushed.

'The usual?' I asked as she sat down on the sofa.

'I'll have whiskey, just a dash of soda. Now, please tell me what the hell is going on.'

I switched on the recorder. Julia listened in silence for a few minutes, and then asked me to turn it off. I'd expected her to become enraged, but she just stared at me, her face calm. Perhaps it was the whiskey. I'd poured a large one, and she'd been sipping steadily.

'Is this the only conversation you've recorded?'

'The only one, I swear. I couldn't think of any other ... insurance ... against your blackmail.'

'Well, if this is what all the fuss is about, I'm not too worried. I don't need you to help me to – wait a minute. Are you recording this?'

'Absolutely not... This is the only recording device I have.'

'What about your consulting rooms. Did you record any of our sessions?'

'No. I never record sessions without permission. And I thought you were seeing me in good faith. But it isn't just the tape, Julia.' I outlined the circumstances of Paul's death, explaining that

Special Branch was involved because it was clearly a matter of national security. I was just about to mention the discovery of the USB when Julia burst into tears. She sobbed uncontrollably for several minutes. I found myself sitting on the sofa, an arm around her shoulders. I feared she might push me away, but instead she leaned into me, her head resting against my shoulder. I said nothing, waiting for her tears to stop.

'I'm sorry,' said Julia. 'The tears just came. I think it was you describing the body, hanging there. It hadn't sunk in. Then it hit me, suddenly it was real. Something I've wanted so desperately. But now it's happened, I feel grief. Only grief.'

'Grief is natural, Julia. You've lost the dream, the hope, of killing your stepfather. Fate has stolen your revenge, or at least the fantasy of it. And that's been your reason for living since you remembered what he did.'

The phone rang. It was Inspector Douglas. 'Doctor Milton. I've just finished listening to the recording in Kirk's file. Kirk's death was on the five o'clock news. If Ms Richmond's heard it, she may have flown the coop. I've just sent a car round to her address. I'm sending a car to collect you now. I want you in my office. And I won't be letting you go until I'm fully satisfied you had no involvement in Kirk's death.' She put the phone down before I could say anything more in my defence.

This was even worse than I'd feared. The now familiar feelings of emptiness returned, this time accompanied by nausea and a sense of dread.

'You look as if you've seen a ghost, George,' said Julia, her eyes now almost dry.

'Listen carefully, Julia. Police Special Branch found a copy of the recording in my rooms. The woman in charge of the investigation, that was her on the phone, she's listened to it. They've sent a car to pick you up. No, not here, your place. But another car's coming here now, for me. You have to make a decision. To run, or stay here with me. If we stick together, they've got to believe we had nothing to do with Paul's death.'

'How do you know I didn't?'

'Your reaction, Julia. Impossible to fake, even for you. And I know how convincing you can be.'

'I'm a lawyer, I've got a reputation for integrity, a good track record. I'd be crazy to run, it'd be an admission of guilt. I'll stay here and go with you. We can face this together.'

The intercom buzzed. 'Jesus, the cops already,' I said. Once I'd confirmed this, I pressed the button that opened the street entrance. Julia and I waited just inside the flat door. We opened it at the first knock and identified ourselves to the two plain clothes men standing on the threshold.

The older of the two introduced himself as Detective Sergeant Briggs. 'I won't caution you formally,' he said. 'This is a Special Branch matter, though I'm with the CID. They're both based at Scotland Yard. That's where we're taking you.'

As we turned off Whitehall into Great Scotland Yard, I felt a powerful sense of foreboding. Less than a week ago, my life had been ordered and stable. The future had seemed secure. Now, I was certain of nothing.

FOUR

Flanked by Detective Sergeant Briggs and his colleagues, we were taken into that part of New Scotland Yard occupied by Special Branch. I saw the familiar face of Detective Sergeant Wills. 'OK, Briggs,' he said. 'We'll take it from here. Thanks for your help.'

Wills escorted us down a corridor and knocked on a door, which was quickly opened. Sitting in the room were Inspector Douglas and two men, one of whom rose to greet us. About my height, but slimmer in build, he looked in his late forties. There was no trace of grey in his straight, light brown hair. His face was thin, and when he turned it towards Julia I noticed a prominent hooked nose. There was an air of vitality about him, and his gaze was forceful and direct.

'This is Superintendent Brock,' said Inspector Douglas. 'My immediate superior in Special Branch.' She invited us to sit. Our chairs, with hers and Brock's, formed a rough square. Wills and the man who had let us in sat by the door.

'I've assumed direct control of this case,' said the superintendent, 'but day-to-day operations will remain the responsibility of Inspector Douglas. The man sitting next to Wills is Commander Richards of Military Intelligence, Section 5, responsible for domestic counter-intelligence and security.'

'Better known as MI5,' called out Richards, evoking a strangled sound from Brock. I couldn't tell if it meant amusement or disapproval.

'He and I are working together on this,' continued Brock. 'You may wonder why Briggs picked you up. We don't always have the resources to do everything ourselves, but we have an excellent relationship with the local CID, who help us when they can. We thought it might be difficult to find Ms Richmond. But as it turned out'– a broad but slightly sinister smile – 'we killed two birds with one stone.'

Inspector Douglas took over. 'I've got two files here. One, courtesy of our friends in the CID, concerns Ms Richmond and allegations of rape against a person she's refused to name. The other contains Paul Kirk's case notes. And a transcript of the recording that was with them. I've made copies for both of you.' She passed them over. 'We'd very much like to hear what you have to say. Especially, Ms Richmond, about where you describe in detail your plans to kill Paul Kirk.'

'Are we being formally charged with anything?' asked Julia. 'If we are, I'd like to contact my solicitor.'

'At this stage,' replied Superintendent Brock, 'we aren't laying charges. And you have my word that this interview is off the record. It's not being taped.'

Julia looked at me. 'George, why don't I try and explain? You can comment when I've finished.'

I nodded agreement, wondering how closely Julia would stick to the truth.

'It's beginning to seem ridiculous, but I really did want to kill Paul Kirk.' Then Julia told her story. It pretty well matched the one she'd told me. When she got to the rape allegations, Superintendent Brock interrupted:

'So you invented the rape to blackmail Doctor Milton into helping you?'

'Yes. I'm afraid I did.'

'But sexual intercourse did take place between you at his rooms?'

'Yes.'

'If we had proof of that, it would add credibility. Doctor Milton, will you agree to provide a tissue sample for matching with the semen recovered from Ms Richmond?'

I hesitated. 'Look. You're putting me in an impossible position. If it's proved that I had sex with Julia, who was my patient at the time, I'll be struck off the register. That's the end of my career.'

'I can guarantee it will never get to the General Medical Council,' said the superintendent. 'Unless Ms Richmond complains about you. But you won't, will you?' He fixed his gaze on Julia, his expression suggesting a command rather than a question.

'Of course not. The sooner I can forget about all this, the better.'

I didn't have much choice. 'OK. You can have your sample.'

'Excellent. We have in-house facilities, lab staff on twenty-four-hour call. Wills will arrange for someone to come over now. They prefer blood, just a few drops. White cells are perfect matching material, I gather.'

He paused, redirecting his attention to Julia. 'Ms Richmond. You've admitted wanting to kill Paul Kirk. Can you prove you didn't? An alibi, for example? Our forensic pathologist estimated the time of death at about one in the morning Based on body and room temperature, that's accurate within an hour or so either way.'

'I slept at my flat last night, alone,' said Julia. 'I went to bed at my usual time, around eleven-thirty, and got up at seven-thirty. But I can't prove it.'

'What about Paul's wife,' I asked. 'Did she notice anything unusual around the time of death? And how did she know he was in his study when she started knocking? Couldn't he have gone out?'

'I asked her the same questions,' said Inspector Douglas. 'They had separate bedrooms. His wife went to bed about ten-thirty. Kirk was in his study, working, when she went to say goodnight. He said he still had a lot to do, and would go on for another couple of hours. Then he'd get up early and finish in time for an important meeting in his office at nine. He hadn't left by eight-forty-five, and that's when she started knocking. When she rang his security staff they confirmed he hadn't arrived at work. Apparently, he often locked his study when he was in it, he said for security reasons. If you're wondering about visitors, he didn't have any that evening. Unless he let someone in after his wife went to bed. There's an elaborate alarm system, by the way. When it's armed, the house is a virtual fortress. No resident housekeeper, just a daily. She has a solid alibi.'

'Just how am I supposed to have done it?' demanded Julia, an angry edge to her voice. 'If he let me in, how exactly did I kill him?'

'We might be able to tell you that after the autopsy,' replied Superintendent Brock facetiously. 'But there's another way you could have got in. One of his windows was open. It faced onto an alleyway. You could have used a step ladder to climb in while he was out of the room.'

'Supposing,' I said, 'the intruder knew enough about Paul's apparatus to loosen the knot on the safety cord? It would have to be tied again after the... accident... but it's theoretically possible.' I noticed that Julia was glaring at me, and I realised I'd just deepened the hole she was in. I changed tack. 'His wife says she's got no key, but if she's lying, she could have done it, or let someone else in.'

'We could speculate endlessly,' said Superintendent Brock. 'But it's pointless until we know the autopsy findings. It's nearly nine-thirty. I suggest we finish now. I'm taking a risk, but my instinct is to believe you, Ms Richmond. You can go home. And you, Doctor Milton. I'll send a car to pick you up at nine tomorrow morning so you can attend the autopsy at nine-thirty. I'd like the four of us to meet again after the autopsy. I'm not sure where, so I'll arrange for you to be collected at ten, Ms Richmond. I know you'll be at home. Now, good night to you both.'

It took less than a minute for the technician, who was waiting in the corridor, to take a sample of my blood. Then Wills led us back to the Great Scotland Yard entrance, where a car was waiting. Julia was dropped off first, and I was back in my flat by nine-forty-five. I still had a land line, so I checked my answering machine. There was one message, from Paul's solicitor, asking me to ring him at home urgently. I dialled at once.

'Adam Spencer here.'

'Mr Spencer, it's George Milton. Sorry to ring so late, but you said it was urgent.'

'No, I'm glad you rang. It's about Paul Kirk. You know he's dead, of course. He instructed me to deliver you an envelope, immediately and in person, in the event of his death. I heard about it on the evening news, and as soon as I'd verified it, I rang you.'

'Have you got it with you?'

'Yes, here in my safe.'

'Can I come and get it now?'

A pause. 'It's late. But you're on Baker Street, aren't you? You can get to my place in about half an hour.' He gave me an address in Wimbledon. 'I'll be waiting for you.'

I arrived at Spencer's home just before eleven. He answered the door almost at once.

'I'm sorry, I can't invite you in. We've got guests. Here's the envelope. I've no idea what's in it. He asked me to keep the whole thing strictly secret. But if the police ask questions, I'll have to be honest with them.'

'I understand. Look, if you do have to tell the police, would you mind letting me know?'

'I suppose that's the least I can do.'

'Thanks. Sorry to have disturbed you. Good night.'

I'd parked in the street. As I was turning to walk back down the gravel drive, I recalled telling Julia that my land line might be tapped. Supposing I was right? Whoever was listening would know about the letter. Could I have been followed tonight?

Instead of walking down the driveway, I crept across the lawn to the garden wall. It wasn't high enough to cover me, but I was able to duck beneath a large rhododendron bush. From there I could observe the street without being seen. At first I saw nothing unusual. Then I noticed a large, dark coloured car parked on the opposite side of the street about forty yards away. Someone was sitting in the driver's seat. I felt a surge of panic. Then I told myself I was being paranoid. In upper-middle class Wimbledon, chauffeured cars were not uncommon. Feeling calmer, I walked out of the driveway and got into my car. As I drove away, the car pulled out. Another surge of panic. I turned left, and the car followed me. I slowed down, and the car slowed down too. I did a U-turn and turned left. No sign of the car. I turned onto the main road and headed for home. I didn't see the car after that.

When I got back to my flat, I was exhausted. I'd almost persuaded myself that the car episode had been a coincidence. Until I looked out of my sitting room window and saw the same car – or a very similar one – draw up about thirty yards away. Then it occurred to me that Superintendent Brock, or perhaps Commander Richards, had arranged for me to be tailed in case I decided to run. I began to relax. I picked up the landline phone, listening for a click or any unusual sound that suggested a wire tap. I heard only the dialling tone. Of course, they may have been able to monitor my mobile, and I had to assume they had the technology. This meant I had to take great care about what I said.

I opened the envelope. Inside were six sheets of paper. The first was a letter from Paul, dated only a week earlier. 'Dear George, by now you will know of my death. The contents of this envelope are your insurance policy. Adam Spencer is totally trustworthy, but he won't lie to protect you, so you can't assume that knowledge of this communication will remain secret. Keep it somewhere very safe. I've included a "dummy" letter which gives false information. You can represent it as the entire communication if you're forced to yield a document. The other contents explain themselves. I'm truly sorry to have put you in this position. Good luck.' It was simply signed with his Christian name.

I looked at the other sheets. My heart started to pound unpleasantly and my temples throbbed. One listed the names and position of three people Paul had persuaded to help in his treasonous data transfer. I didn't recognise any of the names but their status astonished me. A civil servant almost at the top in the Ministry of Defence, another of similar standing in the Home Office, and a divisional director in MI5. As Paul had said, he'd had exactly the right contacts. One in the defence ministry to put the package together, one in MI5 to make sure its transfer was fully cloaked, and someone in the Home Office to help tie up any loose ends. Perfect. Except that now I knew about it.

Apart from the dummy letter, the remaining sheets outlined, with the help of diagrams, exactly what technology had been transferred. I understood almost none of it.

I couldn't see how this knowledge was going to protect me, but it was now past midnight and I was too exhausted to think straight. I had enough wits to separate the dummy letter from the rest of the documents. I replaced it in the envelope which I then taped carefully inside the cover of one of the many large books on the shelves in my sitting room. I then repeated the process separately with each of the remaining sheets. They were now both fairly safe and easy for me to get as I devised a simple mnemonic to help me remember which books I'd chosen. Then I went to bed.

The intercom buzzed at exactly nine o'clock the next morning. I got into the waiting car. The driver said nothing as we weaved through the tail-end of rush hour. Security was high in the mortuary area, and I was taken to the autopsy room by a uniformed guard. I knew the smell from my days as a medical student and house officer: the aroma of newly opened bodies mixed with the smell of antiseptic and an underlying odour of decay. It still evoked a mixture of excitement, fear and revulsion.

As I walked in, I recognised both Inspector Douglas and Superintendent Brock. 'This one's a bit late for psychotherapy, eh Doc?' quipped Brock, trying to put me at ease. 'And a bit past interrogation, I'd say,' I growled back. Douglas introduced me to the chief forensic pathologist, who was going to do the autopsy himself. No-one introduced me to his assistant, a woman whose face was hidden by a surgical mask.

The room was large and Paul's body wasn't the only one laid out on a slab. I avoided looking at the others, although I was surprised at my lack of squeamishness so far. Perhaps, I mused, I was becoming immune to stress, or my body had finally run out of the chemicals needed for a response to it.

The pathologist reported his findings as he progressed, his words picked up by a recording device. First he examined the skin, including the hands, feet and head. Then he and his assistant, with a little help from me, turned the body over, paying particular attention to the neck. 'There is no ligature mark on the neck and no evidence of external trauma other than a few petechial haemorrhages. There is slight bruising to the medial aspect of both axillae compatible with rope constriction.'

The body was turned over again, and the pathologist carefully examined the genital area. 'No sign of seminal fluid or penile tumescence, and no evidence of external trauma.'

He then started the internal examination, which included a close look at the soft tissue of the neck. Samples of most organs were taken for further analysis. 'Well, that about wraps it up,' said the pathologist. 'Let me go and change, and I'll join you for coffee. I'll give you a summary of my findings in non-technical terms, although you'll have got the gist of it already.'

We assembled in a comfortable room just outside olfactory range of the autopsy area. The chief pathologist joined us five minutes later. 'Well, I've no doubt Paul Kirk died of strangulation.

There's little sign of external trauma to the neck – which was protected by a padded collar – but the underlying soft tissue shows clear evidence of damage, mainly haemorrhagic infiltration. The face is congested, with the tell-tale pinpoint bleeds in the whites of the eyes. Other small bleeds on the face and neck indicate rupture of small blood vessels. This pattern of bleeding is the result of congestion above the constricting ligature.'

'There's no sign of any physical struggle?' asked Inspector Douglas. 'I'm thinking perhaps he was strung up by someone else.'

'None at all,' replied the pathologist. 'I think we must assume that he placed himself in the apparatus. Only if he was first totally immobilised could he have been placed there by others. And I don't see how that could've been done without leaving marks on the body.'

'What did you learn from examining the genital area?' I asked.

'There was no sign of any semen, either on the penis or the clothing. And there was no erection. But if there had been, it wouldn't have been proof of sexual activity, because spontaneous erection and even ejaculation sometimes occur in death by strangulation. I've got the full toxicology results, by the way. He was drug free, except for traces of alcohol and a short-acting benzodiazepine, the kind you take to help you sleep. He would have taken it the night before.'

'It's important that we've excluded a physical struggle,' said Superintendent Brock. 'If it was murder, then it was done by loosening the knot on the safety mechanism and then retying it after death had occurred. There's no evidence for this. I'm convinced it was either accident or suicide, and given the apparent lack of sexual activity, inclined to the latter.'

'Unless the tissue sections come up with something totally unexpected, I shall propose suicide,' said the coroner.

'I'd like you to come to my office, Doctor Milton, said Brock. 'There are important matters to discuss. Ms Richmond will be joining us shortly. Since the Spycatcher trial, Her Majesty's Government has learned how very difficult it can be to keep Official Secrets... er... secret. If the verdict is suicide by hanging, there won't be any need to reveal Kirk's autoerotic activities and there won't be a motive for journalists to ferret deeper.'

Superintendent Brock stopped talking as we went through a security point not far from his office. Before we reached it, his secretary appeared, handing him a note. He glanced at it while gesturing for Inspector Douglas and me to sit down.

'Doctor Milton, I took the fairly routine precaution of having a car stationed near your flat last night. You went out, met someone briefly, and spotted the tail on your way back. We assume Adam Spencer gave you some documents. I want them. To be blunt, if you don't hand them over, I'll be contacting the GMC, telling them about your dalliance with Ms Richmond. I've got confirmation here that the semen recovered from her was yours.'

I'd expected some tough bargaining, but nothing as low as this. To my surprise, I didn't panic or get my usual bodily reaction to sudden shocks.

'You'll think me totally dishonourable,' Brock went on. 'But I'm concerned only with national security. To protect it, I believe any means are justified.'

The phone on his desk rang and he immediately picked it up. 'Fine, send her in.'

Moments later, Julia entered.

'Perhaps I can bring Ms Richmond up to date,' offered Inspector Douglas. Brock nodded agreement, and Douglas outlined the chief pathologist's findings and the likely verdict.

'Does this mean I'm off the hook? Oh damn!' said Julia. 'Another pun. They just come out. It's only since I started therapy with Doctor Milton.'

None of us responded to Julia's attempt at light relief.

'Well,' replied Brock, 'since we now think murder is only a remote possibility, we don't really need a suspect. But there's still the matter of your false allegations against Doctor Milton. You're a lawyer, dammit! You know you've committed a serious offence. But I may be able to prevent any charges against you. You see, Doctor Milton has certain documents we need. They concern Paul Kirk. If he doesn't deliver them, we'll be sending the GMC a copy of your rape allegations with DNA proof of intercourse.'

'But you can't do that,' exclaimed Julia. 'We had a deal. You promised to keep the DNA results confidential.'

'I'm afraid they can,' I said. 'And they will if they have to. It will all be incredibly messy. We'll both be struck off for professional misconduct, and you'll face criminal prosecution as well. Our reputations would be destroyed.'

'It's up to you, Doctor Milton,' said Brock, 'Give up the documents and I guarantee neither matter will go any further.'

'It's clear your word means very little. But I've got no choice. You can have the document. It's back at my flat.'

'Document? Is there only one?'

'Yes, superintendent, there's just one, a letter.'

'To be on the safe side, Inspector Douglas will come back with you and collect it herself.'

That was the end of the meeting. In less than half an hour Douglas and I were back in Baker Street. I went straight over to the book holding the dummy letter, and handed the envelope to the inspector. She took out the letter and started to read. Of course I knew that it said nothing about the other material that Paul had given me.

'It's more or less what I expected. We had suspicions that Kirk was up to something, but he was so well protected that we couldn't get any details. Illegal transfer of nuclear technology was one of our hunches, and this confirms it. We thought it involved a Middle Eastern country, but according to this it's one of the newly independent Russian states. And the names of the three other people involved are a bit of a surprise. I know Kirk thought he was protecting you by giving you this information, but I don't see how.'

'He obviously thought his own life was in danger, or perhaps he was planning suicide, though he gave me no hint of it. He feared I'd become a target of espionage groups after his death if it got out that I was his psychiatrist. Especially if there were rumours he'd been selling secret information. Anything sensitive he confided in me might have cash value on the market, and he was worried about rough play. The letter was just to tell me what he'd done. He thought it'd be safer for me if I knew.'

'The logic's a bit obscure, but the story makes sense of a kind. I'll let Superintendent Brock know what you told me. I think you can start to relax. So can Ms Richmond. We'll make sure no charges or complaints are laid against either of you.'

After the inspector left, I fixed myself a gin and tonic. I thought I deserved one. Douglas had accepted the carefully constructed letter as the whole story, and I assumed Brock would, too. I decided to ring Julia with the news.

'Julia, it's me, George. I've handed over the letter to Douglas. She says we can both relax.'

'But do you trust them?'

'Not an inch. But they--' I stopped suddenly, remembering the phone might be tapped. 'They've got what they want. And as long as they've got that stuff on us, they know we'll keep quiet.'

'What are you doing this afternoon?'

'Nothing. Except trying to relax.'

'I've nothing on either. What if I come round?'

I hesitated. I was still angry at Julia, though I understood why she'd been so treacherous and conniving. 'Well... as long as you don't expect me to be a live wire. I'm more likely to fall asleep.'

Julia arrived just before two o'clock. Neither of us had eaten, so we walked to a local café for a snack. Sitting there, I was again entranced by her presence. I knew she was a siren, but I still wanted a relationship with her, a fresh one. This meant burying the old one.

'Julia, I'll be honest. I'm still very angry with you, angry and hurt. But I'd like not to be. I'd like us to become... friends.'

'George, I know I've treated you badly, very badly. But as a psychiatrist you must know that I was... kind of crazy. All I could think of was getting revenge on my stepfather. And you were the key to that. Now, it all seems ridiculous. That unexpected grief I felt when you told me he was dead. It's wearing off, and I'm beginning to feel... more human, somehow. And fresher, cleaner. What I hoped would happen.'

Julia was interrupted by the arrival of our focaccias. We ordered two more glasses of wine. Getting drunk together didn't seem a bad idea.

'What I find most difficult, Julia, is how utterly ruthless you were. You used me without mercy, with no regard for my feelings, my well being, for me as a person.' Suddenly I realised I'd described exactly how her stepfather had treated her.

'George, I feel awful about it, really I do. I have to believe it was a kind of madness. Normally I'm so rational, so controlled. Basically, I'm an honest, straightforward person. It wasn't me who was blackmailing you. It was a ... a desperate twelve-year-old girl.'

I thought Julia was going to cry, but she held back her tears. Instinctively I reached out and took her hand.

'That's how I see it, Julia. But it'll take a while before my feelings stop hurting, before I can start to trust you. That's if you want to go on seeing me.'

'I want to learn to trust you. That's my biggest problem, well, you know of course. Trusting anyone. I've never been able to, not since...'

'Since your stepfather.'

'Yes.'

This time the tears came. We sat in silence until Julia's eyes cleared.

'Do you think I still need therapy, George?'

'I don't know. It depends on what you want. I think now the buried memories have surfaced and Paul is dead... you'll work through the trauma of his abuse. But you'll still be left with problems of trust, intimacy, giving and receiving affection. These are problems that often respond to long-term psychotherapy. Of course, I can't be your therapist anymore. But I can refer you to someone else. What I should have done in the first place.' I gave her a smile which she returned, its warmth rekindling my desire for her.

'Let me think about it. Why don't we go back to your place? Start getting to know each other as normal people.'

At that moment, I'm sure we both believed this could happen. We spent the rest of the afternoon in my flat, doing self-consciously normal things. Reading the papers, even watching the television. The news had broken about Paul's death, but there were no details, and the reports simply mentioned the likelihood of suicide. We snacked again in the evening and, as we sipped a good sauvignon blanc, Julia raised the delicate matter of the night's sleeping arrangements.

'George, I don't feel like being alone tonight. I'd like to stay with you. Tomorrow I've got to work. I know it's Sunday, but normally I spend most of Saturday at the office, so I've got a lot of catching up to do. Quite often I work the whole weekend. They expect a hell of a lot from junior partners.'

I was going to say something about Julia expecting a hell of a lot from herself when I remembered I wasn't her psychiatrist any more. 'I'd love you to stay the night, Julia.'

'No assumptions, George. I still think you're one of the most attractive men I've ever met. But so far our relationship has been bizarre, to say the least. Let's be patient, take our time, see what happens. I want you, really I do. But not now, not yet.'

'You're right. We don't have a relationship yet. Just a history of manipulation and deceit.' I trailed off, noting the edge in my voice. 'And talking of deceit, there's something I haven't told you. We were talking about learning to trust each other. Well, I've just decided to be serious about it. I'm going to show you something that literally puts my life in your hands.' I sounded melodramatic, but Julia took me seriously.

'Are you sure you want to do this?'

'No. But if I want honesty and trust, I've no choice. And you're involved in this mess as much as I am, so you have a right to know.' I went over to the book case and removed five volumes. From each I took the single sheet I'd stuck there, handing them to Julia.

'Oh my God! Then what you gave to Inspector Douglas was a dummy letter.'

'Yes. She seemed to fall for it. I don't know about Brock, though.'

'What if they discover it's a dummy?'

'I haven't thought that far ahead, I daren't. I'm praying it'll work out, all settle down, that they'll keep their promise.'

'All this technical stuff, what does it mean?'

I outlined to Julia exactly what Paul had told me. 'Apart from the Special Branch, no-one else has approached you?'

'No. Almost no-one knew Paul was seeing me. If that became more widely known --'

'Then,' Julia broke in, 'you might be in serious danger. Not just from anyone interested in what you know... but anyone wanting to make sure you keep quiet about it.'

'If it comes to that, I'm sure I can rely on Special Branch to protect me.'

'Can you? What if they find out you've sold them a dummy?'

'Then I might be in real trouble. I could go direct to MI5. Try and contact Commander Richards. His name wasn't on Kirk's list of collaborators, thank God.'

'I hate to say this, George, but can you trust anyone? The Home Office traitor really bothers me. I know the Director-General of MI5 reports to the Home Secretary. I don't know about Special Branch, whether it's the Home Office, the Chief Constable, or what, but they're all in bed together anyway.'

It was just too difficult for me to respond to Julia's concerns. 'On Monday morning I'm going to the office at the usual time. I'm going to focus on my work. Life will return to normal.'

Tactfully, Julia didn't pursue the matter. She gave me back the secret papers, and I replaced them in the same books. We spent the rest of the evening watching television. Then we retired to our separate bedrooms.

I woke to the smell of fresh ground coffee. Julia was in the kitchen, fully dressed and eating toast. I approached her with a smile. We embraced, the contact causing tingles in my skin.

'I woke up in the early hours, George. I was tempted to creep into your room. But instead I went back to sleep and had sexy dreams.'

'I just had the dreams. If you had crept into my room, I'd have kicked you out, of course.'

'Liar!' Julia lunged at me playfully, and we dodged and weaved round the kitchen.

Sitting down, I thought of Celia. We'd never played such silly games together.

'I'm off,' said Julia as she finished her toast. 'I feel really grubby so I'm going home to shower and change. Then I'll go straight to the office, probably stay late. I'll ring you when I get home, if it's the right side of midnight.'

The moment she'd gone I felt a pang of loneliness. Celia has never affected me like that. To distract myself, I wandered out to get the Sunday papers. Since my days as a medical student I'd had the habit of browsing through them on Sunday mornings, sometimes well into the afternoon. It was a comforting ritual, the more so since Celia had left. I bought the Sunday editions of *The Times* and *The Guardian*. Back in my sitting room, I started with the *Sunday Times*. Much of the front page was devoted to an article on Paul Kirk. It focussed on his career, highlighting his achievements. His 'suicide' was not mentioned. The article simply referred to 'his tragic death.'

Mid-afternoon I went for a jog around Regents Park. It was the first time I'd jogged for at least a year, so I mixed it with walking. Perhaps, I thought, I'm finally getting over Celia. Getting on with life again. Maybe with Julia.

After a shower, a microwave dinner, and three glasses of sauvignon blanc, I felt relaxed and mellow. Thoughts of the past week's traumatic events were becoming less distressing. Then the intercom buzzed. I got up and spoke into it: 'Milton, who's there?'

'You don't know me. I've got something for you. From Paul Kirk.'

I didn't panic. 'I need some proof of that before I let you up.'

'Blue velvet. He said you'd know what that meant.'

It was the title of a film that had fascinated Paul because one of the main characters practiced self-asphyxiation.

'OK, that's good enough. The flat's on the top floor.' I pressed the button that unlocked the entrance door.

Paul's messenger was a small, wizened elderly man. His cap was pulled down over his eyes and he'd turned up the collar of his overcoat. His furtive look vanished as I closed the flat door behind him.

'I made sure I wasn't followed. Even if someone saw me come in, they wouldn't know which flat I was visiting. You don't have to know my name. I'm only doing this because I owe Paul a favour. If anything happened to him I was to bring you this.' He handed me a small package.

'Thanks. You're taking a risk. I'm grateful.'

'Like I said, I owe the man. He's dead, but a debt's a debt. Got a back way out?'

'Yes. Through the basement garage, a back door. I'll take you down when you're ready.'

'I'm ready now. The sooner I'm out of here the better. Ain't nothing more I can tell you.'

The door to the basement was little used and needed a hard shove to open it. Regaining his furtive look, the messenger disappeared into the night.

In the package was a well-padded hard disc and a letter from Paul. 'I thought you might need some extra insurance,' it began. 'This policy was meant to cover me, but I won't be needing it now. I didn't tell you, but I had some worries about the technology deal. It was too easy. As if someone right at the top wanted it to happen. So I cheated a bit. All the technical information was put on a special disc. I got one of our boffins – he wasn't in on the deal – to make some changes. He moved data around, deleted some, added irrelevant material. What I sent them looked the real thing, but it's almost useless. They'll have discovered that quite quickly. But by then I'd have known about any double dealing, any failure to make the full payment. If it was safe and clear I'd have handed over the original disc. Now you've got it, together with the data summary – correct by the way – in the envelope from my solicitor. There's another copy of the disc hidden in my house, in a secret compartment in my desk. They'll find it only if they break the desk into tiny pieces. The disc will self-erase if anyone tries to make a copy. On the back of this letter there's a diagram showing how to access the secret compartment.

I've also added the number of my Swiss bank account and the necessary authorisations. You might as well have the money. If you manage to survive all this, you deserve it. There's not much in my estate – I never told you how bad my gambling problem was, and the debts I'd run up - but my wife did well enough out of me when I was alive.'

So gambling debts had been the reason for Paul's need for more money!

I tried to think of somewhere totally safe to hide the disc and covering letter. I couldn't come up with anywhere completely foolproof, so I decided to carry them with me until I'd found a permanent hiding place.

Hoping to get a call from Julia, I stayed up until nearly midnight. By then I was so tired that sleep came minutes after I got into bed.

At work the next morning I stuck to the resolution I'd made on Saturday, determined to get my life back into its usual rhythm. I forced myself to focus on what patients said, pushing aside all thoughts about illegal technology transfers, Special Branch, the GMC, and even Julia.

As I let myself into my flat that evening, I felt good. I'd done some challenging clinical work, and my enthusiasm was returning. My buoyant mood lasted until I walked into my sitting room. It looked as if it has been hit by a tornado. Every drawer had been emptied out, every shelf cleared, every one of my hundreds of books dumped on the floor. I felt sick. Then I ran to the room I used as a study. It looked even worse, books and papers strewn everywhere. The other rooms had all been searched, but much less thoroughly, though most drawers had been emptied out.

I ran back to the sitting room, dreading that they'd found the papers Paul had given me. I searched in the mess for the books

I'd hidden them in. I found one. The sheet of paper was still in place. I collected the other four and checked each of them. Two of the single sheets were still there. I didn't know if the intruders had found the other two or if they were somewhere under the pile of books. I searched. There was no sign of them. By the look of things, I thought, the intruders had shaken each book to dislodge any loose papers. They didn't have time to check them page by page. Since I'd attached each sheet with a piece of sticky tape, only those stuck on loosely had fallen out.

I looked at the three remaining sheets. One was the covering letter from Paul, the others outlined the technology transfer. Thanks to Paul's last communication, I knew they were accurate. So whoever had organised the search now knew what had been transferred. But they didn't know who had given it to whom, and they didn't have the full details. They would certainly want the rest. For the first time since Paul's 'confession' to me, I felt raw fear. I wasn't safe in my flat. They could get in any time. I probably wasn't safe on the streets. At least I could make my flat safer. I looked in the phone book for a twenty-four-hour locksmith and found one located in Battersea. They said they'd send someone round within an hour.

Then I dialled Julia's number. I got her answering machine and left a message asking her to call as soon as possible. I'd expected to hear from her by now. I had her office number, but she'd asked me to keep it for emergencies. Was this an emergency? I decided it was and dialled. No answer.

Anxious about my personal safety, and increasingly about Julia's, I went instinctively to the gin bottle. Then I stopped. If I was going to survive whatever lay ahead, I needed to be sober and clear-headed. Cutting down on the booze would be a start.

I settled for a glass of orange squash. I went through to my study, looking for a clip-board. I found one and attached a pad of paper to it. Back in the sitting room, I tried to outline a plan of action, starting with a list of what I knew. It was very short. I got frustrated and screwed it up. Then the intercom buzzed. It was the locksmith.

An open-faced, blonde-haired man in his mid-thirties, he listened carefully as I told him I wanted to make entry to my flat as difficult as possible. It was impossible to make the street entrance more secure, too many people used it. And for those who knew about it, entrance through the underground garage was easy. We discussed various options. Finally, I decided on a heavy duty dead-lock, a chain, and strong horizontal bolts at the top and bottom. They might still be able to force entry when I was out, but they'd need a battering ram to get in once the bolts were closed from the inside.

It was past eleven when the locksmith finished. 'It's now as safe as Fort Knox, guv,' he said, as I paid by credit card. The bill was outrageous but it was worth it. At least I was safe in my own flat.

I heard the phone ring just as I was finishing my shower. Dripping water, I picked it up.

'George, it's me.'

'Thank heavens, Julia, I was getting worried about you.'

'I left the office about eight. I finally finished the back-log. On the way home I thought I saw a car following me. I panicked, tried to lose it, ended up on the M1. I pulled into a service area, parked, wandered about shops, sat in the restaurant. I didn't leave until it felt safe and I took an indirect route home. I didn't see anything suspicious. I've only just got back.'

I told Julia about the ransacking of my flat and the security measures I'd taken. I'd give her a new key when she came round.

'I'm coming round now, George, whether you like it or not. Tomorrow I'll get a locksmith in myself. Meanwhile, I don't feel safe here. See you in twenty minutes.'

We stuck to our plan and slept in separate bedrooms. 'We'll need all our strength,' smiled Julia, 'to face tomorrow.'

FIVE

The ringing of the phone startled me out of a restless sleep.

'Hello,' I mumbled. It was ten past seven.

'It's Janet. I hope I haven't woken you.'

'Time I was up anyway.'

'The morning paper, George. I know you don't get it delivered. That's why I'm ringing. You're in it. It's not very nice, I'm afraid.'

'Me. In the paper. What's it say?'

'I think you'd better read it yourself. Meanwhile, I'll try and cancel your morning patients. I'm sure you won't be wanting to see anyone. I'll get in early, by eight if I can. I'll expect you as soon as you can make it. There'll be some phone calls. Goodbye.'

'Janet –'

She'd hung up.

I went into Julia's room. She was lying on her side, the blankets pulled right up. All I could see was a small patch of auburn curls. I gently pulled the covers away from her face. She opened her sleep-filled eyes and turned lazily onto her back, smiling up at me.

'Have you come to molest me, George?'

'Not today. It's time to get up. I'm going to get the papers.'

I bought all the quality dailies and a tabloid, *The Sun*. I didn't look at them until I was back in the kitchen, where Julia had already brewed coffee and was making toast.

'You don't usually rush out and buy the papers, do you, George? What's up? Aliens landed in Shepherd's Bush?'

I didn't laugh. I just stared at the front page of *The Sun*. I hadn't quite made the headlines, but the sub-heading was difficult to miss: SHRINK LINKED TO MINISTER'S DEATH. My heart was beating so hard that the print jumped before my eyes. Julia moved behind me to read over my shoulder.

'Christ, I don't believe it. Who's done this?'

When I didn't reply she started to read aloud. 'Harley Street psychiatrist George Milton was treating Paul Kirk at the time of his death. Police investigators have examined his case file. According to reliable sources, Milton knew the risk of suicide was high, but did nothing to try and prevent it. Our sources also revealed that information about unethical conduct with a female patient has been sent to the General Medical Council. Milton will face charges of professional misconduct, and Kirk's widow may file a civil suit against him.'

The article continued with an expert's view of suicide prevention. It strongly hinted that I'd been incompetent to the point of negligence in my treatment of Paul. Julia's name wasn't mentioned, and there was no suggestion that either Paul or I were suspected of selling state secrets.

'It has to be Special Branch,' I said. 'They're punishing me for lying about Paul's letter. But they've lost any chance I'll ever co-operate with them.'

The same material was reported in the quality papers, although none had it on the front page. The similarity of the articles made it certain they were all based on the same leak from Special Branch. I'd read enough about official secrets and D-notices to know that juicy official leaks were often traded off for editors agreeing to keep more sensitive material out of the news.

'How will this affect your practice?'

'Affect it? Destroy it, more like. New referrals will stop immediately, and most of my patients will ask to be transferred to someone else, or just stop coming. As soon as I'm struck off I'll have to finish all my clinical work because I won't have malpractice insurance. I can't risk practicing without it, even if a few misguided souls want to go on seeing me.'

'Oh George, surely it won't be as bad as that. Perhaps the GMC won't deregister you. I could come and give evidence on your beh –'

I cut her off. 'It'll be a waste of time. With DNA proof of intercourse, I'll be struck off whatever you say. The rules are clear. There's only one punishment, and there are no exceptions.'

'But there must be –'

This time the phone cut her off. Frowning, she picked it up.

'Inspector Douglas. For you.'

'You've only yourself to blame, Doctor Milton. One of the three people Kirk named as conspirators was able to prove the allegations false. After visiting your flat on Monday we're closer to the truth, but you still have material of interest to us. Unless you want Ms Richmond to go down with you, you'll give it to us. Hand me back to her, please.'

I gave the phone back to Julia. She listened intently before replying.

'That's totally unreasonable. I won't let him do it. Screw you!'

She put the phone down hard.

'The bastards. I won't let you do it, it's the only protection you have. I'd rather call their bluff.'

'They're not bluffing, Julia. If I don't give them the three sheets they didn't find, they'll destroy your reputation. You'll go down with me. I won't allow that. Anyway, there's something I haven't had a chance to tell you.' I outlined what had happened on Sunday night, showing her the ultra-high-tech disc and covering letter. 'So you see, I've still got plenty of insurance.'

Julia protested for a while, but then agreed to let me hand over the remaining papers. I rang Inspector Douglas.

'It's a pity you weren't honest with us, Doctor. You've paid a heavy price. Everything's been sent to the GMC. It can't be reversed.'

'I know that. But now you can stop harassing Julia.'

'Harassing her?'

'You know bloody well what I mean. Her car's being followed by one of your –'

'Not one of ours. We don't have that much interest in her.'

I filed that away for future reference.

'I'll complete the hand-over on one condition. That you give me the originals of everything the CID's got on Julia. The transcript of the interview when she accuses me of rape, all the related documents, anything that might lead to action against her by the Law Society or the police.'

'I'll have to check that with Superintendent Brock.'

'Why don't you do that now?'

A few minutes later Douglas rang back.

'This is Ms Richmond's lucky day. He's agreed. I can get all the documents right away. I'll be at your place within an hour.'

Julia's relief was tempered by her anxiety about me.

'I don't want to leave you but I have to be at the office by nine. Several important cases are looming, and my work's been a bit off recently. I need to show I'm back on top of things.'

After Julia left, I showered and dressed. Then I rang Janet to tell her I'd be in about ten.

'It's chaos here, George. Not just patients ringing but colleagues, referring GPs, even reporters. Michael's in. He was devastated by the news but now he's helping me out. Of course he's worried about how all this will affect his own practice.'

Tactfully she didn't speculate about her own job prospects.

Inspector Douglas arrived soon after nine. I handed her Paul's letter and the two remaining data sheets.

'This is more like it,' she said after reading the letter. Then she handed me a buff-coloured folder. 'It's all there. All the originals.'

I checked through the file.

'What about the DNA report?'

'That wasn't part of the deal. The original may be requested by the GMC. But all the documents about Ms Richmond are there. She's safe now.'

'I'm not in a position to argue. But there's one more thing. Now the world knows I was Paul's psychiatrist, I may be the target of espionage groups. If it gets unpleasant, can you offer any protection?'

'Officially, no. You betrayed us. Not long ago you'd have been charged with treason. The branch owes you nothing. Personally, I'm sorry it's come to this. If you're in real trouble, contact me. Unofficially, I might be able to help. Now, I must go. My boss waits anxiously for the list of names.'

Events at work that day made it the worst I could remember. Janet and Michael were heroes. Janet fielded all calls on both lines, putting through to me only the calls she or Michael couldn't deal with. Michael cancelled all his bookings and took calls from colleagues and other doctors. The most difficult call came mid-morning. It was from my father.

'George. I've just read the *Daily Telegraph*. There's an article about you. Is it true?'

'Some of it. I know it looks bad, but basically I've been set up. Please don't be disappointed in me. Think of me as an innocent victim, that's very close to the truth. I'll explain it all as soon as I get the chance. If anyone asks you about it, you can tell them I'm not guilty, that the truth will come out. I have to hang up now, there's a queue of people wanting to speak to me. Goodbye, Dad.' I felt a lump in my throat as I waited for the next call.

The ringing of the phone got less frequent after five-thirty and by six-thirty it had almost stopped. The three of us sat down with our coffee mugs and tried to weigh up the day's events.

'There is some good news,' said Janet. 'Many of the patients I spoke to said they wanted to go on seeing you, whatever you'd done. Of course, I had to tell them you couldn't see anyone once you were deregistered.'

'It's an ill wind,' added Michael. 'Several of your referring doctors said they'd start sending patients to me. And several patients asked to be transferred to my care. In the circumstances I agreed, of course. My books are full, almost. If this keeps up, I'll have a waiting list as long as yours ... used to ... ' Embarrassed, he tailed off.

'It's all right, Michael. You've been marvellous today, and I'll need your help for the rest of the week, at least. If you could cancel your bookings tomorrow and Thursday morning, help me and Janet with phone calls ... then you can have my practice, or what's left of it. It won't be any use to me.'

We stayed talking for another hour and then left together. I went straight back to my flat, exhausted.

Julia came round just after nine. After a long and hectic day, she was as tired as I. Her attempts to cheer me up were a waste of time. We sat together on the sofa. Suddenly, I found myself sobbing. Julia put her arm around me and kept it there till my weeping stopped.

'Julia, I never cry in front of anyone, most men are the same. But with you I don't feel embarrassed, it was comforting, almost like ... crying in my mother's arms as a small child.' That started me weeping again. Julia stayed silent, her arm tightening a little around my shoulders.

'I'm partly to blame for all this,' said Julia when I'd finally stopped crying.

'You weren't responsible for Paul's death,' I countered. 'It all started there. If you hadn't given them a weapon to use, they'd have invented one. We know how ruthless they are. They'd have done anything to get what they wanted. I might have been beaten up, threatened with death, killed even. I've lost my career and my reputation, but I'm still alive, for what it's worth.'

'Paul's last letter to you. It mentioned a Swiss bank account. If you need money ...'

'That's far too risky. I daren't approach the bank, not yet. Special Branch or MI5 may be able to monitor such transactions, or at least the phone calls. I just don't know.'

'Well, if you need money to defend yourself, to live on, for anything, I've got savings. Most in shares and bonds, but there's about thirty thousand in cash or at call. You can have that, it's the least I can do. Whatever you say, I know I'm partly responsible for what's happened to you. I feel guilty about it. I want to help in any way I can.'

'I'll need a solicitor to represent me at the disciplinary committee, but it's just a formality. The only decision to be made is how long I'll be deregistered. Unless Paul's wife goes for malpractice, seeking damages for my alleged negligence. But that won't hold up in court. I did everything reasonable to help him.'

'I could represent you.'

'I thought of that. But it's not your field. And imagine if your personal involvement came out.'

'I suppose you're right. Anyway, you have your own solicitor, surely.'

'Yes. Whether he's the right person to come with me to the disciplinary committee, I don't know. I'll see what he says.'

We talked on until ten, then watched the late news. There was nothing about me or Paul's death. That night we slept in my bed. I wanted the comfort of a warm body.

For once I didn't want sex.

Next morning at work I got the letter I was waiting for. It invited me to attend the disciplinary committee of the GMC. They weren't wasting time. It was scheduled for Wednesday next week, just seven days away.

I rang my solicitor, who'd been expecting me to call. He agreed to represent me at the hearing. He thought I might get away with a twelve-month suspension. I said it didn't matter how long, I was finished anyway. He didn't argue.

The rest of the week was a nightmare. Most patients kept their appointments. I said goodbye to all of them. I had more bouts of crying and sobbing, but I managed to keep these private. I got weepy saying goodbye to the patients I'd been seeing for a while.

Some of them were deeply upset, and tears were frequent. About a third said they didn't mind what I'd done, they'd like to work with me until therapy was complete. I had to explain to each one why I couldn't.

Janet and Michael continued to be incredibly supportive. Michael and I arranged quickly and amicably for our partnership to be dissolved. That would yield enough cash for me to meet my immediate expenses. I agreed to vacate the premises with a week of the disciplinary hearing.

I worked all day Saturday doing discharge letters. On Sunday, I was too depressed and exhausted to do anything except flop around. With nothing to keep me busy, I felt the full impact of what I'd lost. I'd helped many patients through loss and grief and knew how overwhelming their pain could be. But this didn't help me manage my own grief. The pain was unbearable. I thought seriously of suicide but fell short of making plans.

Julia did her best. But by mid-afternoon on Sunday, she'd had enough.

'George, I hate to say this, but being around you is ... just unbearable. If I stay any longer, I'll be more depressed than you are. That won't help either of us. Sorry, but I have to go.'

'I'll be fine, really. If I feel like jumping out of the window, I'll ring you first.'

'George, you're making things impossible for me.'

'I'm sorry, I'm being obnoxious. Seriously, I'll be OK. Being alone will help me work through things. Have a catharsis, beat the floor, yell and scream.'

And when she'd gone, that's exactly what I did. I raged at myself for inviting it. I sobbed, I yelled. I moaned, wailed and wept. I beat my fists on the carpet, thrashing my body about like a child having a tantrum. After an hour of this I was drained completely. My eyes stayed dry for a while, and then I had another bout of weeping and wailing. After that I went to bed.

I felt so depressed on Monday morning it took all my strength to make it into work. I'd planned to say goodbye to all my patients by Wednesday, the day of the hearing. Janet had managed to contact almost all of them. For some, a phone call was enough, but several wanted to come in and see me.

Sarah was booked in at eleven thirty. I saw she'd bought Sid with her, and they chose to come in together. They both looked upset.

'Your secretary rang to explain things,' said Sarah. 'She told us this would be the last appointment.'

'I'm afraid so. Once I'm struck off, that's it.'

'Is there any way we could go on seeing you?' Sarah asked.

'I don't see how. I certainly can't do any work for the NHS. I can't prescribe drugs, and the private health funds won't reimburse my fees. Even if I worked as a lay counsellor, I couldn't get malpractice insurance. There's really nothing left for me in the health field, and I've no other skills. What use to anyone is an ex-psychiatrist in his forties?' I hadn't meant to add to their distress, but it just came out.

'I've decided I need to see someone,' said Sid. 'I still have these crazy thoughts about Sarah, I can't seem to get rid of them. I still accuse her of things, and at the time I'm convinced I'm right.'

'It's still a real problem,' added Sarah. 'The only thing that's changed, I won't let Sid's jealousy stop me doing things. But that means we fight more. What's good, though, I didn't have to nag Sid into getting his own shrink – he realised it himself.'

'That's something we can sort out right now. I could refer you to my partner, Sid, but only if Sarah doesn't want to see him.'

'If I can't see you, Doctor Milton, I won't see anyone.'

'Sarah, you've come a long way, but you still need –'

She interrupted me. 'I'm the best person to decide what I need. Ever since that night you came out I've known what the real problem is. I know what needs to be done. Doing it's the hard part. Now I'm going to find out if I've got the guts to do it alone, without you holding my hand. But if I thought, in a real emergency, I could contact you, it might just give me the confidence I need.'

I relented. 'OK. In a real emergency. You can ring me. But not as a patient. As a ... friend.' I almost choked on the last word. I'd broken yet another rule. It had been drummed into me over years of training that friendship and psychotherapy were totally incompatible. Some psychiatrists became friends with patients, usually after therapy had ended. I'd always avoided this, mainly because it seemed to involve a fundamental inequality. As a psychiatrist, I knew the most intimate details of my patients' lives. Only if they knew as much about me could we have a balanced, equal relationship. Without that, friendship was impossible. Or so I'd thought. I realised Sarah was talking.

'... and I promise not to abuse it. It'll be like carrying a Valium tablet in my handbag. For emergency use only. I met someone who'd carried the same tablet around for over five years. You'll be my Valium tablet.'

I managed a smile. 'Well, that's you sorted out. So, Sid, you can see my partner for therapy, if it suits you. What d'you reckon?'

'If you were recommending a carpenter or a builder, I could check his work out, but I can't very well go and ask your partner's patients what sort of job he did. I've got to rely on you. If you say he's OK, I'll take your word for it.'

When it was time to say goodbye, I went with them to the door. I noticed a tear roll down Sarah's cheek, and tears started to form in my own eyes. I couldn't say anything. Sid came to the rescue.

'Doc, you really helped us. More than you realise. What you did, coming out in the middle of the night, I'll never forget that.' He took my hand in a firm grip and looked at me intently. 'If there's ever anything we can do for you. It'll be a chance to repay you. Promise me you'll get in touch.'

'I promise, Sid.' I was moved by his sincerity, but couldn't imagine doing what he suggested.

I walked over to Janet's alcove. 'Did you manage to free me up for an hour at twelve?'

'Yes, George. It wasn't easy.'

I'd been carrying the high-tech disc and Paul's covering letter with me since they'd been delivered the Sunday before last. Finally, I'd decided to put them in a safety deposit box, and had made arrangements to open one at twelve-fifteen today. I arrived at the bank on the dot, and once I'd proved my identity, it didn't take long before I was in the strong room, opening the box I'd been allocated. I felt safer leaving the bank, though I'd only delayed making a decision about how and when to use my insurance.

Back in my rooms, I saw that Sylvia was booked in at four. I recalled she'd been present when Special Branch had arrived last Friday week. I'd told her not to worry. Then she got a call from Janet wanting to change her appointment time. Janet had to explain why it would be the last one.

I expected Sylvia to be angry, and the look on her face as she entered my consulting room told me I was right. I endured her accusing gaze for as long as I could.

'OK, Sylvia. I apologise. I shouldn't have told you everything was fine, that I'd see you next week as usual. But when the police came, I didn't realise ... it would come to this.'

Her look softened. 'If I wasn't angry with you I'd be blubbering all over the place, you know how much I need you. To cut me off without warning after nearly five years. I've seen you every two weeks for all that time. I want to scream at you, call you a fucking bastard, worse, but I know it's not your fault. Shit! Here they come.'

Sylvia's tears flowed for a good five minutes. She wasn't wearing her false eye-lashes today, but there was plenty of mascara to run down her cheeks.

'I know what you're going to tell me, George. You'll find me another psychiatrist, someone really good. Well, fuck you! I don't want another psychiatrist. I want you. After Janet rang, I realised how much you'd helped me, how much I'd got from seeing you. I'm much stronger now. But not strong enough to manage on my own. Not yet.'

I'd yielded to Sarah that morning, and now I yielded to Sylvia. 'This is an unusual situation and I suppose it justifies unusual –'

'Unusual?' Sylvia's scorn-laden voice cut me off. 'You call it unusual? That's the fucking understatement of the fucking year, you pompous git. Extra-fucking-ordinary, I'd say. Once-in-a-life-time stuff. My favourite psychiatrist gets struck off for screwing a patient, and one of his celebrity clients hangs himself. Unusual? Don't make me fucking laugh.'

'What I mean is ... dammit! There are no rules any more. I'm a mess, Sylvia, a total wreck. I know I shouldn't be telling you this, it's unprofessional. But I'm not sure I'll be any good to you. Still, if you want to go on seeing me, we'll do it. Not every week, though. What if you ring me when you really can't cope, we'll talk on the phone, meet if we have to. You won't be my patient; it'll be on a ... social basis.'

Sylvia was out of the room before I'd fully stood up. I couldn't believe she'd been so assertive. Or, judging by the number of obscenities, was it aggressive? It didn't matter, I realised. She'd got what she wanted.

Julia came round that evening. Our relationship was in limbo. I was too fragile and needy to give her anything, and she couldn't provide the emotional support I craved. She wanted to, but nurturing a vulnerable and depressed George Milton triggered her own dependency needs. Instead of affection and warmth, I got brusqueness, bad temper and emotional withdrawal. I understood why, but that didn't help. Finally, we agreed I had to do it on my own. She left about eleven, and I felt an unpleasant mixture of regret and relief.

By Wednesday lunch-time I'd managed to see or speak to all my remaining patients except a handful who were out of the country or otherwise couldn't be contacted. A replacement therapist had been arranged for all who wanted one.

My solicitor picked me up from my flat at two-thirty. I'd been surprised when he offered, and suspected he thought I might not otherwise turn up. The hearing was at three, and we arrived a few minutes early at the GMC building on Great Portland Street.

There were no surprises. My solicitor argued that the patient had set out to seduce me. As I'd feared, this only irritated the disciplinary committee. In their eyes, there was no possible justification for what I'd done. Because of my high professional status and public profile, the committee decided to make an example of me. I was struck off the register for two years, twice the usual penalty for a first offence of this kind. At the end of that time I could apply for reinstatement. Even if it was granted, I'd have to be on probation for a year, working in the NHS under strict supervision. My solicitor wanted to appeal, but I told him to forget it. I was worried they might increase my sentence to three years.

After my solicitor dropped me off, I went straight to the nearest off-licence. I bought three bottles of gin, three of Bacardi, and a good supply of tonic water and Coca Cola. I planned to drink myself unconscious, and, when I woke up, to do it again. I'd never strategically planned a binge before, and wondered what else I needed. I added several bags of mixed nuts and three Mars Bars.

When I got home, I rang Julia at work. I told her I'd be drunk for the next three days and not to call round. She was angry with me.

'I told you not to ring me at work unless it was really urgent.'

'Christ, you're an unsympathetic bitch.'

'George, how often do I have to tell you, I can't handle this kind of shit. Go and get pissed you pathetic sod. I'm working all weekend anyway. Ring me on Monday if you remember my name. If you don't, just ask for the bitch.'

'Julia, I –'

She'd rung off. I poured a very large Bacardi and Coke and sank onto the sofa. My career was ruined, my reputation destroyed, and now I'd just wrecked my only close relationship. Julia was right. I was a pathetic sod. I felt worthless, useless, loathsome.

Getting drunk for the next two or three days wouldn't change that. And I'd have a record hangover. But I couldn't think of any other way to manage the pain of grief and self-hatred, except to kill myself. I wasn't quite ready for that.

My first drink was beginning to work when the land line phone rang. The answering machine was still on and I decided not to pick up the receiver. Until I heard who it was.

'Hello, it's Commander Richards, MI5. I don't know if you remember me, we met in Superintendent Brock's office. I need to speak –'

'Yes, it's Milton here.'

'Thank God, you're in. I can't tell you much on the phone, but I need to see you as soon as possible.'

I groaned inwardly. 'Any clues about what it is?'

'I don't want to alarm you, but it's about your personal safety.'

I wasn't that worried about my personal safety. The way I felt, a fatal accident seemed a reasonable option. And I was still looking forward to drinking myself unconscious. 'To be honest, I was planning on getting myself totally smashed. But if you get round within an hour I might still be able to articulate.'

'I can get round in about twenty minutes.'

'OK. I'll listen out for you.'

I put the phone down and looked hard at my drink. I didn't really want to be drunk when Richards arrived. But I didn't need to be completely sober. I'd finish this one now and take my time over the next. I was about half way through it when I let Commander Richards in through the street-level entrance.

'Would you like to join me in a drink?' I asked the commander as I showed him into the sitting room.

'It's a bit early for me. But I wouldn't mind a cup of tea.'

Not exactly a James Bond, I thought to myself as we moved into the kitchen. Then I looked at the kitchen clock and felt foolish. It was only just past five.

'I'll stick to alcohol. Would you like a biscuit?'

Richards grinned. 'I wouldn't mind something to nibble on, I haven't had time for lunch. But please let's not waste time.'

'Over to you,' I said. 'I've no idea what this is about, remember.'

'First I'd like to say I think you've been very badly treated. Even though you withheld information, they went too far. It wasn't necessary to totally destroy your reputation and your career.'

'Why did they do it?'

'They were worried you might go to the media with what you knew about Paul Kirk, that they wouldn't be able to keep it quiet, even with a D-Notice. With your reputation destroyed, no-one would take you seriously. That's what they thought. That's why they did it, not to punish you. They can't afford such luxuries.'

'But you were involved, weren't you?'

'Absolutely not.' The commander's look was sincere. 'You'll understand my role when you've heard what I came to tell you. I'll start with a bit of background. The main issue is Iran. In 1979, it had an Islamic revolution, bringing to power Islamic fundamentalists who've sworn to export the revolution, not just to neighbouring states but worldwide.

'Now in 1997, the Islamic Conference was held in Tehran. It was a huge success, and since then there have been changes. Even "Great Satan," as the US is known in Iran, has been the object of friendly overtures. But now, with Donald Trump's hard-line stance the danger is as great as it's ever been.'

'The stuff Paul sold to Iran. Is it in the hands of the fundamentalists?'

'We're not sure. Our intelligence network in Iran is weak. We rely a great deal on Mossad. Naturally, the Israelis have a powerful interest in what's going on. Iran still calls Israel "Little Satan" and has vowed to destroy it. But Mossad seem to have clammed up on this one. We don't even know if the technology transfer has been completed, though we assume it has. But we've heard rumours of problems.'

'Do we know what kind?' I was getting very anxious. Was it possible MI5 knew Paul had sold Iran a disc with incomplete and misleading data?

'Before I answer that I need to explain how the Russians are involved.'

'Of course. The Russians. It wouldn't be any fun without them.'

Richards wasn't amused. 'The Russians, for their own reasons, have been helping Iran develop nuclear technology and missile systems. This means Iran will be able to hit targets well beyond Israel. Until now, we assumed the Iranians wouldn't have nuclear weapons for at least ten years. The Russians aren't keen to speed the process up, again for their own reasons. But Iran could have them within two or three years if the technology Paul sold is as potent as we think it is.'

The commander had my full attention. I switched to straight Coke in case I missed anything. 'The thought of Iran being able to launch a nuclear strike against Israel within two or three years ... I can't see the Israelis letting it happen.'

'Spot on,' the commander responded. 'We think the Israelis will escalate their use of advanced weaponry to hit strategic targets in Iran. If they do, any chance of peace in the Middle East will be greatly reduced.'

'Well, so far we've got Mossad, the KGB, and MI5. Oh, the Iranians, of course. Anyone else?'

'I'm afraid so. The Secret Intelligence Service, better known as MI6. MI5 actually functions under the direction of MI6, which deals with foreign intelligence and security. You may recall that MI5 is domestically focussed. The CIA is also involved, though like us it relies a lot on Mossad for intelligence from Iran. But more worrying are the freelancers. International organisations that get hold of nuclear technology, sometimes even bomb components, and sell the stuff to the highest bidder. Or meet specific orders.'

'And of whom among this den of thieves should I be most frightened ?'

'That depends on what they think you've got. And on what you've really got.'

'What do they think I've got? What do you think I've got?'

'I know your history with Special Branch, of course. They believe you've given then everything you have. As you know, Special Branch and MI5 are hand in glove, as of course are MI5 and MI6. Which gives me an edge. Look, I'm going to be totally honest with you, in the hope you'll return it.'

'I'm not promising anything.'

'I wouldn't expect you to. But here it is, anyway. I have high level contacts within MI6, formal and informal. One of them had knowledge of Kirk's technology transfer *before it happened.*'

'But that's absurd,' I exclaimed. 'Paul was approached by someone acting for the Iranians. Well, that's what he told me. If MI6 had known about it, surely they would have intervened?'

'Consider the following scenario,' said Richards. 'Western intelligence organisations, including MI6, are desperate to halt the flow of weapons and nuclear know-how to terrorist organisations.

The KGB is just as keen now they've got their own problems with the Commonwealth of Independent States, to say nothing of the Balkans. What better way than for an agent to masquerade as a key arms supplier? This would give access to other arms suppliers as well as the major terrorist groups. I can't prove it, but I'm convinced that MI6 set up the deal with Kirk to give one of their best intelligence officers credibility as an arms dealer. It was this agent who approached Kirk, claiming to act for the Iranians. MI6 made sure the deal went ahead, but neither Kirk nor the others involved knew this.'

'But there's no way MI6 would risk advancing Iran's capacity to build nuclear weapons.'

'You'd hope not. Once their agent got the disc from Kirk, MI6 planned to alter it in a very sophisticated way, making the data of little use, but ensuring that only nuclear scientists could detect the fraud. By the time the Iranians found they had a dud the agent would have got enough information for MI6 to seriously damage the arms dealers and their clients.'

'I still don't understand why MI6 would take such huge risks. Why not simply create their own disc? Why on earth risk the real one getting into the wrong hands?'

'Because the whole operation had to be totally plausible. Everyone involved had to believe it was the real thing.'

'You've convinced me,' I said. 'It was a brilliant plan.'

'It was,' agreed Richards. 'But it seems to have gone wrong. The disc the agent got from Kirk had already been altered, almost exactly as MI6 had planned. Only Kirk knew the whereabouts of the original disc, but he died before they could get it out of him. Then Special Branch forced you to give them Kirk's documents, and MI6 considered them to be proof that the original data were out there somewhere. They're desperate to get hold of it. And the Iranians will be, too, when they find that they've been duped.'

'And the Russians, Mossad, the CIA?' I couldn't keep the anxiety out of my voice.

'It depends on how MI6 handles things. It may have let the CIA know the plan from the start, though that's unlikely. Its problem now is to keep a lid on things, and to make sure the Iranians don't get the real data. If they do, and MI6 are blamed, there'll be hell to pay. Heads will roll, including the Director-General's. MI6 can't allow that to happen. It needs all the help it can get, and I think they'll concoct a story that gets cooperation from Mossad and the KGB, but which hides the full extent of the disaster.'

'Does anyone think I've got the original disc? Do you?'

'That's why I got here so quickly. We picked up a known arms dealer entering the country on a false passport. As a trade-off, he told us that key dealers, and probably members of terrorist groups, now know of the disc. He mentioned your name in the same breath. Already, members of interested groups are converging on London, presumably to "negotiate" with you. If one group thought another was close to getting the disc, they wouldn't think twice about killing you to prevent it. That could include MI6, I hate to say.

Your life is in grave danger. I want to take you somewhere safe, but I'll do it only if you give me the disc.'

Suddenly I felt the need for more alcohol. I got to my feet. 'Let's go through to the sitting room.' Richards stood next to me by the drinks cabinet as I fixed myself another Bacardi and Coke. 'Sure you won't join me?' He smiled and shook his head.

As I moved toward my armchair, there was a sudden explosion of noise. The window shattered, showering me with glass. I felt a sharp blow on the left side of my chest, and in the same instant Richards hurled himself at me, throwing me to the floor. I hit my head as I fell, and the blow was hard enough to knock me out.

I became aware of Richards screaming in my ear. 'Keep down! Keep down!' He seemed to be sprawled on top of me, so I couldn't move much anyway. Then there was silence.

'I'm going to crawl towards the door,' said Richards. 'When I get there, I want you to do the same. Remember, keep as close to the floor as you can. Whoever shot at you has probably gone, but we can't be sure.'

When we were both in the relative safety of the apartment's corridor, Richards spoke again. 'You were hit. There's some blood. Don't panic, I don't think it's serious. I'm going to ring for one of our vans. But we can't risk the front of the building.'

'There's a lane at the back. We can get out through the basement door.'

The commander tapped digits on his mobile phone, which was answered instantly.

'They'll be here in ten minutes. Now we have to get you downstairs. Can you stand up?'

Getting to my feet set off intense pain below my left armpit. I gingerly touched the spot, which was wet and sticky. My hand came away covered in blood. I felt dizzy, sagging against Richards.

'Put your right arm round my neck,' he said. 'Now, where are your keys, your wallet?'

'In my jacket, the main bedroom. It faces the back, should be safe to go in.' Richards got my jacket and put it gently over my shoulders. We moved slowly towards the flat door. As I opened it, he drew an automatic pistol from under his left arm. We got to the lift and down to the basement without seeing anyone. As usual, the basement door was stuck, and I had to lean against the wall while Richards used his weight to open it. By the time the van arrived, I was struggling with waves of dizziness and nausea. Richards was taking most of my weight.

'We don't need the stretcher,' he called out. 'Just open the rear door.'

From the outside, the vehicle looked like any small delivery van. Inside, it looked like a combined ambulance and communications centre. I lay down on the wheeled trolley secured in the centre of the load space. Someone took hold of my left arm and I felt a sting in the crook of my elbow. Then blackness.

SIX

When I came round I had no sense of where I was. The room was unfamiliar, lit by two standard lamps, each in an opposite corner. A simple plastic shade covered a light bulb hanging from the ceiling. I was lying on a single bed, covered with just a sheet. I seemed to be wearing only my trousers. The top of my head ached badly and there was a nagging pain in my side which reminded me of something. I then remembered.

'Hello, hello.' Silence. I called out again. Still nothing. After my third try, the door opened. It was Commander Richards, dishevelled and bleary-eyed.

'I assume this is the safe place you offered me.'

'Well, I hope it's safe. I don't think we were followed here, but it's easier to tail a van than a car.'

'There's a few gaps. Please fill them in.'

'Someone fired four shots, maybe five, through your sitting room window. One hit you. There was quite a lot of blood. One of our paramedics patched you up. You were lucky. The bullet entered about six inches below your left armpit, glanced off a rib, and went straight out again. Just a flesh wound, but it needed a good cleaning up and about twenty stitches. You'll have a scar, but no other damage. It'll hurt like hell for a while. Lots of bruising. I know from experience.'

It wasn't the time to get into tales of old war wounds. 'I remember you rugby-tackling me to the floor. I've no idea if you saved my life or just gave me concussion.'

'I don't know either. But maybe this one would have got you.'

Richards turned around and I saw a jagged tear in his jacket, across the back of the right shoulder. Below it was a dark stain.

'Jesus. You were hit, too.'

'Just a scratch, a graze, didn't even need stitches. I've had worse.'

'Any idea who it was?'

'You won't like this. I think it was someone from MI6.'

Suddenly I remembered what it was like to feel very frightened. My headache got sharply worse. 'Just a hunch? Or have you got evidence?'

'Mainly simple deduction. It's far too soon for anyone else. It has to be MI6. Someone's panicked, decided to take you out, even though they can't be sure you have the disc. Christ, they must be desperate.'

'Commander, you were going to tell me how you fitted into all this. Now's your chance.'

'I was an intelligence officer for twelve years, a field agent. Then I was badly wounded, put behind a desk for a while. At first I was bored, resentful. Then I found I had a bit of a flair for liaison work. That's been my role for the past three years or so. I liaise mainly with Special Branch, but also with MI6 and GCHQ. That's General Communications Headquarters. In Cheltenham. Huge place, employs over ten thousand people. Anyway, I hear things. I heard about the disc. But I wasn't supposed to.'

'You're in danger yourself?'

'Possibly. Whoever shot at you was waiting on the roof opposite. They'd have seen me go in. An MI6 field agent might have recognised me. I've a bit of a reputation. From my active days. They'll want to interrogate me. After that, they'll decide what to do with me.'

'So we're in this together?' I was alarmed at how hopeful I sounded.

'Not yet. You haven't agreed to give me the disc. Or even admitted you've got it.'

I desperately wanted to trust Commander Richards. He'd risked his life to get me out of the line of fire. Unless ... unless the whole thing was an elaborate hoax. To get me so frightened that I'd confess everything to the man who saved my life. But the tear in Richards meant it couldn't be set-up. Unless...

'I need to be certain I can trust you. Take your jacket and shirt off, please. I want to see the wound. It's easy to rip a jacket. But faking a bullet wound ...'

Richards smiled grimly. 'I'll show you mine if you show me yours. Then I'll expect your full trust and cooperation. Including the disc.'

A bandage covered his right shoulder. I undid it carefully. Underneath lay a piece of Vaseline-impregnated gauze. I lifted the edge, revealing a raw, oozing furrow in the skin.

'Ugh, that looks nasty.'

'You convinced?' asked Richards as I replaced the bandage.

'I'm no expert, but that's obviously a bullet wound.' I waited until he'd turned round to face me. 'It's just sinking in. Real wounds. Real danger. You risked your life for me. I owe you a huge debt, one I'll never be able to –'

Richards cut me off. 'If you give me the disc, I'll consider the debt to be repaid in full.'

I made a decision. I'd give Richards the disc stored in my safe deposit box, but I wouldn't mention the one hidden in Paul's desk, and I'd certainly keep quiet about the Swiss bank account.

'It's in a bank safe deposit. The key's in my wallet. Unless you think it's too dangerous, we can get it tomorrow. Or today? I've no idea what time it is.'

'Your watch is in your jacket pocket. Along with your wallet, and mobile phone. It's half past three in the morning. You've been out for over ten hours.'

By now I was fully awake. I knew I wouldn't sleep if I went back to bed. 'Is anyone else here?'

'No. I'm working alone on this. Normally I'd make sure there was an intelligence officer here, we'd keep watch in turn.'

'Keep watch? I thought this was a safe house.'

'No house is truly safe. This one is supposed to be known only to MI5, but I suspect Special Branch are aware of it, perhaps MI6 too. I was keeping watch by myself, but I must have dozed off just before you called out. I don't usually do that. I must be getting past it.'

'Look, I'm wide awake, let me keep watch. You take my bed. I'll go through to where you were.'

'It's very tempting. Tomorrow will be tricky, I'll need to be a hundred per cent. Can you use a gun?'

'Well, I was in the pistol club at med school. But I haven't touched once since. Actually, I was a fair shot.'

'Let me show you how to use my automatic.'

It didn't take long for Richards to teach me how to work the safety catch and reload the magazine with the spare clip he insisted I took. Then he showed me round what was, he explained, a small detached dwelling in a quiet outer suburb. The rest of the downstairs area was taken up by a single large room and a tiny kitchen. We didn't go upstairs. Richards assured me the alarm system would detect any attempt at unauthorised entry. 'No alarm bells. See that panel on the wall? Anyone tries to get in, you'll hear a low buzz, a light will flash, tell you which room is being breached. If that happens, don't be a hero and go snooping, wake me.'

Richards went into the bedroom and I sat in an armchair facing the alarm panel. I heard Richards talking, and assumed he was using his mobile phone. Then I got up and made coffee in the kitchen, keeping an eye open for flashing lights. There was milk in the fridge, but it was growing a variety of fungi. As I went back to the lounge, Richards came out of the bedroom.

'I've been thinking,' he said. 'If anything happens to me, you'll be totally exposed. Here's a couple of numbers you can ring.'

He handed me two cards. 'But this one's the Director-General!'

'Yes. It's his hotline. I've just got through to him, in spite of the hour. I told him about my contact with you. He denied any knowledge of the disc, but got very interested when I told him you had it and would give it to me tomorrow. If we can't trust the DG, we can't trust anyone. If you gave him the disc, told him everything, I think he'd look after you as best he could. He'd put national security first, of course, even if it meant exposing MI6.' Richards grinned. 'Especially if it meant exposing MI6. There's no love lost between the two DGs, battles over funding, professional turn, that sort of thing.'

I studied the second card, 'And this other contact, Gerry Stein?'

'Mossad, but based in London, not Israel. He's not just a brilliant agent, but a personal friend. If I'm killed, he'll be angry as hell, maybe angry enough to try and find out who did it. That'd mean him giving you some protection, assuming they're after you as well. Working with him, you might have a chance. Now I'm going to get some sleep.'

I resumed my seat in the armchair. Apart from a few magazines, including an old *Playboy*, there was nothing to read. My head hurt worse than my side. I'd wanted to ask Richards where the aspirin was kept, but it seemed too trivial. I sat there trying to make sense of all that happened over the past twenty-four hours, to create some options. But I hadn't considered the after-effects of the intravenous anaesthetic I'd been given earlier. I dozed off.

I jerked awake suddenly, my heart pounding. No lights flashing on the board. I started to relax. Then I heard a scuffling noise followed by a faint thud. It seemed to come from the bedroom. Suppressing panic, I got up, moved to the bedroom door, listened. Silence. I noticed a key in the lock, but the handle turned freely, letting me ease the door ajar and peer inside. One of the standard lamps was on, casting a light on Richards. He was lying on the bed, one leg trailing on the floor. His head and face were covered in blood, a dark circular hole in his left temple. A man stood at the window, helping someone else in. They both saw me at the same time. I slammed the door, somehow finding the presence of mind to turn the key in the lock. Then I ran out of the French windows into the garden.

Blind panic took me over the rear fence, through another garden and then out onto the street. Terror anaesthetised the pain under my left armpit. I ran flat out until I was gasping for breath. Then I hid under a large shrub in a walled front garden. I had a sudden sense of *déjà vu*, recalling the Wimbledon episode an instant later. Soon, I thought, I'll be an expert at lurking in bushes. My watch said fifteen past five. I'd wait here till dawn. Then I'd walk to the nearest main road, get on a bus. But to where?

Forced to keep still, I went back to the thinking I'd started in the safe house. I had to assume agents from MI6 had killed Richards, presumably to stop him exposing the agency's role in the technology fiasco. But what about MI5? Was it purely coincidence that Richards had been killed barely an hour after telling the Director-General about the disc? His assassins had entered without triggering the alarm. This meant either unusual skill or inside knowledge. Then my stomach lurched. I should have been in the bedroom, not Richards. They had meant to kill me. Or perhaps both of us. I wondered what the assassins had been told. Was I still be to be shot on sight? Or questioned first? I shuddered. I was barely coping with the pain from the bullet wound. How would I cope with interrogation? I regretted leaving Richard's gun on the coffee table. At least I still had my mobile phone. But was it safe to use it?

Suddenly I thought of Sarah and Sid. They'd offered to help me. But could I justify putting them at risk? Was there anyone else I could approach, stay with for a few days? I ran through a mental list of colleagues, but I knew none of them would take any risks for me. Why should they? I'd made no attempts at friendship, and now I was a social and professional pariah. My father? No, I thought. That's what they'll expect me to do. Julia? Of course I couldn't stay with her. But I had to ring her, to let her know what happened to me. Warn her.

Soon after dawn, I crept out of my hiding place and peeped over the garden wall. I saw no-one on the street. Judging a left turn would take me further away from the safe house, I set off slowly, constantly looking about for signs of danger. I saw a car turning out of a driveway and hurried towards it. The driver's side window was partly down.

'Excuse me, I need some help. Can you direct me to the nearest main road?'

The driver, a bespectacled woman in her fifties, looked at me suspiciously. She moved to raise the window.

'Wait, please. You'll be saving my life.'

She relented, leaving the window open a crack. 'You go up to the end, turn right, then second left. About half a mile up, you get to Addison Road, where you'll see buses and shops.'

I walked to Addison Road without incident and found a phone box. It was nearly nine o'clock; Saturday morning shoppers were already appearing. I dialled Sarah's number, which I had to look up. A male voice grunted hello.

'Sid? It's George Milton.'

'Doc? Is that you, Doc?'

'Yes, I'm ringing from a call box. My mobile can probably be traced. I need help. But it's dangerous. I'm in serious trouble, I've been shot at. I need somewhere to stay, somewhere safe.'

'I don't care how dangerous it is, Doc. I promised to help you, and help I bleeding well will. Where are you?'

'I don't know exactly. I'll come to your place, but I can't say how long it'll take. I'll try and get a cab at least some of the way. You'll wait till I get there? Oh, what about Sarah? Shouldn't you discuss it with her first?'

'I know she feels the same as me. She'll do anything she can to help you. She's out shopping, on her own, thanks to you, Doc. I'll stay here till you arrive. Then you can explain things.'

I checked the address before hanging up. Then I worked out exactly where I was by wandering around the shops and asking a few questions. There were frequent buses into the city. From there I'd get a cab to Sid and Sarah's flat.

At ten past twelve, I was knocking on the door. It was opened by an excited Sarah. Her face was flushed, adding to her waif-like beauty.

'Come in quick. Sid's told me you're in some kind of danger.'

Sitting in their cosy lounge, I remembered the last time I'd been there. Sid read my thoughts.

'Shoe's on the other foot, eh Doc?'

'Sid!' exclaimed Sarah.

'The Doc knows I'm just ribbing him, don't you, Doc?'

'Sure. It's true, though. Last time I was here you needed my help. Now I need yours. Desperately. I'll explain why.'

I told them almost everything. Even about the second copy of the disc hidden in Paul's desk. If it was extra insurance for me, they might need it, too. But I didn't mention the Swiss bank account.

'So you see,' I went on. 'I'm a live target. If they track me down here, you'll be targets, too. They'll assume I told you about the disc. If you don't want to take that chance, tell me now and I'll go. I won't blame you. To be honest, I'm beginning to feel I shouldn't be here, shouldn't be asking you to risk –'

'Listen Doc,' interrupted Sarah. 'You put yourself on the line for me, came out at night to the middle of nowhere, took me back home where Sid could have flattened you –'

Sid broke in. 'And I might have, Doc. I thought you and Sarah were up to something. I planned to get you inside, and then beat the truth out of you if I had to. But ... well, you know what happened. Anyway, I don't see how they could trace you here, not unless they find out the names and addresses of all your patients and chase every one of them up.'

'My files are locked away very securely. It would be impossible to access them without leaving traces. It's such a long shot, anyway. Even if they thought of it, they'd never give it any priority.'

'Then perhaps we're not in any real danger after all,' said Sarah. 'Have you got a plan, Doc?'

'Yes, I'm working on how to stop you calling me "Doc". I'm not your psychiatrist anymore, remember? And you're not my patient. You're my friend. And so are you, Sid. So please, both of you, call me George.'

This raised smiles and nods of agreement.

'But seriously, Doc, uh George,' persisted Sarah, 'do you have a plan of action?'

'Not yet. First I want to ring Julia. She could be in danger. Can I use your phone?'

'Hold on, George,' said Sid. 'Suppose they're tapping Julia's phone? That means they could trace the call back here. Better use a call box somewhere busy, like a railway station. I'll drive you to the nearest one.'

'It's a nuisance but it makes sense. Let's go right away.'

'I'd like to come along, too,' said Sarah. 'I'll feel safer than staying here alone. I might even be useful.'

The three of us walked into the nearest railway station. I entered a phone booth while Sarah and Sid stood nearby, trying to blend into the background. I got through at once.

'George, where the hell have you been? Why don't you answer your phone?'

'I've had to go into hiding, Julia. I was shot at, wounded, not seriously, thank God.'

'Then it's even worse than I thought. I slept here at the office last night. I've been too frightened to go home. I'd been attending a district court and was in the car park, getting my keys out. This car stopped next to me, two men jumped out and grabbed me, tried to pull me inside, all this in broad daylight. I screamed and fought and God I was lucky, two young women had the guts to run over and help. They screamed, held on to me, pulled and pushed, the men gave up, drove away.'

'Were you injured?'

'Just a few bruises and scratches, nothing I couldn't patch up myself. What about you?'

'Below my left armpit. The bullet went in and out fairly cleanly. Twenty-odd stitches. It aches. Also a bang on the head. That aches worse.'

'George, what's going on? Is this about -?'

I cut her off. 'It's too dangerous to talk now. Your phone may be tapped or bugged. I'm ringing from a phone booth, I'll be off the line long before they can get here. We have to meet. Do you remember, when I told you about your stepfather's death, you made a joke about meeting somewhere?'

'No, I ... wait a sec ... I think I do remember, it was -'

I cut her off again. 'Don't say it, for Christ's sake. Just meet me there. At four o'clock. That gives you'- I glanced at my watch - 'just over two hours. Make sure you're not followed. If there's the smallest chance you might be, call it off. If you're not there by four-fifteen I'll return at five, and again at six. Now, can you do it?'

'Easy. I'll just consult my manual on shaking off private dicks, it will be a breeze. But if I don't make it, ring me on my mobile,

I'll keep it switched on. Uh, here's the number, I never gave it to you.'

I jotted it down, left the booth and walked over to Sid and Sarah. I outlined what Julia and I had arranged.

'So you have to be at Waterloo Station, under the clock, at four o'clock,' said Sarah.

'I'd like to arrive a bit early, look around, just in case ...'

'Makes sense,' said Sid. 'How will you get there?'

'I'll take the train from here. According to the board there's one in ten minutes. But from Waterloo I'll get the tube to Piccadilly Circus, I want to buy another mobile phone. Thinking about it, I'll get two, with different numbers, but both in my name. I'll say one's for my daughter, you can use it. That way we can communicate fairly safely.'

'What do you want us to do?' asked Sarah,

'Well, how do you feel about Julia staying at your place? She can't go back to her flat any more than I can go back to mine.'

'It'll be a bit squashed. The spare bedroom's full of junk, it's got a single bed. We've got an old camp bed, should be room to put that up. You won't mind sharing? Not that there's any choice. You happy with that, Sid?'

'Sounds real cosy, as long as no-one spends too much time in the bathroom.'

'Then that's settled, unless Julia has other plans. I don't know how long we'll need to stay. I'm praying we can sort all this out in a few days, get back to normal. Oh, another thing, if we could use your car. In emergencies, or when you can't drive us.'

'The car's yours when you need it,' said Sid. 'And I'll have a couple of extra front door keys cut so you can both come and go as you please.'

'That's great, Sid. Well, I'll get going now. I'll aim to be back by half past six. If there's a change of plan I'll let you know.'

I had no trouble buying two mobile phones, and I got to the main concourse of Waterloo Station at a quarter to four. I stood by the newsagents, watching the area under the central clock. Julia appeared at exactly four o'clock. I'd seen nothing suspicious, so immediately moved towards her.

'On time for once,' I said.

'Me or the clock?'

'Both of you. Let's go somewhere a bit less public. Want a coffee?'

We walked over to one of the station's cafés.

'I'm staying with a patient of mine and her husband. Ex-patient. In Wandsworth.'

'Come down in the world, have you?'

'Not at all. Parts of Wandsworth are quite fashionable. Actually it's a council block. But one of the newer developments, not a huge eye-sore, it's quite well done, small but comfortable. They've offered to put you up as well, but we'd have to squeeze into the spare bedroom.'

'Sharing a poky flat in Wandsworth with three others isn't exactly my idea of fun. I had enough of that as a student. But I can't go back to my flat, and I don't feel safe at the office, not at night. So yes, I'll accept the offer.'

'They're expecting us back by six-thirty, unless I ring. Do you need to buy anything before we leave town?'

'Some underwear. Blouse, sweater, pair of slacks. Toothbrush.'

'If we get the tube to Leicester Square, we'll have nearly an hour before the shops close. And still get back to Wandsworth by six-thirty. We can get the Southern Region. I feel uneasy about using cabs. I don't know how these things work, but if our description's been circulated...'

Julia and I ended up buying more clothes than we'd planned, although my bullet wound hurt like hell whenever I tried anything on. Julia also bought a new mobile phone. We arrived back to the flat just after six-thirty laden with carrier bags. I'd been worried that Julia would be a bit stand-offish or patronising, but she was warm and friendly, connecting immediately with both Sid and Sarah.

We agreed to order the evening meal from a local Chinese restaurant that home delivered. There was an argument over who should pay, which Julia won amicably by shouting Sid down. Sarah looked impressed. Now, I asked myself, was she modelling aggression or assertiveness? Damned if I could tell the difference.

We got down to business over the food.

'What I don't understand,' said Sarah, 'is how they've connected Julia with the disc.'

'Easy,' I replied. 'Both Special Branch and MI5 know of my relationship with Julia. They have to assume I've told her the story. And there was mention of our relationship in one of the tabloids.'

'OK,' said Sarah. 'We know someone's tried to kill George. How's the bullet wound by the way?'

'Still painful, but I don't think it's infected. I may have torn a stitch or two when I jumped over that fence – Christ, was it really just this morning? My head's a lot better, the lump's gone down.'

'Off the danger list, then,' smiled Sarah. 'Now, Julia. The people who tried to snatch you, did they give any clues about what they were after?'

'Two things come to mind,' Julia replied. 'One's fairly obvious. To find out how much I know. The other is to get to George, offer to exchange me for the disc. Which assumes we have some kind of love thing going.'

'Not necessarily,' I added rather too quickly. 'Anyone who's been told of our relationship might think I'd feel loyalty, compassion, responsibility towards you as a patient.'

'And do you?' Julia's face flushed, her voice rising in anger. 'Is that all you feel?'

'Julia, for Christ's sake calm down. Now's not the time –'

'Oh, yes, it bloody well is,' she cut in. 'If we're going to work together, I have to know how much you're ... committed to me.'

'We can sort this out later. Not in front of Sid and Sarah.'

'We don't mind,' they chorused.

'Julia, what do you want? A declaration of undying love? I can't give you that. I still want a relationship with you. I still find you almost unbearably attractive. But I don't know you, not really, not outside of the consulting room. And George Milton, psychiatrist, he's not there anymore. What kind of man will take his place? I'm just not in a position to make an emotional commitment.'

'Christ, George, sometimes I think you're such a cold fish. You just switch off your feelings, go all blank emotionally. It really pisses me off.'

'Just let me finish. What I am sure of is wanting to stay alive. Twenty-four hours ago I was thinking of suicide. So that's quite a turn around. And you're part of that. Part of wanting desperately to survive and part of actually doing it. What risks I'd take for you, what sacrifices I'd make, I just don't know. I'd like to think you could trust me completely, that I'd even put my life on the line for you. But who knows what'll happen if it comes to the crunch?'

There was silence for a few moments. Then Julia replied.

'Well, I asked for that, I suppose. Don't you want to know how I feel?'

'Of course, I do.'

'I have strong feelings towards you, George. Close to love. You'll probably write this off as transference or some other clinical thing, but these feelings are very real, believe me.'

'Julia, I'm sorry. I had no idea you felt like that.'

'I couldn't tell you, I didn't know it myself even. Fear of intimacy, of rejection, of betrayal and abuse, all that sort of stuff. But now that we're stuck with each other, at least until we get out of this mess, well, the words ... spoke themselves.'

'This isn't a marriage guidance session,' said Sarah. 'It's a war conference. Let's get back to strategy.'

Somehow, Sarah had become the leader of our small group. Perhaps that's why I tried so hard to help her, I reflected. Perhaps I'd recognised intuitively her strength of character, the fierce independence of thought and will hidden beneath her struggle with agoraphobia and Sid's obsessive jealousy.

'One thing's for certain,' she continued. 'You can't just hide. Because they'll find you. It may take a while. But if the stakes are as high as you say they are, hungry, clever and ruthless predators are out there with just one thing on their minds. The disc. The way I see it, you've got to get someone on your side. Now, is there anyone you can trust?'

'Richards, the MI5 man, gave me the names of two contacts. But he was killed barely an hour after talking to one of them. His Director-General. Which has put me off the idea of ringing him. It's too much of a coincidence. Richards was acting alone, or so he said. Only the paramedic who stitched me up and the van driver knew where he'd taken me. He was fairly sure we weren't followed. If we had been, why would they wait eleven hours before trying something? That's how long we'd been there before they got in. And they bypassed a very sophisticated alarm system. That suggests an inside job.'

'And the other contact?' asked Sid.

'A man called Gerry Stein. Of Mossad. The Israeli secret service.'

'Why not ring him now? You've nothing to lose.'

'At fifteen past eight on a Saturday night?'

'Spies aren't supposed to keep regular hours, George. Even if he's out and about, he'll be contactable.'

'What do you two think?' I asked the women.

'I agree with Sid,' said Julia.

'Me too,' said Sarah. 'Why wait?'

'I'll use one of my new mobiles. They can't trace that.'

I dialled the number on the card Richards had given me.

'Stein.'

'You don't know me. Name's Milton, George Milton. It's about Commander Richards. You know he's dead?'

There was a brief silence.

'No, I didn't. Look, I'm with some people. Let me find somewhere quieter. Hold on.'

'He's gone to find somewhere he can talk,' I explained to the others. Then Stein came back on.

'You there, Milton?'

'Yes.'

'Richards and I were friends. Did he tell you that?'

'He did. That's one of the reasons he gave me your name. He thought you'd be interested in finding the killers.'

'So what's your involvement?'

'I was with Richards when he was killed. He'd taken me to – wait a minute, how safe is it to talk?'

'My phone's safe. Is yours?'

'It's a Samsung galaxy A7. I don't know how safe it is, but don't see how anyone could track it, it's brand new.'

'Should be OK unless they're right on top of you.'

'No-one knows where I am. But I'd rather we meet. You interested?'

'Sure. Why not tonight? I can get away in twenty minutes.'

'Wait. I know Richards trusted you. And he proved I could trust him. But I know nothing about him. So I'm not sure I can trust you. It'll have to be somewhere very safe.'

'What about a crowded pub?'

'OK, if I can choose it.'

'Make me an offer.'

'Where are you now?'

'West Hampstead.'

I suggested the lounge bar of a pub just north of Victoria Station, roughly halfway between us. Stein agreed to be there in forty-five minutes. He told me how to recognise him, but I was way too wary to describe myself. Sid offered to drive me. I wanted to arrive early, so we left at once.

We entered the lounge at five minutes to nine. It was crowded, and there was no-one answering Stein's description. We walked to the bar.

'I'll hang about just in case there's trouble. I don't go round picking fights, but I can handle myself pretty well if I have to.'

'Sid, I believe you. I'm glad you're on my side. We won't let Stein know you're with me. What about sitting over there? I pointed to one of the few vacant seats, tucked away in a corner. 'I'll stay by the bar.'

Sid ordered a pint and I ordered a gin and tonic. The first one I'd had for over twenty-four hours. It seemed a lot longer. Sid sat in the corner and I sat on a freshly vacated bar stool. I was about to order another drink when a man answering Stein's description approached the bar. I got up and stood next to him.

'Gerry Stein?'

'George Milton?'

We shook hands. Stein manoeuvred a bar stool next to mine and we sat down. I liked Stein's face. It was broad and open, inviting trust. He was older than I'd expected, approaching fifty, his goatee beard and thick wiry hair both tinged with grey.

'Call me Gerry,' he smiled. I registered an unremarkable middle class accent.

I smiled back. 'George. What are you drinking, Gerry?'

'Whisky and dry, thanks. Now, I made a couple of calls on the way here. Asked some questions about you. You're a hot topic. Something about a disc, a woman, nuclear technology.'

'Jesus Christ, is there anyone who doesn't know about it?'

'Don't panic. I'm very well connected, comes from being around so long. The information's still officially restricted to the highest levels of national intelligence networks, but it's been traded or leaked. Given the stakes, this explains why there's so much interest in you.'

'Richards proved I could trust him. Took a bullet meant for me. He lost a bit of skin, that's all. It wasn't the one that killed him. Can I trust you?'

'He took a bullet for me once, but it wasn't a flesh wound, it ended his active service and we were friends before that. You can trust me because we both want the same thing: to find out who killed him. Then I will settle the score.'

'Look, I know it's urgent, but we've only just met, and there are a lot of details you still need to know. We've made a good start, I think. I feel I can trust you, work with you. But it's late. I've been on the go since three this morning, and I'm running out of steam, not thinking straight. Why don't we meet tomorrow, spend as much time as we need. You could meet Julia. Anyone else you want to bring in?'

'I don't think so. Too dangerous. But you're right. Let's sleep on it. I'll ring you at eight tomorrow morning, we'll meet somewhere safe.'

As soon as Gerry had left, Sid and I walked out to the car. As we drove back, I told Sid what happened. I repeated it to Julia and Sarah.

SEVEN

Gerry Stein rang just after eight. We'd all been up since seven and eaten bacon and eggs. No-one mentioned cholesterol. That was one advantage of being in real danger. You stopped worrying about your diet. I picked up my mobile phone.

'That you, George?'

'Morning, Gerry. How are you?'

'Fine. And I've found the perfect place to meet. A friend's *pied-a-terre* just off Tottenham Court road. Totally safe, and parking's no problem on a Sunday. See you there at nine.'

He gave me the address.

'I'll bring Julia if that's all right with you.'

'What about us?' hissed Sarah.

I gestured her to silence.

'That's your decision,' said Gerry, ringing off.

'Sarah, there's no point in you and Sid putting yourselves at more risk than you need to, than you have already. This isn't negotiable. You're not coming.'

Sarah glared at me defiantly. Sid came to my rescue.

'He's right, Sarah. Anyway, I thought it'd be nice to spend the day together, just you and me, out somewhere.'

Sarah's look softened into a coy smile. 'Sid's made me an offer I can't refuse, George. Sorry, I won't be able to come with you and Julia, after all.'

Sid insisted on driving us to Tottenham Court road before setting off with Sarah. It was a sunny, mild day, so they'd decided to head for Hampstead Heath, which they both loved. At two minutes before nine, Julia pressed the intercom button at the street entrance to the borrowed *pied-a-terre*. Gerry led us into the surprisingly large sitting room of a one-bedroom flat on the third floor. He'd found a coffee machine, from which the aroma was already wafting.

I introduced Julia, and she outlined her role in the affair.

'Here's what I've worked out so far,' said Gerry. 'George contacts the DG of MI6 offering to exchange the disc for a guarantee of safety for both of you, plus the name of John's assassins. Then--'

'But Gerry' interrupted Julia, 'what good will the names do you? You'll still have to find them, anyway, and they were only obeying orders. It's the DG you should really be after. Assuming he admits to being involved.'

'Let me think about it.'

'What kind of safety guarantee should we demand?' I asked.

'That's easy,' replied Gerry. 'Insist on a statement, signed by the DG and properly witnessed, in which he admits sole responsibility for Richard's assassination. You can make multiple copies to be sent to newspapers and opposition MPs if anything happens to either of you.'

We spent until almost noon discussing and dissecting Gerry's plan. Finally, we decided to go ahead with it. The first step was to ring the Director-General of MI6 on his hotline. Gerry told me his name. I keyed in the numbers John Richards had given me.

'Seaforth. I hope this is important, I'm at cocktails with friends.'

'This is George Milton. I have something you want.'

'Ah. Hold on a moment, please. I'll go into my study.' There was a brief silence. 'That's better. Now, just what is it you have to offer?'

'The disc. But first I want to know why you had Richards killed.'

'My dear fellow. I've no idea what you're talking about.'

'If you want the disc, talk. Otherwise it'll go to the highest bidder.'

'All right. Suppose, for legitimate security reasons, I arranged for Richards to be .... decommissioned. What's your interest?'

'It's personal. Now, back to the disc. These are my terms.'

After some shilly-shallying, Seaforth agreed to our requests. The main sticking points were the meeting place and who should be present. I insisted he come in person, and he agreed on condition he could bring two top field agents for protection, and a nuclear technology expert to validate the disc. When I checked with Gerry, he thought this was reasonable. The meeting place was Saint Paul's Cathedral, eleven on Monday morning.

This was Julia's idea. 'It's a place of sanctuary,' she'd said. 'At that time on a Monday morning it shouldn't be too crowded. No-one will interfere.'

After I'd finished talking with Seaforth, Gerry said he'd got a lot to take care of and had to get moving. We left the flat together and Gerry went off on his own. Julia and I had a light lunch in a pub, and in the afternoon we went to the cinema. Afterwards, neither of us could remember what the movie was about; we'd been unrealistic in our hopes it would take our minds off tomorrow's meeting.

We got back to Sid and Sarah's just after dark. They weren't in. We watched television, which distracted our thoughts no more successfully than had the movie. Our hosts returned soon after ten, in high spirits. They'd had a great day. Their relationship, it seemed, was on the mend. I was less sure about Julia and I. In her contradictory way, she'd been a little cool towards me since she'd declared her true feelings about me. Although I understood her ambivalence, it frustrated me. I'd slept alone on the camp bed throughout last night, and tonight was going to be the same. Julia wanted to put off love making until, as she put it, we'd got our lives back.

The next morning, Sarah fought with me again.

'Go to work as usual? Don't be bloody silly. I'm going where the action is.'

Once again, Sid persuaded her to change her mind. 'They don't need us, love, we'd be in the way. And speaking for myself, I need to get back to my routine for a while, try to get my mind off George and Julia's problems. Let's save our help for when it's really needed. This isn't over yet, not by a long chalk.'

We agreed on a compromise. Sarah would drive Sid to work, and then drop Julia and me off at Tooting Broadway underground, where we could get the northern line to Cannon Street. From there we'd go to the bank, get the disc, and take the tube to Saint Paul's.

Getting access to my safe deposit box took longer than I'd expected, and it was twenty to eleven when we emerged from Saint Paul's tube station. We'd arranged to meet Gerry at fifteen minutes to eleven on the steps of the cathedral. He was there waiting for us.

'No sign of the DG yet. I haven't been inside. Could be they got here early, put in some extra protection.'

We'd worked out a basic strategy, but knew we'd have to react to events as they happened.

'Any changes to the plan, Gerry?' asked Julia.

'No. We'll meet them at the back of the nave, sit in a pew if there are no chairs free. Let's go in.'

Previously, entering the central part of Saint Paul's had always brought out feelings of reverence and awe. Today, I felt only anxiety and fear. There were a few chairs free at the back of the nave. People were sprinkled about the pews, and the cathedral was already beginning to fill with sightseers.

At exactly eleven, a group of four men came in from the left. They walked straight towards us.

'I'm Seaforth. Funny place to do business. Have you got it?'

'Yes. Have you got the document?'

Seaforth nodded, brandishing an envelope. His two minders flanked him closely, and the technology expert stood behind him. I'd expected a tall, distinguished man, to fit his public school drawl. Instead, the DG was shortish, plump, jowly and almost bald. Late fifties, I judged. He turned to the man behind him.

'Set up the laptop, check out the disc.' He turned back to me, gesturing towards Gerry, who was standing close to Julia. 'Who's the friend?'

'Just some protection of our own,' I responded.

The boffin sat on a chair and booted up his laptop. I handed him the disc, and he cautiously inserted it. He spent several minutes tapping keys and staring at the screen. The Director-General's minders stuck to him like glue, one never taking his eyes off Gerry. The other's gaze ranged repeatedly across our small group and the area beyond.

'This is it, there's no doubt,' said the boffin.

'Let's see the document,' I demanded. Julia and I read it carefully. It met all our requirements. We completed the exchange.

'Let's all go out together,' suggested Gerry. 'It'll be safer for us.'

'You first,' insisted Seaforth. 'That way we can keep an eye on you.'

We kept the same formation until we were halfway down the steps at the entrance to the cathedral. Then I became aware of figures running towards us from both sides, and of others running up the steps. I heard a rapid sequence of deafening bangs. Realising they were shots, I instinctively reached out for Julia, but she'd turned and was running back up the steps. I tried to follow her, but someone fell on top of me from the step above, knocking me over. I rolled down the steps to the bottom. The firing continued, now mixed with shouts and screams.

I lay motionless for a few moments, dazed. The gunfire stopped, but the shouts and screams continued. I raised my head. Nobody fired at it, so I cautiously got up on one knee. Several bodies lay on the steps. One body, covered in blood, was the Director-General's and I thought I recognised one of his minders, part of his face blown away. I couldn't see Gerry, nor, thank God, Julia. I went into the cathedral looking for them, I knew a security cordon would be formed at any moment, that I had little time. After frantically searching the north and south aisles, I realised they weren't in the building.

I expected to be arrested or shot at any second, but I got back out and down the steps without attracting attention. I walked blindly, at times almost running, until I found myself in The Strand. Here I felt safe enough to go into a coffee shop and sit down. I ordered a cappuccino and tried to work out what had happened and where it left me.

I'd lost the disc; but I still had the DG's letter. Then I realised it was useless. He'd taken full responsibility for the disc. Now he was dead, no-one else would be damaged if his admission of guilt was circulated as we'd planned. As an insurance policy, it had lapsed.

My mobile phone rang. It was Gerry. 'George, I'm leaving the country. No forwarding address. I won't be seeing you again. I'm ringing to explain things.'

'You mean the ... the massacre?'

'I arranged it, George. But it didn't turn out quite as I planned. One thing neither you or Julia knew about me. I'm a double agent, have been for a few years. The KGB. But I'd taken my pay, done nothing, they were getting impatient. It was time I delivered something. Your phone call was the perfect opportunity.'

I tried to talk, then cleared my throat. Gerry went on.

'I contacted my friends in the KGB. Offered them the disc. It would have worked but somehow Sulaiman got to hear of it. He's the head of what's probably the world's biggest illegal arms network. He must have someone in Seaforth's department, very close to the top. And a high-level informant in the KGB. I suppose that's why he's so good at his job. When MI6 and the KGB made their moves, so did Sulaiman's people. That's why it was such a mess. But I shot the DG myself. Not just revenge, I thought it would get some extra brownie points with the KGB.

'Where's Julia, and the disc?'

'I managed to escape with the disc. I told the KGB Sulaiman got it, but one of the Director-General's minders survived, they might think he has it. Or they might think I have it. Or even you. And I've no idea where Julia is, all my attention was on the disc. Perhaps she panicked. Could be hiding somewhere.'

'She'd have contacted me by now. Something's happened to her.'

'I'm sorry. I really liked her. Both of you. That's the only reason I bothered to ring.'

'But now you're leaving me in the lurch. Without you, I'm helpless.'

'Don't be too sure, George. You mustn't give up. Now I bid you farewell.'

'Gerry, don't hang up. Please give me a number, so I can contact you. Or someone else if I really need to.'

'I shouldn't be doing this, really I shouldn't. But hell, I'm out of it now.' He gave me a number. 'He's KGB. Gregor Vingradoff. Perfect English, calls himself Greg. My age, no longer a field officer. Works from the Russian Embassy. Give him my name.' The line went dead.

I sat staring into space for quite a while, my mind refusing to function. Then I rang Sid, who'd taken my second mobile phone to work.

'Sid, can you talk?'

'I'll just go into what passes for my office.' A brief pause, the clatter of machinery in the background. 'How did it go, George?'

'A disaster, it was a set-up. At least four people killed, there was a shoot-out on the steps. It'll be on the news. I'm OK, but Julia's missing. And Gerry's run off with the disc.'

'Shit! Anything I can do?'

'I don't think so. Except let me know if you hear from Julia. There's nothing I can do here in the city. I'll head back to Wandsworth. See you after work.'

I couldn't face the tube again, so I risked a cab. Going over Battersea Bridge – a route longer than the one I'd have chosen – my phone rang.

'Is that George Milton?' The accent suggested Middle East.

'Speaking.'

'You may have heard of me. Harry Sulaiman.'

'I've heard of you.'

Well, I've got something of yours. It has reddish curly hair and is rather beautiful.'

I felt a mixture of relief and anxiety. 'Can I speak to her?'

'One moment.'

'George is that really you?'

'Julia, are you alright? Where are you?'

'I've no idea where I am. So far, I've been treated well. I gave Sulaiman your mobile number. They want to exch –' Sulaiman took over. 'Yes, I want an exchange. Ms Richmond for the disc.' I couldn't admit I no longer had it. 'It's not immediately available. It may take me a while to –'

'Don't play games with me, Mr Milton. I know MI6 lost it, and I know the KGB hasn't got it. My contacts are very reliable. That leaves you and Mr Stein. Yes, I know about your collaboration. Now, don't tell me the disc's fallen down a drain.'

'Well, Gerry Stein's got it, but we're not in direct contact. It could be several days before I can meet him.'

'That's your problem, Mr Milton, but I'm a reasonable man, I'll give you until Wednesday evening, say eight o'clock. If you haven't got the disc by then, it's goodbye Julia Richmond. I may not have her killed. Redheads are in great demand in parts of the Middle East. I'll be in touch.' There was a click and the sound of static.

I seethed with anger. He called me 'Mister,' the rude bastard, why didn't I correct him? Then I saw what I was doing: displacement activity. Focussing on a trivial matter to protect me from overwhelming anxiety about Julia.

Even if I got hold of Gerry, I thought, he'd never give me the disc. Unless ... unless I offered him a truly obscene amount of money. I recalled Paul Kirk's term for what he'd been paid by the Iranians. Perhaps I could get that transferred from his Swiss bank account. But first I had to extract Gerry's new contact number from Vingradoff. I cheered up a little.

I tried Vingradoff's number as soon as I got back to the flat. He answered promptly, and I explained who I was and what I wanted.

'Sorry, old chap, can't help. Stein seems to have disappeared. I've no more idea how to reach him than you have. Anyway, why did he give you my number? It was very naughty of him.'

'I grovelled, to be honest. I was desperate. He'd been helping me ... in a certain matter.'

'May I ask what?'

'It's complicated. And I don't think you can help me at this stage. But now we've made contact, can I ring you again if things change?'

'By all means, dear fellow. And how can I contact you if I do hear anything useful about Stein?'

I wasn't sure how safe it was to give Vingradoff my number, and I doubted he'd be much help, anyway. 'I'd prefer to ring you. Perhaps tomorrow.' I rang off.

I knew no amount of money would help unless I contacted Gerry, and this was looking impossible. There was another option, of course: the second disc hidden in Paul's office. But how could I get hold of it, and in little more than forty-eight hours?'

By the time Sid got back at five I'd roughed out a plan. Sarah was due back at five-thirty, and Sid, in spite of his eagerness to hear what had happened, agreed to wait until she got back before hearing my story. I was beyond telling it twice.

By six o'clock, I'd told them everything and they'd finished their questions. I introduced my plan to get the second disc. 'Obviously, we have to get into Paul's study and safely out again. Now we know a woman comes to the house each morning to clean and help with the house keeping.' I mentioned Julia's fantasies about killing Paul – a fairer description, I thought, than murderous intentions – and that her plans had included kidnapping the housekeeper and stealing her keys.

'Kidnapping's a bit drastic,' said Sarah.

'But we've got to get a set of keys somehow,' I said, 'and she seems the best bet.'

We ordered a home delivery from the usual Chinese restaurant and settled down to detailed planning. By nine, we'd got as far as we could. Sarah was to ring the Kirk household tomorrow morning. She'd try and find out about the regular cleaner. We'd take it from there.

Just before ten we remembered to watch the late news. The killings on the steps of Saint Paul's were given prominence, but were described as an abortive terrorist attack by militant Islamists. Security services, the newsreader said, had followed suspected terrorists to the cathedral, where they were caught trying to plant an explosive device. 'The public can be reassured by British security's early and successful intervention,' said a spokesperson for the Home Secretary. 'There is no reason to think this episode means the start of a new terrorist campaign.'

Impressed by the British government's powers of disinformation, I went to bed.

Next morning, Sarah made the call on my mobile phone at ten past eight. Sid had left for work half an hour earlier.

'Can I speak to Mrs Kirk please?'

'This is she.'

'It's about the housekeeper's job. I heard you were looking for someone.'

'Well, that's not quite true. Who suggested you ring?'

We'd anticipated that question. Luckily, I'd remembered the name of a woman who was a mutual acquaintance of Julia and the new widow.

'Cynthia Slee.'

'I don't remember discussing ... but if I did, Cynthia got it wrong, I'm afraid. I'm happy with the woman from the agency. She's new, of course. The previous woman, I'd had her for over two years, but she left after the ... well, I expect you read about my late husband in the papers, how he died.'

'Yes, it must have been awful for you, I don't know how I'd have coped with something like that.'

'Well, you just struggle on, there's no choice really. I'm sorry I can't help you.'

'Maybe you can. The agency who sent her – sorry, what was her name? – perhaps I could go on their books.'

'Daphne. The agency's very good, you could do worse. Stricklands. But you'll need good references.' She gave Sarah the number.

'Thank you so much, Mrs Kirk. You never know, I might end up working for you one day. I hope so. What are the hours, by the way?'

'Daphne comes in every day from nine to twelve, longer if I've got something special on.'

Sarah ended the call with a sigh of relief.

'Are your middle names Mata Hari, by any chance? You're obviously born to a life of intrigue.'

'Mata who?'

'Mata Hari, though that wasn't her real name. She was a famous – or infamous – secret agent in World War 1. Had affairs with top government and military officials, sold their secrets to the Germans. The French shot her as a spy.'

'I sincerely hope no-one's going to shoot me!'

We both managed a laugh.

At eight-twenty, Sarah rang Stricklands, not expecting the agency to be open yet. But she got through at once.

'My name's Sarah Kelly. Daphne told me to ring, said she was very pleased with you, loves the job you got her at the Kirk's. I want to get on your books.'

'Hold on a mo. I'll put you through to Sabrina, she'll be able to help you. She's the one who deals with Mrs Kirk.'

'Hi Sarah, it's Sabrina. I gather Daphne Roberts recommended us to you. We're a small agency, but growing fast. Always looking for new talent. Can you come in and talk with me?'

'I'd love to. What time?'

'Well, today's out. Booked solid. What about tomorrow, half past three?'

'That's fine. Look forward to seeing you, then. Oh, before you go, I've mislaid Daphne's phone number. Got it handy by any chance?'

'We don't usually ... but since you know Daphne. Hold on, I'll check the file.'

Sarah wrote down the number and rang off.

'I'll take the day off work. Ring in sick. You need Mata Hari on this one.'

Although I didn't want to put Sarah in even more danger, I knew she was right. 'It's too late to nobble Daphne this morning,' I said, 'even if she hasn't left home yet. But we can find out her address, drive around, see if she lives alone, that sort of –'

'We might be able to do that with a phone call,' Sarah interrupted. 'Let me give it a try.'

Sarah rang the number she'd conned out of Sabrina.

'Daphne Roberts speaking. Look, I'm just on my way out.'

'Yes, you're off to the Kirk's, aren't you.'

'Who is this?'

'My name's Sarah. This won't take a sec, I've just moved to London, and I'm new on the books at Stricklands. They've offered me a job, but I've nowhere to live. They said to ring you, they thought you had a spare room.'

'They should have checked with me before giving out my number. Yes, I do have a room, but it's small, not much more than a broom cupboard. But if you're desperate.'

'Can I come and see it today? If we suit each other, I could move in tomorrow. I've got excellent references. Oh, is there anyone else sharing?'

'There's just me. I usually finish the Kirks at twelve but I'm meeting a friend this afternoon, we're going shopping. I'll be home five-ish. Six o'clock suit you?'

'That's perfect. What's your address?'

Sarah jotted it down and rang off.

'Now, George, you'll have to give me something to knock her out. Next morning, I'll ring Stricklands pretending to be Mrs Kirk. I'll say Daphne rang in sick, that I'm ringing for her as she sounded so poorly, and that they don't need to send anyone else.'

'She'll need to be out till you get back from the Kirk's. This means a second dose. So we need someone else to help. I have someone in mind.'

Sarah agreed to give it a try.

'There's some phenobarbitone in the fridge in my rooms. It's old but it keeps well. It's the perfect drug.'

'Tell me about it, just so I know what I'm doing.'

'It used to be widely prescribed as a tranquilliser. But it's highly addictive, and was sometimes fatal in overdose. Been replaced by the benzodiazepines, like Valium. Two hundred milligrams should keep her out for up to eight hours, although someone will need to keep an eye on her. She'll wake up feeling hung over, but that should be all.'

'How will you get hold of it?'

'Ring Janet, ask her to meet me with it.'

'But if the phones at your rooms are tapped ... No, there's a better way. I'll go round myself. There's no reason anyone should suspect me. I'll give Janet a note from you, walk out with the goods. And don't say it's too dangerous. I *want* to do it. I'm enjoying all this so much, even the danger. I feel alive, more alive than I have for years. Who will you ask to help?'

'Sylvia. Another patient. Ex-patient. I arranged to go on seeing her. On a social basis. Uh, a bit like you.'

Sarah bristled. 'I thought I was the only one. Me and Sid that is.'

'She's the only other.'

I looked up Sylvia's number and keyed it in. It wasn't quite nine o'clock. She won't be up, I thought. Her sleepy voice told me I was right.

'Sorry to wake you, Sylvia. It's George Milton.'

'George, I'm so glad you called. I rang you, got your answering machine, didn't know what to say, so I hung up.'

'I understand, I do that myself sometimes. How've you been?'

'Much better than I thought I'd be. I rang to ask your advice, it wasn't an emergency, not really.'

'What about?'

'Well, I've met this man. He's been in prison but he's lovely, really he is, gentle as a lamb. I wanted to know what you thought.'

'Sylvia, are you free this morning? I'd really like to see you. It's very urgent. I need you to do something for me.'

'Me do something for you? That's a turn up! As it happens, I've no engagements this morning. You're welcome to come round here.'

'I'll be with you before ten.'

I wrote a note for Janet. Sid had left the car, so Sarah dropped me off at Sylvia's on her way to Harley Street.

When Sylvia opened the door, I saw she hadn't had time to put on her false eyelashes. But she'd gone to town with the rest of her make-up.

'George, lovely to see you. Come in. Cup of tea?'

We sat with our cups at a small table in her kitchen.

'What I'm going to ask you, you don't have to do it, Sylvia. It could be dangerous. Very dangerous.'

'Try me, George.'

'OK. Well, let me explain the background.'

I found myself telling Sylvia everything. Half-way through I realised that in a strange way we'd reversed roles. I was pouring out my story, she was listening intently, asking the occasional question, making the odd comment. It was called active listening, she was very good at it, but I'd never noticed before. Then I explained what I needed her to do.

'You're asking one hell of a lot of me, George.'

'Sylvia, I know. Like I said, you don't have to do it. I won't reject you if you say no. It won't affect our agreement.'

'I'll do it. On one condition.'

'Name it.'

'I want you to meet my new boyfriend. Come out with us somewhere so you can get to know him a bit. Suss him out for me. You see, everyone tells me I'm crazy going out with an ex-con. But I love him. I just don't know what to think. Will you do it?'

'Of course, I will. As soon as all this is over.'

'No, George. I can't wait that long. One day this week please?'

'OK. If I'm still around.'

'You will be. You've got me helping you now.'

We spent another hour or so discussing details. I made sure Sylvia knew enough about phenobarbitone to administer it safely, if it was needed to keep Daphne unconscious.

'That's it, then,' I said. 'Sid and I will pick you up at half past seven tomorrow morning. Let me give you my mobile number in case you need to contact me.'

I risked a cab back to Wandsworth. Sarah had got back twenty minutes before me.

'Any problems with Janet,' I asked.

'Well, as soon as I showed her the note she got quite worked up. But it was mostly about you, wondering how you were. She could see from the note you were in a spot of bother, but I told her it was nothing you couldn't handle. I said you would have rung her, but it was too risky. Sent her your love, hope that's OK.'

'And the phenobarb?'

'I put it in the fridge. Expiry date's over a year ago, but I remember you said it keeps well.'

We walked to the fridge. There was enough phenobarbitone to knock out an elephant.

'These are thirty-milligram tablets, Sarah. Let's crush seven and wrap the powder in a twist of grease-proof paper. Then crush three lots of four tables in case Daphne needs more. The powder will dissolve quickly, but make sure you put it in tea, coffee, any drink with some kind of flavour. Otherwise, she might notice a bitter taste.'

'I've never spiked anyone's drink before. Should I practice on you?'

'Sarah, like I said, you're a born Mata Hari, just play it by ear.'

'Thanks for the confidence boost, George.'

Then we went shopping for the things we'd need tomorrow.

EIGHT

We picked up Sylvia at the appointed time and got to Daphne's place at just past eight. Sarah said that Daphne was still asleep, which reassured Sylvia. It was eight-forty when we got to the Kirk residence. Sid was able to find a parking spot close to the front door. The meter limit was two hours. If I took longer, he'd keep driving past until he found another space. We couldn't risk attracting the attention of a parking warden.

At nine o'clock, I was in the alley adjacent to the window of Paul's study, my small step-ladder positioned below it. When I heard Sarah arrive, I edged closer to the front door. Sarah rang the bell. The door opened. I strained to hear.

'Mrs Kirk, I'm from Stricklands. Daphne rang in at eight, she's sick, they asked me to cover for her.'

'No-one rang me.'

'I'm sorry, they usually do, but things are pretty hectic some mornings.'

'Never mind, come in.'

Just before eleven, the window of Paul's study opened. Sarah craned out. 'It's all clear,' she hissed. 'Come on up.'

Within seconds, I was up the ladder and inside. Paul's desk stood exactly where I'd seen it last. I felt surprisingly calm.

'The door wasn't locked,' said Sarah. 'I'm supposed to be doing the bedrooms so I'd better leave you to it.'

I'd memorised Paul's diagram, and I found the secret compartment almost at once, but it was so narrow I couldn't get my fingers inside. There was a letter opener on the desk and I used it to gently probe the narrow space. I felt resistance and applied some upward leverage. The corner of an envelope appeared, and I pulled it out. Inside was the disc.

Once my feet were firmly on the ladder, I pulled the window down in case someone came into the room before Sarah had a chance to return and secure the window lock.

I put the ladder in the boot of the car and we drove off. Sarah would stay until twelve unless she could leave earlier without raising suspicion. We'd agreed with her to drive round to Daphne's as soon as we left the Kirk place. On the way, I rang Daphne's land line. Sylvia answered, saying it wasn't quite going to plan but she was OK. We got there shortly before noon.

'Come in quick,' said Sylvia. 'I need a bit of help.' She took us through to the sitting room. Daphne was lying on the sofa, waving her arms about and singing, the words incoherent but the melody recognisable as the 'Londonderry Air.' She made a lot of noise hitting the high notes. 'Oh Danny boooo...y,' she wailed as I squatted next to her. I checked her pupils and they reacted normally.

'Any problems with the neighbours?' I asked Sarah.

'Not so far. But she didn't get like this till ten. Maybe they'd gone to work by then.'

'How much phenobarb has she had?'

'A total of ... let me see ... ten tablets. She had six at around ten last night and another four at about five thirty this morning. I was going to give her four more to shut her up.'

'I think it's safe to give her four more. She should be more or less recovered by early evening.'

'Maybe,' said Sylvia, 'we should type out a note explaining what happened, so she doesn't worry about the twelve hour gap in her life. And I'd like to leave her five hundred quid as compensation.' Sylvia had the cash, which I said would be reimbursed by Julia or me. Sylvia used Daphne's desktop computer to type what I dictated, adding a few touches of her own: 'You've been given a harmless dose of phenobarbitone so that someone else could take your place at the Kirk's this morning. Some personal property was recovered, but nothing was stolen, Mrs Kirk was told you were off sick, but the agency doesn't know. Just carry on as normal. No harm's been done to anyone, including yourself. It won't happen again. I hope the money will help you get over it. It's important that you understand that what we have done is of the utmost importance to the safety and security of our country.'

My mobile rang about half an hour after we dropped Sylvia off and got back to Wandsworth. I hoped it was Sulaiman, but it was Sarah.

'I'm ringing from a call box. I got away a bit before twelve. It all went pretty well, I don't think she suspected a thing. In fact, she was so pleased with me she said I could have the job permanently if Daphne left.'

'Well done, Sarah, you've been fantastic.'

After we picked her up, she told us how it went with Daphne. 'I arrived at her place at six as planned. We got on very well, and Daphne was happy for me to move into her spare room.

'She loves rum and Coke, and I popped out for another bottle of rum when we'd emptied Daphne's half-full one. It was easy to add the phenobarb to an extra strong drink at around ten, and by ten-thirty Daphne was lying on the sofa, out cold and snoring her head off.' I congratulated Sarah again, and then reminded everyone that tonight was the deadline for delivering the disc to Sulaiman.

His call came mid-afternoon. But it wasn't what we'd expected. 'Mr Milton, there's been a change of plan. Your friend Gerry Stein has offered me the disc. One of my people is meeting him shortly. I'm afraid he's sold you out. Which means I don't need your help any more. And Ms Richmond has become ... well not exactly a liability. I'm working out what to do with her. She's got to know rather too much about me. I just couldn't resist her company, you see.'

I didn't panic. Instead, I felt an icy calm, and my mind became clear and focussed.

'Supposing the deal with Stein falls through. You might need me then.'

'I very much doubt it. You've no influence over him. And I've got total confidence in the courier I've sent to Par-'

Sulaiman stopped abruptly, realising he'd said too much.

'Supposing there's another copy of the disc?'

'What nonsense are you spouting now, Mr Milton?'

'I'm not saying there is. But supposing one did exist, and I was able to get hold of it?'

'Then you might still be of some use to me. And I might continue to enjoy the companionship of Ms Richmond. But this is just a fairy tale, the mouthings of a desperate man.'

'Until you have Stein's copy of the disc in your hands, you have to give me the benefit of the doubt. Anyway, you've nothing to lose by keeping me dangling a bit longer.'

'All right, Mr Milton. Until I get Stein's disc.'

Sid and Sarah had picked up enough to know what was going on, so I made my next move at once, keying in Vingradoff's number. As before, he answered immediately.

'George Milton here. You know Harry Sulaiman?'

'Of course. He's one of our main ... interests.'

'Well, he seems to have been indiscrete with me. One of his people is meeting Gerry Stein, who's handing over the disc. This courier is either in Paris or en route. You could check passport control for known couriers, get him or her followed.'

'And what do you want in exchange for this little snippet, my dear friend?'

'Help in getting Julia Richmond back from Sulaiman. Unharmed.'

'No promises. But I'll do my best. Now, I've some calls to make. Keep in touch.' He disconnected.

We sat waiting for the phone to ring. Just after seven we got a call from Sulaiman.

'Are you clairvoyant by any chance, Mr Milton?' For the first time I heard anxiety in his voice. 'The woman I sent to Paris, somehow she was followed, intercepted. There was gunfire, she was killed. Stein was hit, but managed to get away, he seems rather good at that. With the disc of course. I suspect KGB, if only because my contact has gone strangely quiet. So my deal with Stein is off, Mr Milton. You and I are back in business. What exactly are you offering?'

'I can get you another copy of the disc.'

'How do I know you're not bluffing?'

'You don't. But if I got hold of one copy, why not another? Bring a laptop, with one of your experts. It'll take just a few minutes to check it out.'

'When do you want to meet? And where?'

'Somewhere public. Just you, your technology expert, a minder or two. And don't forget to bring Julia. I'll have a friend with me.'

I thought of a pub at the Elephant and Castle. It had a huge public bar which shouldn't be too crowded on a Wednesday night. Sulaiman agreed to meet me there at nine.

Then I rang Vingradoff. 'I know you were able to intercept Sulaiman's courier. But did you have to kill her?'

'George, my dear fellow, all's fair in love and war. Anyway, she was known to be a vicious, sadistic woman.'

Vingradoff's clichés amused rather than irritated me. I guessed they were part of his attempts to sound like an ex-Public School boy. 'I gather Stein was wounded, but got away.'

'Fraid so,' replied Vingradoff.

'Are you interested in picking Sulaiman up?'

'Not really. We can do that more or less any time. It won't help. Better to keep him in circulation, find out his contacts, what he's up to, catch him in the middle of something big.'

An idea was forming in my head. 'Listen. You owe me for putting you onto Stein and the disc, even if you blew it. I need a gun.'

'Normally I'd have to say no. But I have a gun that's just become an embarrassment. You want it delivered? It's hot, of course.'

I couldn't see any harm in letting Vingradoff know where I'd be. It must have got around by now that I no longer had the disc, that Stein had it. This meant I was no longer in real danger, unless someone in MI6 still wanted to shut me up. So I named the pub in the Elephant and Castle, gave a time, and rang off.

'Sarah, I need a hard disc. And the use of your computer.'

We got to the pub just before eight, which I remembered was the original deadline for the exchange. 'Meeting spies in pubs is becoming a bit of a habit,' said Sid. 'Next time, we should use a strip club, like they do in the movies.'

Sarah was about to make a suitably scathing response when we spotted the KGB man standing just inside the door. I identified myself and he handed me a small parcel. 'It's all there. Ammunition, too. Good German gun.' He disappeared.

'If I take the gun out in the middle of the pub I might be mistaken for a local.'

Sarah sniggered but Sid didn't think it was funny. 'Some of my best mates live around here,' he said.

I asked Sid and Sarah to find a table with enough chairs to seat our guests when they arrived. Then I went into a toilet cubicle, put the seat cover down, and sat on it. When I was confident about handling the gun, which was similar to the one Commander Richards had shown me how to use, I rejoined my team.

'We've been very good,' said Sarah. 'Sid's drinking a pint of shandy –'

'Tastes like weasel's piss,' he interjected, grimacing.

'And I'm on Coke. Not that kind,' she giggled when Sid mimicked snorting cocaine from a beer mat. What are you having, George?'

'A Coke, same as you. No, sit down, I'll get it.'

We sat there sipping our drinks, Sid and Sarah trying to ease the tension with jokes and repartee. I managed a laugh or two.

Just before nine I saw Julia coming in through the main door. My heart started pounding. She came over to our table followed closely by a group of four men, one carrying a small case. It was easy to recognise Sulaiman. He was wearing an exquisitely tailored grey suit, and he walked with studied elegance. His two minders flanked him closely, reminding me of the recent visit to Saint Paul's.

Sulaiman, Julia, and the man with the laptop sat down at the table. The two minders stood close behind them. There were no niceties.

'The disc,' demanded Sulaiman.

My gaze was held by his sepia eyes. His smooth olive skin made it difficult to judge his age. Late fifties at least, I guessed. His squat build suggested physical strength. I handed the disc over to him and he inserted it into the laptop himself. The operator's fingers moved rapidly over the keyboard. Suddenly a look of horror appeared on his face. 'It's impossible, it can't be ... the disc is self-erasing.'

'You bloody idiot!' I yelled. 'You tried to save it into the A-drive, didn't you?'

'No, no, I'm sure I --'

'You'd better be sure,' cut in Sulaiman, 'or the disc won't be the only thing erased this evening.'

Sweat poured from the operator's brow. His fingers continued their movement over the keyboard, now with desperation. 'It's gone. But I may be able to recreate the file. Let me take the disc back to my lab, work on the problem.'

Sulaiman stood up abruptly. 'I smell duplicity. Ms Richmond stays with me. Until I've worked out exactly what went down tonight.'

I stood up and faced Sulaiman, opening my jacket and placing my right hand on the butt of the automatic, which I'd stuck in my waist band. 'I know how to use this, Sulaiman. Julia will stay exactly where she is. You and your men will walk out, all together, without turning round.'

I looked for a change in Sulaiman's expression. I saw only a tightening around his mouth and the throbbing of a blood vessel in his left temple.

'If you've double-crossed me, Milton, I promise you'll pay.' Then he turned and walked out, signalling his men to follow.

'It worked,' breathed Sarah.

Julia's face looked blank with shock. She struggled to speak. 'George ...' A pause. 'George, is that a gun in your pocket, or are you just pleased to see me?' What started as a hoarse croak ended as a remarkably good imitation of Mae West. At that moment I knew I never wanted to be parted from this brave, resourceful, and beautiful woman.

I became aware of laughter. Sarah's with a hysterical edge. I joined in, the tension now broken.

'So you traded me for the disc,' continued Julia. 'Am I really worth it?'

'To me you're worth ten discs. But the real disc is right here.' I smiled and tapped my breast pocket.

'Let me tell Julia how we did it,' pleaded Sarah. 'It was George's idea. One of our neighbours is a bit of a computer freak. We got him interested, didn't tell him the truth of course, and he did what we wanted. Which was to recreate the very first part of the original disc. We knew it'd self-erase if he tried to copy it. But he found a way of making the blank disc look convincing. Especially the bit that said 'You have performed an illegal act. This file is now erasing itself.'

'And when they look at the disc and the laptop's hard drive in the lab?' asked Julia.

'They'll see it's a fraud,' I replied. 'There's not the slightest doubt about that.'

'You think Sulaiman meant what he said about getting even?' asked Sid.

'I'm the best person to answer that,' Julia responded. 'I've got to know the man a bit, see him operate. For some reason he liked me to be around. He's utterly ruthless, a cold and calculating man who tries to keep all emotion, all feeling, out of his business dealings. Except in the matter of personal pride. He's got a massive ego. Any threat to that, real or imagined, he'll go to endless lengths to get even, to get revenge. So you're in even greater danger now, George, than you were before. What I don't understand, why didn't you give him the real disc?'

'Two main reasons,' I replied. 'The most important, we'd be utterly defenceless, powerless without it. Once it gets around that there may be two copies of the disc, we'll be in danger again, although Gerry Stein will take most of the heat. Having one of the two originals gives us huge bargaining power. The other, well I was pretty sure we'd get away with a double-cross and I couldn't resist giving it a shot. I figured the technology expert would focus so hard on the contents of the disc, he'd work the keyboard automatically. With me shouting at him, he'd get flustered, believe he'd really made an error, help confuse things long enough for us to get you back. Now, we'd better get out of here.'

On the way back to Wandsworth, Sid kept turning suddenly, retracing his route, going down small lanes that only locals and cabbies knew were there. He kept this up till he was sure no-one was following us. Julia had plenty of time to tell us how Sulaiman had kidnapped her.

'I was dazed, stumbling about just inside the cathedral entrance. Someone called my name, said to follow them. I just assumed they were friendly. We went back down the steps, I couldn't see you George –'

I cut her off in my anxiety to explain that I hadn't run out on her. 'I was lying at the bottom of the steps, dazed.'

'Well, not being able to find you made it worse, I just stopped thinking, got into his car. I saw I'd made a big mistake when the man in the front passenger seat introduced himself as Harry Sulaiman. But like I told you on the phone, he treated me very well. At times I found myself strangely drawn to him.'

'Ugh!' exclaimed Sarah. 'How could you? The man's revolting.'

'But you don't know him,' replied Julia. 'When I was with him, he was like a ... a sort of static whirlpool, drawing me towards its centre. And he was polite, attentive, knowledgeable, enjoyed talking about the sort of things that interest me.'

'Stockholm syndrome,' I said, surprised at the edge to my voice. Surely I wasn't jealous of a murderous arms dealer? 'The name comes from a bank robbery in Stockholm. Hostages were held for several days, and when they were finally released they'd taken sides with their captors, saw everything from the bank robbers' point of view. Technically it's known as identifying with the aggressor, it's a psychological defence mechanism, probably aids survival.'

'Well, thank you, Professor Milton,' said Julia scornfully. 'Thank you for your most illuminating lecture.'

I realised I'd slipped into pompous mode. Sid and Sarah were tactfully silent. Mercifully we arrived at the flat a couple of minutes later, nearly an hour after we'd left the Elephant and Castle. By the time we'd sat down in the sitting room, the atmosphere had thawed.

'Well,' said Sarah, 'it's nearly ten-thirty and I'm totally knackered. We should probably do some planning, but I vote we leave it for the morning. Anyone want a hot drink before bed?'

Sid had more energy than anyone else, so he volunteered to make hot chocolate. We drank this with wheatmeal biscuits and then went to bed. I'd hoped to hop in with Julia as reward for rescuing her, but she was still very cool towards me, although she'd stopped calling me professor. I slept on the camp bed as usual.

We were all up by seven the next morning, Thursday. Sid and Sarah wanted to take the day off work, but during breakfast I managed to persuade them to stick as closely as they could to their usual routine. I argued safety, but I had a hidden agenda: I wanted to be alone with Julia.

As soon as they'd gone, she came and sat close to me on the sofa.

'George, I'm sorry I was a bit off last night. It's just, well, I was upset about what you said about me and Sulaiman. A bit close to the bone. Anyway, I'm over it now. I want to say how brave you were, standing up to that evil bastard and his lackeys. I don't know what plans he had for me. But you probably saved my life. Right now, there's only one way I can thank you.' She nuzzled against me and began stroking my thigh.

'Julia, you know how desperate I am to make love with you. But I want it to be a mutual thing, not just you saying thanks,

'Don't worry, George, darling, I want you as much as you want me. Can't you tell?'

I wasn't sure that I could, but I took her word for it. She led me into our cramped bedroom. Our love-making was very different from the last time. Then it was just having sex, sublime though it was for me. This time, there was both passion and tenderness. I felt fiercely aroused, and the touch of Julia's skin was almost unbearably erotic. The experience felt completely mutual. If it wasn't, Julia was the greatest actor since Marlene Dietrich, who I'd been in love with since seeing the original *Blue Angel*.

'Penny for your thoughts, Georgy baby.'

'Georgy b- I cut off the impulse to escape from this intimate moment. I surrendered to child-like playfulness and snuggled up to Julia. Then I decided that for once in my life I was going to be honest about what was going on inside my head. I told her about my problems with intimacy, and my jealous streak.

Julia responded with a long, soft smile. 'Now we've explored your inner scars, George, what about the outer ones? How's your bullet wound?'

I guess she'd been reminded of it while we were making love. 'I've been keeping an eye on it, changed the bandage once, no sign of infection. It's probably time the stitches came out. Let's see ... I was shot last Friday and tomorrow's Thursday. That's nearly six days.' I pulled the gauze away. 'I can reach most of the stitches, but three or four are too far under my arm. Can you do those for me?'

'My mother wanted me to be a doctor, I nearly went to med school. But I'm not good with blood and gore. One of the reasons I chose law.'

'There shouldn't be any blood, Julia, not unless you cut me with the scissors.'

'All right, show me what to do.'

'Just watch.'

I found a pair of nail scissors with sharp points, and a pair of eyebrow tweezers. Then I carefully cut the first stitch and pulled it out.

'Ugh, it's revolting,' complained Julia. 'But I've survived kidnapping and a few other traumas, so I guess I can handle this.'

She took the last few stitches out as if she'd been doing it for years. The wound had healed well. It wouldn't give any more trouble.

'Do you realise, George, this is the first quiet moment either of us has had since ... at least last Friday. I've been putting it off, but I can't any longer. I have to ring the office. I'll just tell them I've been very ill, confined to bed, unable to ring. That I can't say when I'll be back. They'll just have to cope.'

When Julia finished her call, I rang my father. I don't know what I expected, but he was his usual distant self. He seemed to have forgotten I'd been struck off. I told him I was getting by, not to worry about me. He didn't seem very interested. After the call I felt inexplicably sad.

I knew Julia's natural father had died a few years ago, and that she was alienated from her mother. We'd talked about it a little during therapy. 'I still feel really angry with her,' Julia had said. 'But hearing you talk to your father, I thought suddenly about contacting my mother. She lives in Swiss Cottage. I can look the number up.'

'I'll go through into the kitchen, give you some privacy.'

'Thanks, George.'

About forty minutes later, Julia joined me at the kitchen table. Her eyes were still red and moist with tears.

'I'm so glad I did that. I had no idea ... how much she ... missed me. She sort of understood why I hadn't contacted her for so long, not since my father's funeral. I never told her about the sexual abuse, of course. At first I was too frightened of my stepfather's threats, and then, you know of course, I managed to bury all memory of it. Well, I finally told her. She was upset, but not really surprised, said she'd guessed something like that had happened, Paul was such a strange man.'

'She said strange, not evil, wicked?'

'Exactly my reaction. In fact I asked her the same thing. She said she'd never thought of him as evil, more weird. And selfish, domineering, a man who made up his own rules, marched to the sound of a different drum. Always got his own way.'

'Did you get a chance to talk about why the marriage ended?'

'No. But we're going to meet and talk ... and talk and talk. I said things were very difficult at the moment, that I'd contact her again as soon as I'd sorted it all out.'

The mobile phone rang.

'George, it's Sarah. I've been kidnapped.'

'Sarah, this isn't a good time for jokes.' Or, I thought, trying to compete with Julia.

'I'm not joking, George. It was Sulaiman. At lunch time, in a lane behind the office, they grabbed me, pushed me into a car.'

'How the hell did they find you?'

'On Wednesday evening, after we met him, he put three cars on us. We shouldn't have stayed in the pub, it gave him time to get organised. Anyway, Sid finally lost all three of them, but not till we were almost home. Apparently, they drove around blindly for a while, looking for him. Then, chance in a hundred, they saw our car parked on the street. So they just kept an eye on it until someone got in. Which was me and Sid. They followed me to work, after I dropped Sid off, so they know where he is, too.'

'Any idea of where you are? And why on Earth are they letting you call me?'

'It's crazy. They didn't search me, just took my handbag. I had your spare mobile phone tucked away in the breast pocket of my jacket. It's so small they didn't notice it. And even crazier, I know where I am, almost exactly. Near that East End marina, yacht haven, whatever they call it. I don't know the address, but it's near the old St Katharine's Dock.'

'I know it. On one of my favourite walks, along by the Thames.'

'If I stand on a chair I can see almost the whole marina. Obviously, I'm in one of those buildings next to it. You heard from Sulaiman yet?'

'No. Now listen. Keep the phone switched on, I charged the battery overnight, it should be good for another eight hours at least. Not that we'll take so long to rescue you. Are you being watched?'

'There's a guard outside my door, and sometimes I hear talking, so there may be two. This place looks very secure. Sulaiman obviously uses it as a warehouse. You may have trouble getting in.'

'What kind of lock on the door?'

'Hold on, I'll check. It's a Chubb, looks like. And there's an alarm system, turned off while we're inside.'

'OK, we'll be there as soon as we can.'

I immediately rang Sylvia.

'Sylvia, it's George Milton. An emergency.'

'Another one?'

'Even trickier. Another kidnapping. Sarah this time. Can you contact Charlie? We desperately need his help.'

'He's here now. Want to talk to him?'

'Perhaps you could just explain who I am first.'

'I've already told him about you. And about our adventures. Here he is.'

'Charlie Adams here. What's up, Doc?'

I flinched inwardly at his use of my least favourite expression. 'Charlie, I gather Sylvia's filled you in on what's been happening. Well, now Sarah's been kidnapped by Sulaiman. We've no chance of getting her back without your help. I'm assuming you know a few tricks I don't.'

'Any friend of Sylvia's. What do you need?'

'Have you got a gun?'

'Blimey. Who you planning to knock off?'

'These people are armed, and they're unpredictable. I've got an automatic. Two guns would be better than one. And we'll need a set of skeleton keys. For a Chubb lock.'

'The piece I can manage. Chubbs, well, they can't be picked, not without an x-ray first. Unless you're dead lucky. I'll have to blow it. I happen to have a little piece of Semtex handy.'

'Great. Now transport. We don't have a car. Can you pick us up?'

'No problem. Want me to bring Sylvia?'

'She's best out of it. Too dangerous. Anyway, she's done more than enough already.'

'I'm going to have trouble persuading her.'

'Tell her we need back-up, reserve troops, something's bound to come up we didn't think of.'

The phone rang as soon as I'd finished talking to Charlie.

'Sulaiman. I have Sarah. You know what I want in return.'

I feigned shock. 'How ... if you've harmed her ...'

'She's being well cared for, but she's not with me now, or you could talk with her. Is she worth the disc to you?'

'Yes, she is. Where do you want to meet?'

'This time I'll choose. No more pubs. And no address, in case you ring one of your friends. Just keep your phone on, I'll direct as you drive.'

'Listen, Sulaiman, the disc's in a bank safe deposit, it'll take me at least two hours to get it out. Three o'clock at the earliest. Ring me then. Better still, give me a contact number and I'll ring you as soon as I've got it.'

Surprisingly, he gave me the number. 'This time, Milton, no tricks. Just you and Miss Richmond. I see anyone else, the deal's off.' A click and then static.

'I told him the disc's in the bank to buy us some time. We've got until three to get Sarah out. We'll have to pick up Sid on the way. Christ, how will he react when we tell him?'

'When *you* tell him, George. But do you have to? Why don't we rescue her first, then tell Sid?'

'Because he'd never forgive us, especially if anything went wrong. Anyway, we'll need his help. Now, it's ten minutes to one. Charlie should be here by a quarter past one. That gives us nearly two hours. Half an hour to get to the East End. We can do it, damn it!'

Charlie arrived on time, alone. I liked him at once. Bit of a rogue, lots of Cockney style, a number one hair cut but you could still see he was blonde. Dimples in his narrow cheeks when he smiled, disarming you. He was thirty-three, Sylvia had told me.

I rang Sid with the news just before we picked him up from work. He was more agitated than I'd ever seen him. After asking a few terse questions, he'd been silent.

By ten to two we'd parked as close to the yacht haven as we could. It was part of the East End's incredible transformation since the last of the docks had closed in 1982. The old warehouses had gone. In their place were exclusive apartment blocks, offices, shops and cafes. But somewhere very close, Sulaiman had managed to preserve a bit of the old. He had a warehouse.

I rang Sarah's phone. 'Can you talk?'

'Yes. Where are you?'

'At the marina. Near the main entrance. Can you pinpoint your location?'

'I think so. Let me stand on the chair. You see that big catamaran at the far end, nearest you that is. And the blue-painted building, you must be almost in front of it. Well, the mast of the cat and the main door of the building are lined up, so a bead in that direction should take you right to me.'

We persuaded Julia to stay in the car as the getaway driver. Finding Sarah's prison wasn't difficult. The building had been modernised but was still recognisable as an old warehouse. There were no windows at the front, just a large steel roll-up door. Round the other side we found windows too high for us to see in. And a door. We had no strategy, and not enough time or information to work one out.

Why don't you knock, George, say you're Sulaiman?'

I knew I'd lose my resolve, and probably control of my bladder, if I hesitated. So I did what Charlie suggested. The door opened.

'I wasn't expecting you back so –'

With astonishing speed, Charlie moved forward and hit the man on the side of the head with the butt of his gun. He buckled forward and Charlie caught hm. The three of us manhandled him inside, propping him up against the wall. Sid called out Sarah's name. A muffled shout came from a door in the far wall. Charlie examined the lock while Sid reassured Sarah, telling her she'd be out in two shakes.

'It's a Chubb all right. The door itself isn't reinforced. It'll blow fairly easily. But we shouldn't need the fireworks, let's find the key.'

We searched the unconscious man, but found no keys that fitted the lock. We looked in obvious places, but the key eluded us. So Charlie set the charge, shouted a warning to Sarah, and crouched down with Sid and me behind a packing case. He triggered the detonator. There was a sharp crack, but the door didn't budge. We went over and put our shoulders to it in turns, but it stayed shut. Charlie noticed a piece of old mast, used as a decoration, standing against a wall.

'That'll make a great battering ram,' he said.

After three attempts the door crashed open. Sarah rushed forward and hugged Sid. Then she hugged me. I introduced Charlie. 'He's the man who made the bang. Without him we couldn't have done it.' She hugged Charlie.

The man Charlie had hit started groaning. 'He's coming round,' I said. 'We don't want him contacting Sulaiman before I do. We'll have to tie him up, gag him. And we'd better be quick.'

While Sid, Charlie and I tied up the guard with lengths of cord we found lying around, Sarah explored the warehouse.

'Look at this,' she called out. She'd lifted a trap door. 'There's steps going down to the water. That must be how he gets his stuff in and out, I bet on some luxury yacht. No-one would suspect.' Then she lifted the lid of a crate, one of several. A yell. 'Come and look at this, will you?'

I left Charlie and Sid tightening knots and peered into the crate. Inside was what looked like a guided missile and its launching device. I called Charlie over. 'Any idea what this is?'

'Yeah. Looks like a heat-seeking missile. Terrorists love them, great for knocking out choppers. Pricey, real pricey, very hard to come by.'

Behind us we heard the sound of a key being put into a lock. In an instant Charlie was next to the entrance door, back pressed against the wall. He signalled the rest of us to duck behind a crate. The door opened, and a tall man entered. Charlie swung at his head with the but of his gun, but his target saw the movement and jerked away. There was a scuffle which Sid, Sarah and I quickly joined. Even with four of us, subduing the man was a huge struggle. But we were able to tie him up securely.

Julia drove us back towards Wandsworth. She was disappointed to have missed the action, but Charlie said she was well out of it. 'It's quite a while since I've done this sort of thing,' he added. 'And I've just realised I don't enjoy it anymore.'

'You mean you used to enjoy whacking people on the bonce then?' asked Sarah cheekily.

'Well, not exactly. But it was ... part of my trade.'

There was an awkward silence. I glanced at my watch. It was only two-forty, but I rang Sulaiman.

'I've got the disc, didn't take as long as I thought. Some directions please.'

'Where are you now?'

'Southwark.'

'That's very convenient,' responded Silaiman with a tinge of suspicion. 'I had in mind somewhere in the East End. So, drive down Jamaica Road. I'll ring in five minutes with further directions.'

'Sulaiman insisted Julia and I come alone,' I said. 'So, if it's all right with you, Charlie, we'll drop the three of you off and continue in your car.'

'What I don't get,' said Charlie, is why you're still meeting the sod. You've got Sarah back. What's the point?'

'Because we have to finish things between us,' responded Julia. 'I know Sulaiman. He won't rest until he's got even with George. And his idea of getting even, well, killing George wouldn't be enough. Probably a bit of torture first.'

I suddenly felt nauseous. 'Julia!' I exclaimed. 'What are you talking about?'

'I spent a lot of time with this man, remember. If we don't finish things now, he will find a way to make you suffer horribly before he kills you, and that might involve me.'

'You're crazy to go to this meeting,' said Sarah. 'He'll probably shoot you both. For fuck's sake call it off. Arrange a different time, place, with some back-up.'

I looked at Charlie. 'The gun you took off the guard at the warehouse. Give it to Julia, show her how to use it. Julia, find a place to park.'

Sulaiman rang again just as we stopped. He gave us further directions. We were heading for his warehouse. I prayed it wasn't the meeting place. Charlie showed Julia how to use the gun, an automatic not unlike the one I was carrying. Then he, Sid and Sarah got out of the car.

'We'll go and pick up my car from Sarah's work,' said Sid. 'Then we'll wait to hear from you. Good luck.'

Sulaiman's next call made it clear we were going to meet somewhere close to his warehouse, but not in it. 'I'll be waiting in a car. A white Mercedes. You'll see it on the left as you drive along.'

He'd chosen a road that was closed to traffic at one end because of a reconstruction project. We saw his car parked in front of a half-renovated building. It was cordoned off and deserted, but the single chain preventing access had been pulled back. We drove up close to the Merc and stopped. Sulaiman wound down the window. 'We'll go inside the building.'

Julia and I got out. We followed Sulaiman and two of his henchmen inside. The driver stayed in the car. I noticed it was the man who had carried the laptop at our last meeting.

Sulaiman seemed to know the building.

'Perhaps this is one of his legitimate projects,' I whispered to Julia.

He led us into a large room at the rear. As I walked in, his two henchmen drew guns, pointing them at my face. Sulaiman came up close to me.

'I'm a bit out of practice, Milton, but I wanted to do this myself.'

He then proceeded to search me, making it as humiliating and intrusive as he could. He extracted my gun, my keys and wallet, and of course the disc. Julia was left alone. There are times, I thought, when a bit of sexism isn't unwelcome. With this sentiment came an awareness that my mind was clear and my body free of its usual signs of acute anxiety. I felt slightly detached from it, and the world looked slightly unreal, almost as if I was watching a scene from a movie. With no conscious help from me, my body was preparing itself for action.

'I'll take this outside and get it checked,' said Sulaiman. 'Don't take your eyes off him for an instant,' he added, looking coldly at the two gunmen. They stiffened, raised their guns slightly, inched closer to me.

Sulaiman returned in a few minutes. 'The disc checked out. Now Milton, I'm not used to being double-crossed. And certainly not by a rank amateur.'

I prepared to grovel, but somehow it came out wrong. 'Sulaiman, I don't blame you for being pissed off, but be reasonable, put your –'

'Shut up, you treacherous worm.' He looked at the younger of the two gunmen. 'Shoot him in the belly. Then in the groin. Then we'll see what he has to say.'

Instinctively, I threw myself at Sulaiman, who was standing six or seven feet to my left. He was strong, but I had the advantage of height. I got my left arm round his neck, and with my other hand I forced his right arm up behind his back. At the same time, I twisted him round so that he was between me and the gunmen. I sensed Julia close behind me.

'Shoot the woman,' yelled Sulaiman. The gunmen began moving to the right, but Julia moved to the left, keeping Sulaiman and me as a human shield.

'Split up, you fools!'

The gunmen stopped and then began to move away from each other. Julia and I couldn't shield ourselves from both of them.

'Boss, I've found something you-'

The laptop operator stopped talking as soon as he entered the room. I saw both gunmen look at him. Then there was a deafening bang next to my left ear, and three more in quick succession. The younger of the two gunmen buckled to the floor, and the other clutched at his shoulder, dropping his gun. Julia moved forward and picked it up, handing it to me. I released Sulaiman, pushing him towards the gunman who was still standing. He stumbled, sagged, leaned against the injured gunman, gestured defeat with his free hand. Then he suddenly moved behind the gunman, grabbing his injured arm and forcing it up and back. There was a scream of agony. The man with the laptop let out an involuntary cry and began backing out of the room. I thought he might have the disc, so I yelled at him to stop. Instead, he turned and began to run. I didn't want to shoot him, so I hit his head as hard as I could with my gun. He didn't fall, but began screaming at the top of his voice, dropping the laptop and clutching at his head. Stunned, he staggered into Sulaiman. This gave me the chance I needed. I fired at Sulaiman and kept on firing until he fell to the floor.

Only Julia and I were standing. The injured gunman had collapsed, whimpering with pain and clutching his shoulder. Three other bodies lay still.

'The disc's in the laptop,' called out Julia. 'I'm taking it out. Now let's go for Christ's sake.'

I dialled the number of my second mobile phone. Sarah answered. I was very brief, said we were both fine and on our way back to Wandsworth. Then neither Julia or I spoke until we were driving through Southwark.

'Julia, you were just … unbelievable. You saved my l-'

'And my own,' she cut in. 'When I fired the gun, it was pure instinct. The gunmen were distracted, and I just found myself shooting at them. It seemed unreal, almost like-'

'Almost like a scene from a movie.'

'How did you know that's what I was going to say?'

'Because I had exactly the same experience. It's some kind of survival mechanism, a pre-programmed alternative to blind panic.'

'It seems to have worked rather well. For both of us. If you hadn't kept your cool, shot Sulaiman …'

We chatted on, still dazed and feeling slightly unreal, the conversation disjointed, until we got back to the flat.

The others had returned only a few minutes earlier. Sylvia was on her way over to join us. When she arrived, Julia and I had to tell our story all over again. And then everyone wanted to hear it one more time. We all felt like heroes. Then suddenly a reaction set in. Julia and I were overwhelmed with tiredness. After making our excuses, we squeezed into Julia's narrow bed. Sleep claimed us within moments.

NINE

Julia and I woke late on Friday morning. We'd both tossed and turned all night, and I'd reluctantly escaped from her restlessness to the camp bed.

'I had this horrible nightmare,' said Julia. 'Sulaiman appeared as a bloated, zombie-like creature. I tried to run away from him, but my feet wouldn't move, I was rooted to the spot. I haven't had that kind of nightmare since my teens. I woke up just as he was sinking his teeth into my neck. It was so vivid, so real. I think I cried out in terror.'

'I think you did. And it's vampires who do the neck-biting thing. Not zombies.'

Julia managed a faint laugh. 'I thought I heard you cry out a couple of times. Nightmares, too?'

'Yes,' I replied, 'but they were all jumbled up, fragmented. Sulaiman was there, though.'

In the kitchen we found a note saying Sid and Sarah had gone to work. Sylvia and Charlie had slept on the floor and left early for Charlie's place, thinking we'd like some privacy.

We felt a little better after breakfast, though we were still a bit dazed and emotionally numb. Julia kept getting flash-backs from the day before.

I was startled by her coffee cup hitting the table. 'Oh God!' she exclaimed. 'I just had this vivid image of the man I shot. I saw his face, his eyes were staring straight into mine.'

I couldn't help slipping back into my psychiatrist's role. It stopped me having to sort out my own chaotic thoughts and feelings.

'Remember he was going to kill you. It was self-defence. You really had no choice.'

'But he was a human being. He probably had a wife and kids.'

Julia started to sob. I put my arm around her. She went on sobbing, chest heaving, for at least ten minutes. Afterwards she felt better. The guilt was less acute, the flashbacks less frequent and intrusive.

'I don't feel the least bit guilty about killing Sulaiman. In fact, I felt rather proud of myself. But I do feel guilty about the laptop man. I hope he's still alive.'

'I've realised, George,' said Julia, 'we just have to stop thinking about yesterday. We'll never, ever make sense of it, it's too far outside our ... normal experience. We just have to try and let go of it, get on with things. Take stock, try and make some plans.'

'You're right, of course. Well, we don't have to worry about Sulaiman, anymore, but there are still people out there who think we have the disc. So, we have to stay out of sight until we can get them off our backs or get some kind of help.'

'That warehouse,' said Julia, 'MI5 would surely be grateful if we told them where it was, assuming they don't know already. Maybe that would get them back on our side.'

'Maybe,' I responded. 'But who can we trust?' 'We could try Superintendent Brock. He may not know about the second disc, in fact I don't see how he could. He'll know about Stein escaping with the original, but he won't have heard anything else. Not unless he or MI5 had a source very close to Sulaiman.'

'Then we'll just have to play it by ear. As long as we both tell the same fibs.'

I rang Brock who dropped everything when I told him we had important information. He suggested we meet in his office as soon as possible. Scotland Yard still seemed a safe place, but I declined the offer of a car to pick us up. We weren't ready to tell Brock our location, and I wanted to put the disc back in the safe deposit box before the meeting.

Brock rose as we walked into his office. 'You know Inspector Douglas, of course, this is Commander Jennings, MI5. He's er ... well, he's taken Commander Richards' place. Damn shame. About Richards, I mean. A good man. So is Jennings, of course, aren't you, old chap?' A clumsy attempt at a smile.

We told Brock about the warehouse and he immediately sent Inspector Douglas off to deal with it in person. Then he got onto the disc.

'We know you arranged to hand the disc over to the late Director-General of MI6. We also know you involved the Mossad agent Gerry Stein, and that he managed to run off with the disc. After shooting the DG. Then you both disappeared. Well, since the ah ... episode at Saint Paul's, we've discovered that the late DG planned the whole disc thing himself. Paul Kirk was to be the dupe, the fall guy. But Kirk was too wily. He took control. Well, almost.' He paused.

'Go on,' said Julia, 'we're all ears.'

'You'll be pleased to know we've uncovered the truth about Kirk's death.'

'You mean it was suicide after all?' I asked, unable to keep the urgency out of my voice.

'No. Let me tell you what we've managed to piece together. The late DG became aware that Kirk had passed off a fake disc, and of course he was desperate to recover the original. Kirk probably suspected the DG's involvement, and that's one of the reasons he created the fraudulent disc, although as we shall see, it backfired on him. The DG rang Kirk late the night he died, saying he had to see him at once, a matter of national security. He and one of his top field officers got round to Kirk's place about midnight. We know all these details, by the way, because the field officer told us.'

'And now,' said Julia, 'he's been ... 'decommissioned,' like Richards.'

'Oh no, my dear girl, he's very much alive. In fact, he's been promoted. After all, he was just obeying orders.'

Julia and I exchanged looks, raising our eyebrows in unison.

'Now,' continued Brock, 'on with the story. The DG confronted Kirk, who admitted everything. But he refused to hand over the disc, threatened to expose the DG instead.

'Voices were raised, but his wife had taken a sleeping pill apparently, and wasn't disturbed. Kirk took a gun out of his desk, the field agent managed to grab it. At that point the DG decided to shut Kirk up. Permanently. They'd already worked out a contingency plan for this, and the agent was prepared.'

'But how did they do it?' asked Julia. 'There were no marks on the body, no signs of a struggle.'

'They pushed his chair tight up against the desk, trapping his legs in the desk well. The DG held Kirk's arms down, and the field officer strangled him. He used a silk scarf. Applied in the right way it wouldn't leave evidence of manual strangulation. You see, they'd planned to make it seem like suicide by hanging. But they knew a skilled forensic examination might suggest murder.

'When they were searching for the disc,' continued Brock, 'they found Kirk's apparatus. It was the perfect cover for their crime. They hooked him up, assuming that his death would be judged an accident or suicide.'

'Obviously, we're cleared of all suspicion over Kirk's death,' said Julia. 'But what about the disc?'

'Stein recovered from his injuries quickly. Then he tried to sell the disc back to MI6 but instead of buying it they asked us to help out. That's how I got involved. We brokered a rather complicated deal that included Mossad and the KGB. Stein was offered a small cash payment and, more importantly, a written promise, signed by all the agencies involved, to leave him alone.'

'Then the slate's clean?' asked Julia.

'Absolutely,' replied Brock. 'In fact, we'll end up owing you if your tip about Sulaiman's warehouse pays off. Assuming it does, I'll do everything in my power to make sure you're both left alone from now on. News of the disc's destruction will be networked. And regarding false allegations of rape, Ms Richmond, I will personally make sure the file is not just buried, but destroyed. You'll both be safe, able to get on with your lives again. Well, that about wraps it up. Leave me a contact number, I'll ring you as soon as I hear from Douglas.'

Julia and I weren't quite ready to go back to our own homes; we still didn't fully trust Brock. So we asked for a car to drop us off at Victoria Station. We walked to the nearest café.

'I can't believe it's all over at last,' said Julia. 'After all the murder and mayhem, even the office will be an anticlimax.'

'At least you've got work to go back to. I'm unemployed. Unemployable. And fast running out of cash. I've still got a bloody great mortgage to pay.'

'George, darling. We've talked about this. I can help you out. And there's that money in the Swiss bank. Maybe it's time to try and get hold of that.'

'I wouldn't know where to start.'

I've got a colleague at work, a financial specialist. I'll talk to him if you like.'

'Does that mean you're going back soon?'

'If I don't they'll give up on me. Assume I'm unreliable, haven't got what it takes. I disappeared last Friday, didn't contact them till Wednesday. If they've swallowed my story about being too ill to ring, they'll be wondering about my health. Questioning my suitability for a full partnership. I have to go back on Monday, try and undo the damage. At least I won't have to worry about those false rape allegations coming back to haunt me.'

I felt an unexpected pang of loss. 'I'll miss being with you. The past week's been traumatic, but it's been exciting and challenging, too. And it created a closeness between us, a bond, that feels ...'

I stopped suddenly, a lump in my throat.

'George, darling. What's the matter?' She reached over and took my hand.

'I don't know, Julia. But suddenly I'm really scared. Not of being shot or beaten. It's a different fear, almost a panic. Oh God, I'm so frightened of losing you.'

'But you won't, George. No way. I need you, love you, more than I can express in words. For the first time in my life, I feel I can trust someone. Really trust. You were willing to risk everything for me. No one can give more than that. I'll never lose that feeling for you, because it's based on ... well, not just on words, but on what you did.'

I started to feel less panicky. 'You really feel that way towards me?'

'Sweetheart, how many times do I have to tell you? You know how incredibly difficult I find it to express affection. Saying I love you is about the hardest thing in the world for me, I'd rather walk across hot coals.' She smiled and held my gaze for a long moment.

I smiled back. 'Then I've nothing to worry about. Except unemployment, social ostracism, and poverty.'

We weren't in a hurry, so we decided to go by tube to Waterloo and take the Southern Region. We were back at the Wandsworth flat by a little after one-thirty. Soon after that I got a call from Superintendent Brock.

'Hello, Milton. I've just been talking to Inspector Douglas. She was excited about the warehouse. Seems it's the key to Sulaiman's European operations. He smuggled arms in a luxury yacht, used a dinghy to get them into the warehouse, it's got direct access to the river through a tunnel. We found cocaine as well.'

'So he was into drug smuggling?'

'Not as a major part of his business. Part of a barter system, we think, drugs instead of cash. Anyway, what you've given us is more than enough to clinch our deal. I'll do what I promised. This time, I won't let you down. Oh, there are a couple of other things. Douglas found two men at the warehouse, bound and gagged. They're proving singularly uncooperative. And we've just heard that Sulaiman's been found dead, along with another man. A delay in identification, or we'd have known sooner. I don't suppose you could help us with either of those matters?'

'Negative on both counts, Superintendent. I'm sorry.' I rang off before he could ask any more awkward questions.

'Well, Julia, it seems we really are in the clear. By tomorrow it should be safe for us to resurface, go back to our own homes. Unless you'd care to move in with me, or have me move in with you.'

'You haven't seen my flat, George, it's a lot smaller than yours. Two would be a squeeze.'

I sensed evasion. 'But my place is more than big enough.'

'George, darling. I need my own space. We live barely ten minutes drive from each other. For me, loving someone doesn't necessarily mean co-habiting.'

I flinched inwardly at her use of a term I found cold and clinical. 'Never ever?'

'Of course not, darling. I'm totally committed to you. Who knows what will happen in the future? I believe our relationship will get even better, deeper. And that's exactly why I don't want to live with you, not yet. Living apart, each time we meet will be a bit special. We won't lose that freshness we have around each other, or that touch of mystery that keeps relationships intriguing, invites surprises. And most of all, we won't take each other for granted.'

I started to feel rejected. 'Well, you've obviously thought about this. I can see you won't change your mind.'

'Give my idea a try, George, you might get to like it. And you won't have to share your bathroom.'

'But I've got two, remember.'

'I think I meant it as a ... metaphor. For not having to share the pettiness and trivia of everyday life. No arguments about who puts the rubbish out, n--'

'But there's a garbage chute.'

'George! Don't be so obtuse, so pedantic.'

We both laughed.

I was still struggling to accept what Julia had said when Sid came back from work. Sarah arrived soon after. When we told them about the deal we'd made with Brock, they expressed a mixture of relief and regret.

'We'll miss having you around the place,' said Sarah. 'But it'll be nice to, well, you know, be able to walk around in our undies.'

'Let's ring Sylvia and Charlie,' suggested Sid. 'Get them round for a party. We deserve a celebration. A bloody big one.'

'Brilliant idea,' I responded. 'I'll go and get some booze. And some snacks. We can order a take-away later.'

By seven, the party was in full swing. Sylvia approached me with a conspiratorial look.

'Remember your promise to check Charlie out.'

'Check him out? I don't need to check him out. The man's a hero. I'd trust him with my life.'

'But there's a few weird things about him.'

'Such as?'

Sylvia looked around to make sure Charlie wasn't in earshot.

'Well, he likes to ... put it up my bottom.'

For a moment I didn't know what she meant. 'Oh, you mean anal sex. He likes anal sex.'

Sarah looked around again. Charlie was still talking animatedly with Julia. 'Yes,' she whispered, 'anal sex.'

'And how do you feel about it?'

'I don't like it. Especially when it hurts.'

'What about uh, regular sex. Does he ever...?'

'Oh yes, he likes that, too. In fact, I think he prefers it, judging by the noise he makes. He told me he learned to enjoy anal sex in prison, that he really feels the need for it sometimes.'

'Let's go into the kitchen,' I suggested. 'We'll have a bit of privacy.'

We closed the door and sat down at the kitchen table.

'I know you really love Charlie,' I continued, 'and you're frightened of losing him. But does that mean doing things you don't like?'

'I guess I've always been so desperate to have a man in my life, I've done whatever he wanted, put up with all kinds of shit. Even beatings.'

'Is that still true?'

Sylvia stared at me, her eyes suddenly widening in surprise. 'No. It bleeding well isn't!'

'So what's changed?'

'Well, I've got to say nice things about your therapy, haven't I?'

'No, you don't. I'm not your psychiatrist, anymore. You can say what you like, I'm tough enough to cope.'

'The truth is, it was a huge help, especially the group. Once I was cured of my delusion, I was able to start facing up to my real problems. You helped me understand a lot about why I was the way I was, why I behaved the way I did. But I still found it almost impossible to actually change anything. Until you asked me to help you. After that I started to move.'

'Have you worked out why?'

'More or less. I've thought a lot about it. Mostly it was the sheer nerve of it. Looking back, it was a huge gamble, I would never have backed myself. But you backed me, and you won.'

'No, Sylvia. You won. All by yourself, with no help from me or anyone else.'

'Anyway, I started to feel better about the way I was. Oh yeah, another thing. When you asked me for help, I realised you were just another human being, not the superman I'd painted you. That I couldn't expect you to perform miracles, wave a magic wand, fix up all my problems. I had to do that myself. All you could do was offer a bit of help and encouragement. And of course, I had to stop seeing you, which forced me to realise I could manage without you. So lots of things, really. Then I met Charlie. Which I wouldn't have done unless I'd built up the confidence to go out that night.'

'And how does Charlie fit into all this?'

'Well I fell in love with him. You know how that changes the way you feel about, well, about everything. But I can see now I related to him in the old way. Clinging to him. Looking up to him, doing everything he wanted, never arguing with him. Laughing at his jokes.'

'And now you realise you don't need that kind of relationship anymore. Not with me. Not with Charlie. Not with any man.'

'Exactly. I suppose that's why I wanted to talk to you. I thought I wanted to talk about Charlie. After you'd sussed him out, of course. But I really needed to talk about me.'

'Yes,' I responded. 'And now you've got to make some difficult decisions.'

'And I know what they are. No more anal sex for a start. And if he doesn't like it, he'll just have to find someone else. I don't need him to make me feel alive anymore, to make me feel like a real woman. I can start doing those things myself. Now, I'm going to get totally smashed.'

'I'll join you. I've been sober far too long.'

But I didn't get smashed. I no longer felt the need for the numbing effect of alcohol, for oblivion. Losing control of myself, laughing inanely at fatuous jokes, telling my own incoherent stories, needing help to walk straight, waking up hung over, struggling to fill the gaps in my memory of the night before. None of this appealed to me in the least. So I drank mainly soft drinks. Instead of getting drunk, I watched the others doing it.

By way of entertainment, Charlie offered to show us how to pick locks using his set of skeleton keys with built-in lock pick. I proved to be a good student.

'If I wasn't going straight, George, I'd offer you a partnership. Natural talent.'

'Well, I am looking for a new career, but I'm not quite ready for a life of crime.' I wandered over to Julia.

'I notice you're not drinking,' she commented.

'I've lost the taste, somehow. Maybe had enough of making a fool of myself. Is that Coke you're drinking?'

'Just Coke. I've lost the taste, too. But for different reasons. Life feels kind of precious at the moment. I don't want to blurr it, tune it out.'

'That's close to the way I feel. It's bizarre, but I feel more alive now than I have for years. Even though I've lost everything.'

'Not everything, George. You still have me. And an obscene amount of money in a Swiss bank account.'

'Assuming Paul wasn't exaggerating. And assuming I can ever get hold of it. But no amount of money will replace what I've lost. My profession, my calling. My whole identity was tied up with being a psychiatrist. Now I'm a pariah, I've been shat out of society's arsehole.'

'Well, darling, you're in remarkably good nick for a man who's lost his entire raison d'être.'

'And on top of that I've been persecuted, hunted, shot, and I've killed someone. Not bad for a man who swore the

Hippocratic oath: "First, do no harm". So why the hell am I feeling so good?'

'Apart from being around me?' said Julia, smiling.

'Even allowing for the Julia effect,' I replied with a smile.

'George, has it ever occurred to you that being a psychiatrist wasn't actually very good for you?'

'Not while I was one. I kept so busy I never had time to think about anything except work. Which I thought I enjoyed. Well, most of the time. Since I stopped, though, I've been having these alarming flashes of insight. Mostly to do with how I've managed to avoid my own psychological problems by focussing on those of my patients. Even worse than that, I was living my life by proxy, at second hand. I fed off my patients. I had no real substance of my own, just what they gave me, what I extracted from them.'

'Including me?'

'Especially you, Julia. You are beautiful, intelligent, free-spirited, independent with an outstanding career ahead of you. You had strength, the strength of someone who'd fought to survive. But you were also vulnerable, defensive, walled off emotionally. And full of rage towards the man who had abused you, destroyed the safe, predictable world of your childhood. It wasn't just your physical beauty. You had all the qualities I lacked. I thought I had them, but I didn't, not really. They were illusory, stolen from my patients. But now I've stopped living life by proxy. It comes from the things we did. We've been brave, resourceful. For perhaps the first time, I feel truly alive.'

We were interrupted by a sudden roar from Sid, who had staggered to his feet.

'A toast. To George and Julia. Here's wishing them a happy future together. May they never have disc trouble again.'

Julia stood up. 'Now that it all seems to be over at last, I guess it's time for a few thank you's. First Sid and Sarah. We'll never be able to repay you for what you did, and for your ordeal at the hands of Sulaiman.'

Sarah rose, steadier on her feet than Sid. 'I won't pretend I wasn't scared. But once you knew where I was, I knew I'd be out in no time. So it never really sunk in that I was in danger, kidnapped by a ruthless murderer.'

'I'd like to say something,' said Sid, sober all of a sudden. 'I hope I won't regret it. But this is a special moment. It's about Sarah and me. Well, about me really. I've always had this problem with jealousy. George helped me work out why, but didn't stop me being that way. Checking up on Sarah all the time, cross-examining her, accusing her of having affairs. The feelings got worse when she went back to work but I managed to control them a bit better. I knew if I didn't, she'd leave me.' He paused for a moment. He had everyone's attention, but I sensed he needed some encouragement. Sarah came to his rescue.

'Go on, love.'

'Well, this sounds crazy, but when I heard Sarah'd been kidnapped, all I could think about was ... was her being fucked by Sulaiman. And enjoying it. Then by some of his gangsters. And enjoying that. Instead of wanting to save her, I wanted her to be punished, killed even, for betraying me. And then suddenly it was as if an electric shock ran through me. I had this thought, almost like someone had planted it in my head. Just before we got to the yacht haven.'

'I remember you were quiet,' interrupted Charlie, 'didn't say a word the whole journey.'

Sid paused again, losing his stride.

'The thoughts,' said Sarah, who'd been listening with rapt attention.

'It was almost like a voice in my head,' Sid continued, 'telling me it wasn't the end of the world if Sarah had sex with someone else. I didn't own her. And if it happened, she'd tell me. And we'd sort it out. Then my feelings changed. I wanted more than anything to rescue Sarah, to be with her, to comfort her, specially if she'd been...'

'And you still feel the same way?' asked Sarah a little breathlessly.

'I still feel the same way. It's taken a kidnapping to do it, but I think I'm finally cured.'

Sid sat down, and Sarah perched next to him, putting an arm round his shoulders. Her eyes glinted with tears.

How extraordinary, I thought, that the challenges we've faced, and the acts of courage they've summoned from us, have done what therapy failed to do, perhaps never could. I was about to say something along these lines, something that wouldn't sound pompous, I hoped, when my phone rang.

'George Milton.'

'I know about the second disc.' A woman's voice, accentless. 'And I want it.'

I froze. 'I can't talk here. Hold on a moment.'

'Who's ringing at this time on a Friday night?' demanded Julia.

'I'll explain later. I'll just go into the kitchen.'

I closed the kitchen door behind me. 'I can talk now.'

'I've taken over Sulaiman's organisation. He didn't tell me about the disc, a secretive man. But I found out. We have to meet.'

Dear God, I thought, here we go again. 'When and where?'

'Tonight. My flat.'

'But it's past ten. And I hardly think your pl-'

'Dr Milton,' the voice cut in, 'I've got Sulaiman's files. I know where you are, who you're with.' She gave me the address of the Wandsworth flat. 'So you see, I can get to you any time. Or Julia, Sarah, uh, Sid I think his name is.' She gave me an address close to Regent's Park, not that far from my place. I said I'd be there in half an hour.

I gave an edited version of what had happened, insisting that there was nothing to worry about. Then I was on my way.

TEN

The flat was in one of those exclusive blocks facing the park. Way out of my league, I thought, a notion confirmed when I was ushered into a huge lounge decorated and furnished with at least my annual income. That didn't include the paintings, my viewing of which was interrupted by a young man who explained he had to check me out for weapons. He removed my mobile phone, but he didn't take my wallet and keys. He withdrew when a woman entered through a door at the far end.

She was no more than five feet tall, with a tiny frame. Fine ash blonde hair drawn back tightly into a bun. A narrow face, features delicate except for a long, slightly hooked nose. Clear green eyes, smooth pale skin. No makeup. Mid-forties, I judged.

She introduced herself as Naomi Freeman. 'Please call me Naomi.'

'George.'

'The disc. I'd like to explain why I'm so keen to own it.'

'Apart from the money?'

'That was my predecessor's sole motive. But I have another. Would you like a drink, by the way, something to eat?'

'I'm not hungry. But a soft drink would be nice.'

Naomi made a sign and a manservant stepped forward. He'd been waiting just inside the door through which I'd entered. Another stood by the far door. She murmured instructions.

'I want to deliver one copy of the disc to the Iranians, and another copy to the Israelis. For a price, of course. When the Israelis realise Iran will have the capacity within three years or less to hit them with nuclear missiles, they'll be forced to act. Tensions in the Middle East will escalate, and I'll be in a perfect position to supply the extra arms needed. To be frank, since the special branch raided our warehouse in the East End, I have a serious cash flow problem. I really need this one.'

'But there's only one disc now, and it can't be copied. Not without the right technology.'

'I can arrange access to that.'

'And if I refuse to give you the disc?'

'There's no reason why you should. Consider what could happen in the Middle East if my plan doesn't go ahead. Israel will eventually make a pre-emptive strike against Iran anyway, but without the perfect excuse the disc provides. When that happens, the whole Middle East is likely to be plunged into warfare. It would be chaos, I'd have no edge over my competitors. My plan makes it much less bloody, much easier to control. And will solve my cash flow problem.'

'An arms salesman – person, sorry – concerned about saving lives. That's a bit rich. You really expect me to believe it?'

'I won't use the tired old arguments. But I do care. Especially about Jewish lives. I take my faith very seriously.'

I'd been outmanoeuvred. I couldn't think of anything to say. Maybe she was telling the truth.

'I'll pay you for the disc,' Naomi continued. 'Not as much as it's worth on the open market, of course, I can't afford that. But you'll be able to pay off your mortgage, and–'

'How did you know about my financial ... situation?'

'It's all in the file, George. I'm willing to offer five hundred thousand pounds. That covers your mortgage with a bit left over. You could sell your flat, buy a smaller one in town or a house in the suburbs, have enough to live on until you got your life back together.'

'It's tempting. But can you guarantee my safety, my friends' safety, after I've handed over the disc?'

'George, I'm not like Sulaiman, nothing like him. I'm not a murderer. I'm a business-woman. Anyway, what motive could I possibly have? Once I've got the disc, you're no threat to me.'

'I'll need time to think this through, maybe discuss it with someone who-'

'No!' She cut in harshly. 'I'm sorry, I can't allow that. I must have a decision now.'

'You still haven't told me what you'll do if I refuse.'

'Simple. I'll let MI6 know about the second disc. And everyone else with an interest. You'll be back to square one, safe nowhere. You and your friends.'

'Then I've no real choice. But I want the money in cash, and the hand-over in a safe place.'

'Agreed.'

'The disc's in a bank safe deposit. I think the bank opens on a Saturday morning. If you can get the cash by then, we could do it tomorrow, use the bank premises for the hand-over.'

'The cash isn't a problem. We'll do it tomorrow, the sooner it's done the better for both of us. Now it's well past eleven. I still have work to do, but there's no reason why you should stay up, I'll have you shown to your room.'

'My room? I don't remember asking to stay the night.'

'Merely a precaution. A necessary one. Others may still be wanting to do business with you, or stop you doing it with someone else. Now that I've got you, I'm going to make sure I keep you. Just for tonight, of course. There's no point in arguing. You can call your friends. Just don't tell them where you are. Make something up, use your ingenuity.' She indicated a land line phone on a nearby table. 'Now, please excuse me.'

I looked around. The paintings and opulent décor no longer gave me any comfort. I tapped in the number of my second mobile phone. Sarah answered.

'George, we're still up, waiting to hear from you.'

'Can I speak to Julia?'

'I'll hand you over.'

'Julia, I'm having to stay with the arms dealer, just for tonight. Please don't worry. Just explain things to the others.'

I rang off before she could respond.

'Doctor Milton, allow me to show you to your room.'

One of Naomi's minions had quietly come up behind me. Without protest I followed him out. He showed me into a large room with a king-size bed, an ensuite bathroom and a walk-in wardrobe. Spartan in comparison with the lounge, it was still five-star accommodation.

'I'm sure you'll be comfortable. But if you need anything ...' He pointed to a button near the bed. Then he left. I heard him turn the key in the lock.

I was physically tired, but very anxious and wound up. I thought a bath would relax me a bit. From force of habit, I emptied the pockets of my jacket before hanging it up. Along with my own keys I pulled out the ones Charlie had shown me how to use. Obviously I'd forgotten to hand them back to him. My watch said eleven-thirty. I'd wait half an hour and then try to open the door. It had a standard ward lock, the easiest to pick.

Before tackling the door I practised on the window, which was secured by a small ward lock. I selected a fine probe bent at the end and inserted it. After ten minutes or so of fiddling there'd been no rewarding click, so I gave up. The window was on the third floor, so even if I opened it I'd have to find a way of climbing down.

A few minutes after midnight I started on the door lock, trying to remember exactly what Charlie had shown me. I used the skeleton key rather than one of the probes. Just as I was beginning to despair, there was a sharp click. Cautiously I turned the doorknob and pushed. Nothing happened. Then I pulled gently. The door opened. I turned the bedroom light off.

The corridor was lit by a low wattage wall-fitting at one end. I turned away from it, following the corridor round to the right. I came to the huge lounge, walked gingerly through it and opened the door at the far end. I realised the flat was even larger than I'd thought. This part was clearly a business area. I walked past an office with two desks, each set up with a computer and printer. I crept further down the corridor. Then I heard a voice. Stopping at once, I tried to work out where it was coming from. A metre or so on the corridor turned left. I peered round the corner. The voice came from a door on the right, slightly ajar, contoured by a thin strip of light. I walked silently towards it and peeped into the room.

Naomi Freeman was sitting at a large desk, her back to me, a phone to her ear. She was listening intently. Then she spoke.

'But I told you, he's agreed to sell me the disc. For peanuts. He believed it, the story about preventing bloodshed by forcing an early pre-emptive strike.' A pause while she listened. 'I've got three firm offers. One from Iran, another from the Taliban and another from an extreme right wing group in the US. The Taliban's offer is the highest, but the situation in Afghanistan means their funds aren't guaranteed. The Iranian funds are cleared, but I'm concerned about a double-cross. The US group won't double-cross, I'm pretty sure. We have a good working relationship and they'll need us in the future. And they have the cash. They're offering fifteen million, five less than the Taliban, but I think we should accept it. Unless we get a better offer.'

I suddenly felt dizzy. Fearing I might fall, I reflexively shifted my feet. The floorboards creaked. Naomi stiffened, her free hand moving under the desk. She continued talking and I wanted desperately to hear what she said. But I knew she's pressed some kind of alarm button, so I turned, hoping to get back to my room before I was discovered. I heard running feet. Then two men appeared. They gripped my arms and I didn't struggle. Naomi opened the door of her office and gestured us in.

'Cuff him and sit him down there.'

She pointed to a stylish wooden chair. My arms were forced over the back of it and I was pushed into a sitting position. Cold metal rings closed round my wrists. I couldn't move without getting acute pain from the pressure of the chair back under my armpits.

'I assume you heard enough to-'

'I heard enough to make me sick,' I cut in. 'And if you think I'm going to give you the disc now, you're crazy.'

Naomi got up and moved behind me. I noticed she took care to avoid getting in range of my feet, which were still free. She's done this before, I thought, the back of my head tingling unpleasantly. She leaned forward and spoke softly in my ear.

'You will give me the disc, George. In fact by the time I've finished with you, you'll be begging me to take it.'

She stood up. 'Take him back to his room. Strip him, get him in a bath robe, put the cuffs back on, tie his feet to his wrists. Then bring me everything you find in his pockets.'

Back in my bedroom I pleaded to keep my underpants on but ended up stark naked while one of the men got a bathrobe. They tied my ankles together with some thick cord, and then they used another piece to link my ankles to the handcuffs. I could stand up and maybe hop about a bit, but I couldn't do much else. They left me lying on the bed.

A hand was pulling at my shoulder. 'Wake up, Doctor Milton.'

I opened my eyes, trying to focus on the face above me. In spite of being trussed up like a turkey, I'd dropped off.

'Time to get up,' the voice persisted.

'I can't. Not without some help.'

'Then I'll untie you.'

I was rolled over onto my stomach and the rope removed from my ankles. The handcuffs stayed on. After some wriggling I got my legs over the edge of the bed and managed to sit up. Then I felt a hard, stinging slap on my cheek. I fell back onto the bed.

'That's just to remind you this isn't a game, Doctor Milton. Now stand up and come with me.'

I allowed myself to be led into a small windowless room with bare walls and a tiled floor. In its centre was a heavy wooden chair with chunky arms and a solid, square back. There was also a sink, a large glass-fronted cabinet and a table with a white enamel top.

Several cardboard boxes were stacked against one of the walls. There was a smart black briefcase on the table.

'This used to be a bathroom. But now, any excretory functions that occur here are involuntary. Should you have such an accident, Doctor Milton, don't worry. They kept the tiled floor.'

I was getting very frightened, but I wasn't ready to show it. I tried defiance. 'If you're trying to scare the shit out of me, you'll have to do a lot better than this, you arsehole.'

My captor raised his right hand and I braced myself for a second blow. But he lowered his fist and called out a name I didn't catch. Another man entered the room.

'He's being bolshy. Help me secure him.'

I struggled. My reward was another blow to the face, this time with a fist. It dazed me and by the time my head cleared, my wrists and ankles were strapped tightly to the chair. 'I'm sorry, I didn't introduce myself. Willy Travis at your service. Call me Willy.'

I saw a face with high cheek bones and deep-set grey eyes. Creases round the mouth, a prominent jaw clenched firmly when not in movement. Jutting brow, a flattish nose bent slightly to one side. An unpleasant face.

He turned to the other man. 'You can go now. Close the door and wait outside. I'll call if I need you.'

Turning back to me he smiled mirthlessly. 'I prefer to work alone. Now, Doctor Milton, George, let's get down to it. Your hostess Naomi Freeman has explained the background. Told me you have something of hers, won't give it back.'

'That's bullshit. It's not hers. And I'll never give it to her. She's selling it to the highest bidder, doesn't give a damn what it's used for, doesn't care that thousands will die, maybe tens of thousands.'

'I'm afraid I don't care about that either, George. But I do care about my reputation. And that's as good as my last performance. I have to get results. You know what I want, of course. The name of the bank which holds the disc in its strongroom. And the access code. I assume this is the key. It was found in your wallet.' He held up the key to my safe deposit box.

'You don't understand, do you? I'm not going to be responsible for the deaths of countless innocent people. I couldn't live with that. Whatever you do to me, I'll never tell you.'

'George, George, you're being irrational and I'd say a touch melodramatic. I'm going to help you think straight, get some perspective. I can be very persuasive. Now listen, if you give the disc back to-'

'I told you, it was never hers. Let's get that straight, at least.'

'I won't make an issue of it, George. If you give the disc to Naomi, your responsibility ends there. It's up to her what happens then. Up to her entirely.'

'But I know what she plans to do. Sell it to a right-wing group in America. We've already seen how ruthless these people can be, bombing federal buildings, a child care centre, killing and maiming children. Give them a nuclear bomb, they'll use it. I'm sure of that. When that happens, I'll be responsible, I'd rather die than have that hanging over me for the rest of my life.'

'Perhaps we can persuade her to sell it to someone else.'

'Sure. Like the Taliban or the Iranians. If the Taliban get a nuclear bomb, they won't hesitate to use it to consolidate their power. In Jihad, Holy War, the end justifies the means. Many thousands of innocent Afghans will die. If Iran gets it and they build a nuclear bomb within two or three years, well, I don't need to spell that out.'

'I can see that words are going to be a waste of time, George. Let me show you the alternatives.'

He walked over to the table and opened the black briefcase. He drew something out and thrust it towards me. It was a fine metal probe that came to a needle-sharp point.

'I have considerable knowledge of anatomy,' he said with a touch of pride. 'The distribution of nerves, their function, is a particular interest of mine. With this little thing'– he waved the probe under my nose – 'I can find and penetrate any major nerve within an inch of the surface. As a doctor you'll know how painful, how exquisitely painful, that can be.'

My mouth was too dry for a response. Travis put the probe back carefully and withdrew another instrument.

'Now this,' he said with a smile, 'is something I keep in reserve.'

I shuddered involuntarily. It was a dentist's drill.

'There's something about teeth,' he continued sadistically. 'For some reason, the nerves to their roots are extraordinarily sensitive. For pure pain, pain that penetrates to the very core of one's being, it's difficult to beat drilling into the root of a healthy tooth. But it's messy and can be bloody. Requires a dental clamp to keep the mouth open, and an assistant. That's why I keep it in reserve, as a last resort. Unless the subject is expendable. Then I can really use my skills, be truly creative. I don't have to worry about causing too much damage. Are you expendable, George?'

I still couldn't speak, but I managed a croak. Travis brought me a drink of water and held it gently to my mouth. After I'd taken a few sips he began to stroke my face.

'Such a nice face, George, such a handsome face. Not ugly like mine. I'd enjoy making you look more like me. Are you expendable, George?'

'No, I'm not bloody well expendable. You'll need me to do things. Like sign an authority. Even if you have my PIN, the bank won't let you open my deposit box without a letter from me. When I rented the box, I requested maximum security. They'll probably want to talk to me on the phone, could even insist I come along in person. So you'll need to keep me presentable.'

When Travis had shown me the dental drill, my resolve began to fade. If it wasn't my worst nightmare, it was very close to it. But I wasn't going to let him know.

'Nothing you do to me with that drill could be worse than the dentist I had when I was a child. No fluoride then, lots of sweets. Each visit I needed one or two fillings. He never gave me an injection or gas. The pain was unbearable. I don't know how I survived it. But the worst thing, he always gave me a bar of chocolate as a reward. Made sure I came back regularly.'

'What a tragic tale. Chocolate I don't have. Injections I've got a few. But I don't use them much. I've tried sodium amytal and other so-called truth drugs, but they just don't work for me. So I stick to what does. Pain, pain and more pain. And mutilation, of course. Slow, careful, creative. But not in your case, alas. Well, not right away. As you said, they might need you at the bank. So we'll start with this.'

A bolt of searing pain erupted in my left elbow and spread down my arm. I screamed. I told myself it was the surprise as much as the pain.

'Bull's-eye. Ulnar nerve's one of my favourites. Good old funny bone, ho ho ho. Scream too much, I'll have to gag you. Floors here are thick, but too much noise and they'll wonder what channel we're watching.'

I screamed again. I just couldn't help it, the pain was so sudden and excruciating. Travis put a ball gag in my mouth when it was clear my own efforts to suppress the noise weren't working. Still I refused to give him the access code.

'You're an obstinate man, George. I admit I'm surprised. I thought you'd be a pushover, all piss and wind.' He called out a name, and this time I caught it. Jamey came back in at once.

'Go and ask Ms Freeman if she'd be kind enough to join us.' He looked at his watch. 'If she's not up yet, arrange for her to be woken.'

Travis turned back to his briefcase, inspecting and rearranging the contents. He stopped as soon as Naomi entered.

'He's being difficult, Naomi. I need your advice. Can I cut him, or will you need him later? He says the bank might want him to come in person.'

'They shouldn't. Not if we have his PIN and a letter of consent. But it's possible. So don't disfigure him.'

'Then it's the drill. Ugh, I hate the mess, I don't like working in people's mouths. And I'll need an assistant. Someone who's not too squeamish.'

'I'll be delighted to assist you, Willy. My father wanted me to be a dentist, you know, but I felt the same way as you. Do you have rubber gloves my size? I've got very small hands.'

Travis took out the ball gag. I clamped my mouth shut. After failing to prise it open, he removed the dental drill from his briefcase, plugged it in and turned it on.

'George,' he breathed, bringing the drill close to my face, 'if you don't open your mouth, the drill bit will go straight into your right eyeball. You'll have to wear a patch to the bank.'

He brought the drill so close to my right eye it blurred into a shadow. I opened my mouth.

'That's better,' said Travis. 'Now we'll put in a clamp.'

Naomi helped him screw a dental clamp onto my lower gum. When Travis was sure I couldn't bite down on his fingers or the dental mirror he used to guide him, he started to drill into one of my right lower molars. As he got closer to the pulp, the pain increased. I couldn't open my mouth wide enough to scream. Instead I emitted a piercing whine that competed with the sound of the drill. I started to sweat, I prayed for oblivion, a dulling of the senses, but my consciousness stayed clear and sharp. I couldn't bear the pain any longer, but I wouldn't give up the disc. The sound of the drill stopped, and with it the pain.

'Had enough, George?'

I nodded.

'We'll leave the clamp in, just in case you change your mind. Sign this. And jot the access code down here.'

I signed wrongly, then paused. 'Just give me a moment. To remember it.'

The six-digit code was based on my ex-wife's date of birth. I'd never forget it. I wrote down six numbers.

'The bank's open from nine-thirty to twelve on Saturday,' said Naomi. 'It's nearly nine. I'll leave now. There's no need for you to stay. Doctor Milton won't give us any more trouble.'

'I hope not. But if you do need me again, just ring. I'm fairly free this weekend and I'd love to do some more work on him. In fact, there's nothing I'd like better.'

Travis spent a minute or two tidying up and packing his briefcase. 'That tooth, George,' he said as he left, 'might just survive. Otherwise it's a root canal job. Pricey. Hope you're insured.'

I knew Naomi wouldn't get really rough until I was no longer needed. If the bank told her my signature and the access code were enough, then she'd have just one thing on her mind. Getting my correct signature. That meant Travis could really get to work on me. Pain was one thing. Having my face cut up, maybe an eyeball popped, that was something else. Once he started on that, I knew I'd sign anything.

Somehow I had to escape, even if it meant jumping out the window. Broken legs were nothing compared to what Travis had in mind. But my limbs were still strapped tightly to the chair and the dental clamp was still in my mouth. I couldn't call out, but I could moan. I sounded like a sick cow, but it made me feel better. At least I was doing something.

The door opened and a face appeared. 'George Milton?'

I stopped moaning and nodded. A young man walked furtively into the room. He wore wire-framed spectacles with round lenses and his clothes were badly matched. His wiry black hair stood straight up from his scalp, and it looked as if he'd cut it himself. The impression was classically nerdish, but his brown eyes shone with intelligence and he moved smoothly and precisely.

'I'm Fred, Fred Walker. I've come to get you out of here. There's no time to explain. You'll have to trust me.' He undid the straps while he spoke. After trying several keys on the handcuffs, he found one that worked.

I stood up and grunted, pointing to the dental clamp.

'We'll sort that out later. Just cover your mouth if we pass anyone. First we'll get your clothes.'

We got back to my room undetected and I dressed quickly. I'd given up trying to talk, relying on grunts and gestures. All the contents of my pockets had been taken, but I saw the skeleton keys lying on the carpet close to the wall. I'd dropped them there after picking the door lock. I put them in my pocket.

'There's a fire escape at the back,' said Fred. 'We're very close to it. Let's go.'

The door to the fire escape was locked. It was a Yale.

'Damn! They're supposed to keep this unlocked. Health and safety regulations.'

I grunted and waved the skeleton keys. Then I attacked the lock, but without much hope. Yales were way beyond my expertise.

'Let me have a go,' said Fred after I'd fiddled about for what seemed an eternity. 'We'll try, uh, this one.'

A moment later there was a click. The door opened. 'Beginner's luck,' grinned Fred. We clambered down the metal stairs and didn't stop walking until we reached the crowded safety of Marylebone Road. Fred waved down a cab, gave an address in Hammersmith. Twenty minutes later we were there. I followed Fred down some steps into a dingy basement flat.

'OK, let's get that thing out of your mouth. Sit down over there.'

Fred's manner was anything but nerdish as he inspected my mouth. 'Standard dental clamp,' he said with authority. 'It'll hurt a bit. I just have to loosen these screws. I'll need a small pair of pliers.'

After removing the clamp, Fred helped me through to the kitchen. I was unsteady on my feet. He gave me a glass and I rinsed my mouth out over the sink. The cold water sent a surge of pain through my injured tooth.

'Thanks,' I said, 'but before I start to show my full gratitude, I need to know why you rescued me.'

'Of course,' replied Fred. 'Let's go back into the lounge. You look as if you could use a drink, I know I could. We've got whisky, gin, vodka, Bacardi.'

'I'll have whisky. Straight.' I wondered what neat whisky would do to my tooth.

'Cheers,' said Fred. 'I don't usually start drinking this early, but in the circumstances.... Now, some explanation. First and most important, you're safe here. This place isn't my home. It's registered as a business and I've carefully hidden my links with it. No-one will look for us here.'

'I've heard that one before.'

'You've been through a lot, I know. I don't expect you to feel safe, or to trust me. Not until you've heard me out. This flat is our headquarters. Me and three others, Ray, Tony and Barbara. Basically, we started as computer hackers, but we've come a long way since then. We're legitimate, have our own software company.

'How did you get involved with Naomi Freeman?'

'That goes back about two years. The four of us, no, three, Barb joined us later, we were really into computers. Could write programmes, hack into mainframes, we really knew our way around. There was, like, fierce competition between us, healthy at first, then it got a bit out of control, we started taking too many risks. I hacked into Sulaiman's computer, but he traced the break-in back to my PC. Looking back, I was incredibly stupid. But the challenge of breaking into the computer of an international arms dealer. Irresistible. Well, Sulaiman sent a couple of his heavies round, I was sure they'd kill me, but they didn't lay a finger, just invited me to come with them and meet their boss. Of course, I thought they were taking me somewhere out of the way, then the concrete boots. After a bit of persuasion to find out what I knew. But I really did meet Sulaiman, and he made me an offer–'

'You couldn't refuse.'

Hackneyed though it was, the phrase made Fred laugh, and I couldn't help joining in. It broke the tension between us and we both relaxed a little.

'I had no choice, of course,' continued Fred, 'but the deal was a fair one. I'd join his organisation, strictly on probation, and help him access his competitors' information systems. In other words, I'd be a professional hacker. Starting pay was barely enough to survive on, but if I did well, the sky was the limit, he said. My complete loyalty was taken for granted. He didn't need to spell out what happened to traitors, double-crossers. Or if I refused to join him.'

'And this happened about two years ago?'

'Give or take a month. Is that important?'

'Not really. I was just thinking, you survived that long, you must have been crucial to him. He was taking a big risk, you knowing everything about his set-up.'

Fred looked embarrassed. 'Well, I was very good at my job, if that's what you're getting at. But he knew I'd never betray him. I had scruples, of course, about what I was doing.'

'What kind of scruples?'

'I kept in close contact with Ray and Tony. I trusted them with my life, so I told them what was happening. They went ballistic. Accused me of selling out. You see, we were kind of leftish, against the multinationals, that sort of thing. Which I believed in then. Ray and Tony helped me find a way of easing my conscience.'

'Which was?' I didn't bother to hide my eagerness for more.

'First they wanted me to be a kind of double agent, pass information to the authorities. I refused, said it was a death sentence. Then we came up with the idea of using Sulaiman's information ourselves, building up a global picture of the arms dealers and their customers. I'd smuggle data out and we'd enter it into our own system. We didn't think beyond that, but we hoped to somehow use the information for good. Without getting me tortured and dumped in the river. We haven't yet found a way of doing that.'

'You still hope to?'

'More than ever. Especially me, it's the only way I'll ever be able to forgive myself for working with Sulaiman.'

'What are your....resources? I mean the business, the four of you.'

'It's complicated. I'll explain the background first. I started to earn real money with Sulaiman. I was a brilliant hacker before I joined him, and I just got better. I hate to say it, but the growth of his power over the past two years, his becoming perhaps the biggest dealer, he couldn't have done that without me. He knew what his competitors were up to, what the national security agencies were doing, almost before they did.'

'Doing so well,' I ask suspiciously, 'how come you put it all at risk by rescuing me?'

'When Sulaiman was killed, everything changed. Naomi Freeman took over and she had it in for me. We'd never got on. Sulaiman insisted the data I came up with was for his eyes only. Naomi tried to wheedle things out of me, I always refused. She got really angry with me, the more so when I refused to work with her after Sulaiman's death. I didn't think she would go as far as Sulaiman had threatened. I bugged her office, found out she was planning to kill me. But only after extracting the information she needed. By torture if necessary. Then I discovered you were there, so I acted on impulse. Thought if I could get you out, hide you, I'd have something to bargain with. You were to be my life insurance.'

I became suspicious again. 'But surely it all depended on me still having the disc. What if I'd already given it to them?'

'I'd nothing to lose. I had to disappear fast. If I left with you and the disc, bull's-eye. And I thought you might be useful even without the disc, though I didn't have time to work out how. Of course, there was an outside chance you had another copy of the disc.'

'Makes sense. Uh, you were going to tell me about your resources.'

'Like I said, Sulaiman paid me good money. I put it all into the business. Which I now own about three-quarters of. We made some bad decisions, also we were a bit unlucky. Invested a lot in creating and marketing a software package, someone came up with a similar product, undercut us. Lawyers said we might get them on copyright but it was marginal. And we couldn't afford the legal fees. Just escaped bankruptcy, now we're fighting back. So resources: cash, nil; computer equipment, some; talent and ambition, megabytes.'

I suddenly remembered that Naomi had my mobile phone. I panicked at the thought of her answering a call meant for me. Especially one from Julia.

'Can I use your phone? I need to warn people about Naomi. There's a problem, though. Might be a tap on their phone, allow someone to trace the call back here.'

'Impossible. We still do a bit of hacking from here. Both our land lines pass through a series of filters. Makes tracing the source of our hacks almost impossible. Also stops phone traces.'

The switchboard operator at Julia's office put me through to her extension.

'Julia, it's George. You haven't tried to ring me, have you?'

'No, but I was just going to.'

'Don't use your mobile to contact me, and don't let anyone else. I'll explain when I see you. I'm ringing from a phone that can't be traced. Hold on.' I asked Fred if I could give Julia his number. He nodded. After she'd read it back to me, we arranged to meet at two in a café near her work.

Then I rang Sid and Sylvia to tell them I was OK. I gave them Fred's number, saying I didn't know how long I'd be there or when I'd be back at Wandsworth.

'How hard,' I asked Fred, 'will Naomi look for you once she finds you've scarpered?'

'It'll be a priority. I deleted all my files, all the data I built up over the past two years, but she was able to copy about half of it before I did so. I've got it all on USB's, of course. I copied the last lot this morning.'

He patted his breast pocket. 'She'll know, of course, and she'll do anything to get it back. How hard will she be looking for you?'

'How much do you know about me?' I countered.

'Quite a lot. Mainly from MI6 files.'

'You can hack into them?' I shook my head in amazement.

'And GCHQ, MI5, Special Branch, but KGB's tricky. Idiosyncratic systems, bizarre programmes, unpredictable. Mossad's easier, so are most of the Middle Eastern intelligence agencies.'

'That's unbelievable. I thought all those computer systems were impenetrable.'

'Not to a true superhacker. Don't forget I've been doing this for years, full time for the past two. I've learned passwords, access codes, bypass systems, not just by hacking but from Sulaiman's contacts. And a few of my own.'

'You said you came close to bankruptcy. Why haven't you hacked into banks and transferred funds to your accounts?'

'You've been watching too many Hollywood movies. It's one thing to hack into a system passively, collect information. It's something else to enter new data, manipulate files, give instructions, create output. And big financial systems are particularly well protected.'

'All that information you've got. It must be worth a fortune.'

'Sure. But only to the bad guys. And we're trying to be good, remember?'

'You see the national intelligence agencies as bad guys? Surely they'd pay well for what you've got, use it for good purposes.'

'I'm not so sure. They all try and break into each other's computer systems, some have superhackers like me. Maybe it's no longer possible for any organisation with a huge computerised database to keep all its secrets. Information is everything. Often, it's thought better to allow a terrorist or arms group to keep functioning, monitor its activities, study its communications. That way it can be predicted, controlled to some extent. Close it down, it'll just spring up again under a new name.'

'Like the Hydra of Greek mythology. Cut one head off, two take its place.'

Fred grinned. 'Yeah. Anyway, I can't tell the good guys from the bad, anymore. And it's not a matter of ideology. Not like the Cold War. Unless you think multinationals and economic rationalism are the new enemies. Ray and Tony do.'

'And you?'

'Not anymore. Survival of the fittest, that's what I believe in. I learned that from Sulaiman. Which reminds me. We were talking about what I got on you from MI6 files. And from other sources.'

I was amazed at how much Fred knew. There were plenty of gaps, especially about Julia's role. I told him everything. It had sunk in that he'd probably saved me from a horrible death, or at least a great deal of pain. Now his own life was in danger and he wanted me to help him. I was still in a lot of trouble with Naomi. This meant that Fred and I had the same problem. It made sense for us to trust each other, work together. Much more sense than his initial impulsive and impractical notion of using me as insurance. His flat was the ideal place to stay. When I suggested that Julia should stay, too, Fred agreed.

ELEVEN

Julia was already in the café where we'd arranged to meet at two. She looked tired and drawn, but raised a smile when I sat at her table.

'How's things at the office?' I asked, knowing she'd just returned after her sudden disappearance.

'It was busy, most of us come in on a Saturday, though not all day like me. On the surface they've accepted my story about being too ill to ring. But of course some of them suspect an emotional crisis. It helped that I'd been working so hard. Nervous exhaustion's an acceptable compromise between a genuine physical illness and a nervous breakdown. Anyway, I've put in a good morning's work and I'll be staying late tonight.'

'Julia, I don't think it's safe for you to go back to your flat, yet.'

'But I've been back. I left Wandsworth early this morning. No sign of anything unusual. It was so good to use my own bathroom, get into some decent clothes.'

I gave Julia a detailed explanation for my sudden departure the night before, skimming over the torture scene and focussing on Fred and his set-up.

'So you and Fred are going to work together,' she responded, 'but you haven't got a plan yet.'

'Not yet. Any ideas?'

'Give me a break, I'm still taking it all in. From what you've said, this Naomi Freeman is even more vicious and nasty than Sulaiman. So maybe you're right, it's not safe to go back to my flat yet. But I can't face another night at Wandsworth.'

'We can stay at Fred's. There's a room set up for overnight use, quite civilised. And it's safe. He says it's impossible to trace him to that address. It's registered as a business.'

'I hope he's right. It means buying some more clothes and things, like when we stayed at Wandsworth. Unless we risk getting our stuff from there.'

'Not with Naomi on the prowl.'

'We could do the shopping now. If you don't mind taking mine back to Fred's flat in Hammersmith. I don't want to cart it back to the office. And I really must go back to work.'

We finished our shopping by four-thirty. Julia went back to her office and I took a cab to Hammersmith, loaded with carrier bags. Fred had given me keys and the alarm code, but he was there to let me in.

'You met up OK?' he asked, helping me with the bags.

'She was there waiting. And she's coming here tonight. At least half these bags are hers. I'm sure you'll get on together.'

'I've rearranged things a bit, let me show you.'

We went on a tour. He'd set up the lounge so he'd be comfortable sleeping on the sofa. The overnight facility now looked more like a bedroom, and the bathroom was clean and tidy. Fred's efforts in the kitchen had been less successful, but he'd stocked the fridge with frozen food and bought milk, butter and bread.

'Well done,' I said. 'What about showing me the business area?'

Fred unlocked a door in the far wall of the lounge and keyed an alarm pad.

'Separate alarm system,' he said as we went through.

The rear of the flat had been turned into a single large room, with its own toilet facilities. The windows were barred, and there was no back door. Powerful fluorescent lights shone down on three long, widely spaced work tables. Shelves and storage cupboards filled most of the walls. The tables were almost empty.

'Not a lot of equipment,' said Fred with a hint of apology. 'But what we do have is really good. We've still got some powerful machines.'

'Could you make a copy of the disc?'

'I'd have to see it. But I'd be surprised if I couldn't work out a way of doing it. Don't tell me you've come up with a plan.'

'Not really. But some ideas are beginning to percolate.'

'Don't be shy, George. Share them.'

'Well, we have to assume that Naomi has carried out her threat that if I betrayed her, she'd inform MI5 and the arms dealer network that I have a second copy of the disc. Now, I have a question: the Internet. How much do the arms dealers, their clients, use it to do business?'

'Until recently, not much at all. But encryption software is now very effective, and so is security on the Internet. Secure websites are more and more common, and sometimes they're very difficult to get into. And of course there's the Dark Web. So, what's your plan?'

'What I'm thinking is some kind of auction. Advertise the disc online. Lure the key players to a real-time auction venue, then have Special Branch arrest them. Solves all our problems. Assuming Naomi attends in person.'

'If we can organise it that way.'

'Before we take it any further, let me explain how the arms dealers use the Internet. For a start they all use very sophisticated encryption software to protect their sensitive files and e-mail transmissions. There's a problem with this. You can transmit encrypted e-mail only to people who've sent their public code key to a restricted server, or directly to you: this tightly constrains the number of people you can correspond with.'

'So we can't rely on e-mail alone. We'd miss a lot of potential customers.'

'Not a lot, because I'm part of the network. Although Naomi will have warned them off. Our best bet is to set up a website and create hyperlinks with the arms dealers' websites. They all have a mixture of secure and open pages. The open pages are designed to attract you to the site. Secure pages contain the sensitive information, such as weapons available and price lists. You have to send your security certificate, or digital ID, before you can visit them. Some sites are very exclusive.'

'Supposing I wanted to buy, say, a Uzi submachine gun. Could I do it on the Internet?'

Fred grinned. 'There are three versions of the Uzi. The standard one, a mini, and a micro. The micro isn't much bigger than an automatic, but what a punch! So you'd have to be specific, know exactly what you wanted. And a routine search wouldn't help. You'd have to know the site addresses. Even if you ordered one and paid for it with bitcoins, delivery would be the main problem. Not in the US so much, but certainly here in Britain. Europe's a bit easier.'

'Supposing,' I said, 'we set up a website that included some highly secure pages giving an outline of the disc's contents. Back that up with a selective e-mail campaign. Maybe duplicate it on the Dark Web, for those who use it instead of the regular internet. Could we persuade the dealers to attend a real-life auction?'

'Only if we explained that detailed inspection of the disc had to be done in real life, not in cyberspace. But it needs very careful planning. And it would cost money. We'd have to book an auction venue, accommodation for the clients. Too much to do alone. Have to bring in one of my partners.'

'Which' Suddenly a vivid image lit up the inside of my head. The face of Travis, huge and grinning. Then the noise of the dentist's drill, mixed horribly with the sound of my screams. For an instant I thought I was back in Naomi's torture chamber. Then I heard Fred's voice, and the room came into focus again.

'You all right, George?'

I shuddered. 'I'm not sure. The most frightening thing just happened. For a moment I was back in Naomi's flat, being worked on by Travis. It was so real, soundtrack as well. I'm still shaking.'

'There's a name for this, isn't there?'

'Post-traumatic stress disorder. PTSD. I've seen plenty of people with it. But I never imagined I'd ... be like one of them.'

'Does this mean we'll have to change our plans? Will it stop you ... uh, functioning?'

'I don't think so. Depends on how it develops. Only very severe persisting symptoms are likely to make me ... unreliable.'

'Is there anything you can do to fix it?'

'The best way seems to be critical incident debriefing. Must be done as soon as possible after the traumatic episode. Encourages people to relive it, work through their feelings. If they manage to do that, it stops them repressing stuff, helps stop PTSD developing. Of course, it's often more complicated than that. Victims of major assault, armed robbery, violent home invasion, anything life-threatening, they have to work through issues of trusting others, fear of it happening again. Front-line soldiers, of course, have high levels of PTSD.'

'With you, George, it's a case of physician heal thyself. What are you prescribing?'

'I'll wait and see. Already I've noticed that I avoid thinking about Travis and what he did to me. It's just too hideous. But thoughts, images, sounds, even smells, keep trying to push their way in. Or suddenly blast through, just like then. It could all settle down. Too early to say. Meanwhile, let's get on with planning the auction.'

The phone rang. It was Julia.

'George, I'm leaving the office. Much earlier than was planned, it's only just six, but I can't concentrate. Everyone's gone home. It's scary here alone. I'll drive. Be with you in half an hour.'

'Be careful, Julia. Especially walking to the car. That's when you're most vulnerable. If you can't park close to the flat, ring and we'll come out and get you. But you should be OK, parking's good around here. Oh, if you think you are being followed, don't come anywhere near the flat. Stop somewhere safe and ring. We'll work it out from there.'

Julia's call prompted me to ask Fred if he'd been in contact with any of his business partners. 'I rang Ray, Tony and Barbara before you left this afternoon, while you were shaving and showering. Told them I'd left Naomi's employment in difficult circumstances, couldn't say more on the phone. Asked them to keep away from the business until I'd got things straightened out. They've got other stuff they can do, enough to keep them busy for a day or two.'

'But we'll need one of them to help us, you said.'

'Yes, Barb's the best bet, I thought I'd ring now, get her round tonight. That's if you can cope.'

'I'm still pretty shaky and I can't help feeling anxious, waiting for the next flashback. But it won't stop me doing whatever's necessary. Why don't we organise some food, eat when Julia arrives. Then as soon as Barb gets here we can do some serious talking. You hungry?'

'I could use something,' answered Fred, 'haven't eaten all day.'

'Me, too. What do you reckon? Microwave dinner or get a take away?'

'I live on microwave dinners. Take away'd be a change. There's a good curry house quite close, they home deliver. I happen to have a menu.'

I knew Julia loved a good curry as much as I did. I chose for her and ordered while Fred used his other phone to contact Barb.

'Order a beef Madras, hot, for Barb,' Fred called out. 'She'll be round by six-forty-five.'

I went into the kitchen to brew some coffee. I made it strong. It threatened to be a long night. We were sipping it when Julia rang the front bell.

She wasn't the hugging type and neither was I, but we embraced with a naturalness that surprised me. Then I introduced her to Fred and got her a coffee. A few minutes later Barbara and the curries arrived at the same time.

Barbara was about Fred's age, but there the resemblance ended. Straight, glossy and well-cut black hair matched her attractive Asian features. When Fred introduced us, she smiled, her black eyes sparkling.

'Call me Barb,' she said. I liked her at once.

There was just room for the four of us to sit round the kitchen table. Fred offered alcohol, but no one accepted. We needed clear heads. He began to outline the plan he and I had thought up, but stopped when he remembered Julia and Barb needed briefing on the day's events.

'Tell me more about what Naomi did to you,' said Julia, looking at me with concern. 'It wasn't Naomi herself. Well, she joined in towards the end. She got this man in, Travis. He arrived early in the morning, I don't know what time exactly.'

At that moment, I decided to give a full account of what had happened, hoping it would serve as part of the debriefing process I knew I had to go through. I explained this to the others, warning them it'd be harrowing. Barb was hesitant at first. Then she smiled and said:

'In for a penny, in for a pound. We can call it team building.'

'If you really think it'll help,' said Fred. 'But let's finish eating first.'

It was even more difficult than I'd expected. I had another flashback, so vivid that I reflexly raised my arm to my face, cowering away. I started moaning. Julia moved to sit beside me on the sofa, but I gently removed her arm from my shoulders.

'I've got to experience my feelings in full force. I can't do that with your arm around me. Much as I'd like it.' I smiled at her. She smiled back warmly, letting me know she understood. 'But I need to feel safe. So it's really important that the three of you stay close.'

It took over two hours, but I relived the whole episode. I wept a lot, and screamed a couple of times. There was more moaning. Julia knew enough from her own experience to prompt me when necessary, forcing me to keep hideous images in my mind when I craved to obliterate them. When I'd finished, I was totally drained, and so were the others. In providing a safe framework for me to work through my feelings, they'd had to share my suffering. I didn't know if I'd done enough to fix the problem, but I couldn't do any more, at least not till tomorrow. It wasn't yet ten, but my body ached for bed.

'Barb,' I said, 'I know this was the last thing you expected tonight. Thank you for putting up with my rantings and ravings. I am eternally grateful.'

'George, I think it was very brave of you to go through with it. Glad to have been of help. You're going to bed and I'm exhausted, so I think I'll be off. I'm only ten minutes' drive away.' She looked at Fred. 'What time do you want to start tomorrow?'

'We've got so much to do,' he replied. 'And we haven't even had a chance to discuss the plan. The earlier the better. I know it's a Sunday. Is eight o'clock totally ridiculous?'

'That's fine by me. And you two?'

Julia and I nodded. Then we all walked with Barb to her car. We were concerned about safety, but our main motive, I suspected, was to prolong the sense of closeness that had formed between us.

The night seemed one long dream about Travis and what he did to me. But the images didn't have the nightmare quality that would have woken me up repeatedly. They were frightening, but I jerked awake in horror only once, the image of Travis' grinning face fading quickly as my eyes found familiar objects. This time I allowed Julia to comfort me. We ended up making love, but for me it was therapeutic rather than passionate. I suspected Julia didn't really feel like it, but to my surprise I wasn't offended by the idea of sex as solace.

Barb arrived a little after eight. She'd had breakfast and was ready to go. We were just finishing coffee and toast. I felt as if I'd been awake all night, but I was much less anxious than I'd been the day before. Julia and Fred claimed to feel alert and refreshed.

After discussing the auction plan and getting broad agreement on it, we moved through into the work room at twenty to nine, setting up one of the long tables as our operations area. Fred positioned a portable whiteboard where we could all see it.

'OK,' he said, 'let's start off with a division of labour. Match skills and tasks. There's not much Barb doesn't know about the Internet. I suggest she works on setting up our website and sending out e-mails. I'll carry on with the disc. Julia, this is beyond the law, of course. But we might have some legal issues to deal with. More immediately, we'll need someone to manage the real-time side of things, perhaps you and George can do that and of course liaise with Special Branch.'

'We've already been a great help to them with Sulaiman's warehouse,' I said. 'Our direct line to Superintendent Brock is still open. I'll take responsibility for ensuring that he knows every detail. I'm certain that he'll approve of our plan, now that we actually have one. Brock will involve MI5, of course. Some of them and Special Branch can double up as security guards. That'll save us some cash!'

'Then let's start with the Internet,' continued Fred, writing the word in capitals on the white board. 'Barb, over to you.'

'The way I see it,' said Barb as she moved to the white board, 'we have a big problem. How to sell something without revealing exactly what it is. How can we auction the disc unless we prove it delivers what we claim?'

'That hasn't been a problem so far,' replied Julia. 'Only its creators have seen exactly what the disc contains. But we know that Naomi had offers of up to twenty million dollars, sight unseen.'

'Don't forget,' I broke in, 'that Kirk created a technical summary of the disc's contents. Special Branch extracted this from me, then they and MI5 gave the disc official endorsement, as it were. That was enough for Sulaiman and his competitors to start fighting over it.'

'You didn't make a copy of the summary?' asked Barb.

'No, it all happened too quickly.'

'Can we create our own summary?' asked Julia. 'Make it convincing without giving too much away?'

'I think we can,' Fred replied. 'I know it's possible to copy the disc. I did some work on it last night, after you'd gone to bed. Give me another day and I'll be able to make as many copies of the disc as you like. And let Barb set up a website that includes, say, the first quarter of the data. Highly secured, of course. Accessible only after we've personally checked digital IDs. And we can stay anonymous as long as we want to. But we'll have to reveal ourselves at the auction. Unless we bring in auctioneers, and I don't think that's realistic.' No-one disagreed. 'All right,' Fred went on, 'I'll get back to the disc. Barb, you'll need everything I downloaded from Sulaiman's computer. It's all there.' He pointed to a small pile of USB's. 'You'll find they give you most of the public keys you need and many of the hyperlinks.'

'There's one other thing,' I said. 'We need to decide whether to auction just one copy of the disc or several. If we sell only one, whoever buys it will spend whatever it takes to make more copies. They'd have the choice of selling them. I don't know how the market works. Can you help us out here, Fred?'

'If we sell just one copy of the disc, that'll be reflected in the price. It's not realistic to set a reserve, but obviously twenty million dollars is the right ball park. If we sold two copies, I think the price would fall dramatically. No, it's got to be just one. And I'll make it even harder to copy than it is now.

No-one argued with Fred, who started getting equipment out of a cupboard. Julia and I went back into the lounge. We began to focus on arranging the real-time auction. First, we needed to know the likely number of participants.

'I'll pop through and ask Fred,' said Julia. Just as she said that there was a shout from the work room. I ran through. Fred was sitting at a computer, face flushed, muttering to himself. Barb was standing next to him.

'Come and see,' he called out. 'I think I've done it.' We peered at the screen. 'See that? It's the self-erase instruction. The key to the whole thing. I just need to find a way to cancel it and the disc's safe. Could be a while yet. But it's a real breakthrough.' I asked Fred about the likely numbers at the auction. 'At least twenty. Plus hangers-on. I suggest booking for forty. We probably won't know the final number until the start. People change their plans at the last minute.'

'Can we do much on a Sunday?' I asked Julia. 'I'm thinking if we can't, why don't we take the afternoon off, try and relax. Spend some time together, just you and me.'

'Sounds good,' replied Julia. 'Let's check it out with the others.'

We decided to see a West End movie, wander about a bit, and then have a meal in a good restaurant. We'd be safe in the crowds.

I had a couple of flashbacks in the cinema, but they weren't that distressing. Julia didn't even notice. Afterwards we walked around Soho, enjoying the bustle around us, rejoicing in a sense of the every day, of being in the world again. The restaurant was superb, and the occasion verged on the romantic. I said I felt we were reconnecting, but Julia disagreed.

'For me, it's more a part of connecting for the first time. Things have changed. You having PTSD is somehow crucial. Along with me helping you to cope, sharing common experiences around it. It's as if we're now truly equal. I'm no longer your patient, no longer dependent on you for ... for ...'

'For all the things you never got from your own father, things you thought you could get from me as a therapist.'

Julia looked thoughtful. 'That's part of it, perhaps. I'll work it out for myself, I guess. Insights will keep popping up.'

We got back to Hammersmith soon after eleven. Barb and Fred were still working. They reported no major breakthroughs, but steady progress. Julia and I went to bed.

Waking on Monday morning I realised I'd had a fair night's sleep. No nightmares, just a few turbulent dreams.

'You didn't toss and turn nearly as much,' said Julia when she realised I was awake.

And I hadn't had a flashback since yesterday afternoon. Maybe I was over it.

Barb had stayed the night, sleeping on the sofa. Fred had pulled two armchairs together and slept rather uncomfortably on them. They both looked bleary-eyed, but were in good spirits.

'Almost there,' said Fred.

'And the website's pretty well set up,' said Barb. 'Just fine tuning now. I want to do the e-mails this afternoon, but first I'll need an auction date and venue.'

'We've had the go-ahead from Superintendent Brock, so we can organise that this morning,' said Julia. 'But the first call I have to make is to my office. I've decided that what we're doing here takes priority. I'll never feel safe until Naomi's dealt with, none of us will. We'll never know when she might strike. I can't go back to my flat, and I don't feel safe anywhere, not at work, not even here. I can't live my old life until she's no longer a threat. Even if I have to kill her myself.' She grinned sadistically. 'I'll ring the office at eight-thirty, tell them I'm sick again, won't be in for the rest of the week.'

'Makes sense to me,' I said. 'Now, an auction date. Fred, what do you suggest?'

'As soon as possible. I'd say this Friday, early afternoon. That's nearly a full working week. It's a matter of giving people enough time to assess the data on the website, decide on what they're willing to pay, raise the funds if necessary.'

Julia and I found it much more difficult than we'd expected to book an auction venue and matching accommodation. In the end we settled on a conference room in the Hilton International at Heathrow. Luckily they weren't busy, and had eleven rooms free on the day of the auction. We were able to book another nine at the Forte Crest, and five more at the Sheraton Skyline. We knew many people would make their own arrangements, others would fly in and out on the same day. But we had to offer hotel rooms as part of the package. Julia had enough money to cover all the booking costs and insisted that she did so. In reality, there was no other source of funds.

By six we'd done as much as we could. Fred, with a shout of triumph, had finally deactivated the self-erase mechanism around two o'clock. He'd made two copies of the disc and was working on one of them, trying to make it impossible to copy. As planned, the first quarter of the disc's contents was now in secure pages on our website, and e-mails had been sent to everyone on the list that Barb had compiled. We just had to wait.

The next two days were far busier than we'd predicted. We had several hundred visits to our website on both days, and a huge amount of e-mail. We'd been almost too successful in our advertising, and attracted people who were interested in buying anything from Semtex to cruise missiles. Fred had decided to allow access to our secure pages only on the basis of a digital ID that he himself approved. He'd already listed many of those seeking clearance, but the unfamiliar ones who weren't obviously crazy had to be checked out. This took a lot of time.

E-mail requests for extra information had to be dealt with as well. We responded only to those people who'd already accessed our secure pages. But we took anyone who'd got that far very seriously. We wanted the maximum number of bona fide customers at the auction, and we worked very hard at achieving this.

Questions about secrecy and personal safety were common. Several bidders were worried about being arrested by the British authorities once they had taken possession of the disc. We stressed that our internet security was high enough to ensure that the police and MI5 would not know about the auction. Julia's legal training proved invaluable here. She was able to put together an impressive looking summary of the disc's origins and legal status.

Julia argued that Paul Kirk had been the original owner, and that he'd put my name on the document.

Other clients were worried about the risk of violence from rivals or unsuccessful bidders. We had to be able to prove to these people that our own security arrangements were good enough to give them full protection. Julia had just enough money to pay for security guards.

We needed only two because Brock and MI5 provided four more. Posing as security guards was the ideal cover for their true nature. Her funds didn't extend to paying for the accommodation we'd booked, so we knew we'd have to bluff.

Busy as we were, Julia found time to ring her mother and I rang my father. As usual, he showed little interest in me, and I ended the call feeling sad and dissatisfied. I rang Sid and Sarah to tell them we were tied up with a make-or-break project but would try and visit them next week.

On Friday, we left for the Hilton International at ten. Julia drove me in her car and Fred took Barb in his. We were in the booking manager's office soon after eleven.

The auction was scheduled for one-thirty, but we'd booked the conference room for a full day. Our own security staff were due to arrive at twelve. Both had asked for lunch to be laid on, and paying for this and other details had taken us to our budget limit. But if it all worked out, we'd be twenty million dollars better off by tea time.

'I'm concerned about the number of security staff you seem to be bringing in,' said the booking manager, a tall slender woman in her early thirties. Far from looking concerned, she exuded a bland indifference.

'Oh, we don't really need them,' said Julia. 'It's to make our clients feel important. Part of creating the atmosphere. Anything we can do to get them spending.'

'And what exactly are you auctioning?' persisted the booking manager.

'Technology,' replied Julia. 'I'm afraid we can't say any more than that, it's secret. Another reason for having plenty of security.'

The booking manager switched to the matter of payment. 'You've paid a booking fee, of course. The balance is due today. I've got a note here from the reservations manager. He's wanting to clarify who'll be responsible for your guests' bills. Fourteen have booked in under your account name. But most of them have said they won't be staying the night, just using the hotel room for the day. As a base.' She looked at us expectantly. 'Uh, the balance, we really do need to ...'

'You'll take a company cheque, of course,' said Fred with a brashness that should have put the booking manager on her guard. He flourished a cheque book. The company account was already at its overdraft limit, but if the auction was successful, funds could be transferred before the banks closed. The booking manager looked carefully at Fred's cheque before accepting it.

She took us through to the conference room. 'All the equipment's been checked, but most people want to test it themselves, have a dry run.'

The room was larger than we needed. I counted eighty seats, laid out neatly in rows of ten, with an aisle down the middle. According to our latest figures, thirty-eight people were attending. We knew some of them were personal bodyguards, and some were obviously MI5 and Special Branch. Given our hopes for massive arrests, we would have been worried if all the registrants were bona fide. Fred estimated the number of potential bidders at about twenty, which was close to his original guess. We assumed that Special Branch had secured the building.

Barb set up her laptop on a low table at the side of the small dais that we'd use as an auction platform. She connected it to the large television screen which would show the introductory video she and Fred had put together. It included carefully selected images of the disc's contents. Then she connected the laptop to the phone socket so she could deal with any last minute e-mails. Her computer would have a crucial role immediately after the auction. It was to be used for the electronic transfer of funds to an offshore bank account set up by Fred. Only when he was satisfied the full amount had been paid in would the disc be handed over to its new owner.

When everything was connected up and running, Julia stood on the dais behind a portable lectern. Fred and I sat in the front row facing her. We'd had no trouble agreeing that Julia should be the auctioneer. Some brief role play had shown she was a natural.

Our security guards arrived just after twelve. Both were in the same uniform, and each had a variety of dangerous-looking objects hanging from a thick leather belt. The senior of the two, who introduced himself as Frank, was more interested in lunch than discussing security.

'We've come all the way from Peckham,' he said. 'Took us nearly two hours, road works on the motorway, of course. We need refreshments.'

'Lunch is laid on,' said Julia. 'The booking manager will take you over. Please make sure you're back in half an hour. We could have some early arrivals.'

It was a quarter to one before they came back. I smelled beery breaths but wasn't game to say anything. They obviously thought this was going to be an easy day. I hoped they were right.

'Anything you want to run through?' asked Frank, directing his questions to me.

I gestured to Fred. 'He's the man to talk to.'

Frank shifted his gaze to Fred. 'Not expecting any trouble are you?'

'Of course not,' Fred lied smoothly. 'But let's assume a worst case scenario. Some of our clients have their own bodyguards, and a few of these could have smuggled in hand guns. We can't ask you to search them, our clients wouldn't allow it. If someone starts shooting, how will you handle it?'

'Well we don't have guns, of course. This isn't America. But we have nightsticks, Tasers and stun guns.'

'Just remind me of the difference between a Taser and a stun gun,' asked Fred.

'They both work on exactly the same principle,' he replied. 'Although they run off just a couple of nine volt batteries, they transmit an electric shock of up to two hundred thousand volts. But because the current's very low, it's quite safe. It's specially designed to interrupt nerve impulses so people can't use their muscles, lose coordination, feel dazed, fall to the ground. Stun guns rely on direct body contact, but Tazers work at up to fifteen feet. They fire a couple of probes that penetrate clothing but don't have to make direct contact with the skin. The probes are attached to a fine wire and the current passes down that. Same result as the stun gun.'

'So if someone pulls out a gun, you'd fire a Taser, they'd collapse in a heap.?'

'According to the manufacturer's blurb,' replied Frank. 'Anyway, since we're not allowed guns or capsicum spray, this is the best we can do. Now, let's have a look at the layout.'

Frank, Fred and I walked slowly round the conference room, Fred consulted a note pad from time to time. Then he sat down. Julia and Barb joined us.

'Having two separate doors is a bit of a problem,' said Frank. 'We can close the main one, but we can't lock it. Fire regulations. So I'll have to station one of us there. The other will be on the single door at the far end, where everyone should come in and out. I know we can't search anyone, but we can delay suspicious looking customers. And make it obvious we'll stop anyone trying to leave in a hurry. Sound OK?'

'We're in your hands,' Fred replied. 'This is what you get paid for.'

By ten past one, both guards were in place. Frank was on the door at the far end.

We had given him photographs and personal details of each registrant. Barb and Fred had approved a late applicant, so there were now thirty-nine attendees. Only those who met all identification criteria would be allowed in. Fred was standing nearby in case of problems.

The first registrant arrived at one-fifteen. From then on there was a steady flow. By one-thirty, only five of the thirty-nine registrants had failed to turn up.

Julia mounted the dais and walked to the lectern. She spoke into the built-in microphone. 'Ladies and gentlemen. Welcome to our auction. The start will be delayed for five minutes to allow for late comers. Please accept my apologies.'

Three more registrants were granted entry over the next few minutes. At one-thirty-eight, Julia formally began proceedings. She started with the introductory video. Then she asked for questions.

A blonde haired man of about forty raised a hand. 'It's clear from what you've shown us that the disc contains very interesting nuclear technology. You claim it's sufficient to allow anyone with the right materials to build an atomic bomb. Before bidding I'd need absolute proof that the disc contains everything you claim.'

'We anticipated that,' replied Julia. 'The highest bidder will be allowed to study the disc's entire contents. Here in the auction room, using one of our laptops. And we'll give the two next-highest bidders the same opportunity, in case the top bidder fails to proceed. If there are no more questions, we'll start the auction. Do I have a bid at five million pounds?'

There was total silence. I was standing next to the dais, on the opposite side from where Barb sat with her laptop. Fred was watching from his position by the entrance door. My heart started to pound, my legs felt weak. Supposing there were no bids?

In the third row from the front a hand went up.

'I have five million. Any advance on five? Am I bid six?'

Another hand went up, this time in the fifth row back. Naomi Freeman was sitting in the back row.

'Six million. And seven. Come, ladies and gentlemen, you all know what this disc is worth. Let's have some real bidding. What do I have? Nine million? And ten over there. That's more like it. Do I see eleven? Yes, eleven, to the woman in the back row.'

Naomi Freeman had entered the bidding. Then a fresh bidder came in, offering twelve million. He and Naomi pushed the price up to fifteen. I started to relax a little. Another new bidder came in at sixteen million. Then there was a pause.

'Sixteen million, to the gentleman in the front row. Going once, going twice ... sixteen and a half am I bid? Sixteen and a half?'

Julia was doing very well, I thought, although she shouldn't be revealing where the bids were coming from.

'I have sixteen and a half. We'll take it up half a million at a time. Am I bid seventeen? Is that a bid, Madam? Thank you. I'm bid seventeen million. And a half. Eighteen. Eighteen I'm bid. Any advance on eighteen? Going once, going twice … I'll take quarters. Eighteen two-fifty, am I bid eighteen two-fifty?'

Naomi Freeman raised her hand.

'Eighteen two-fifty I'm bid. Do I see eighteen five?'

The bidder in the front row raised his hand.

'I have eighteen five. I'll take hundreds. Any advance on eighteen five?'

Again, Naomi raised her hand, followed by the man in the front row. At eighteen million seven hundred thousand, a hand was raised in the second row. A new bidder. The tension mounted. Now it was a three-way contest.

The bidding got to nineteen million and stuck there.

'We're in the right ballpark, ladies and gentleman, but the disc's worth more than that, you all know it is. This is your last chance. Nineteen million. Going once, going twice, going three times … gone. To the lady in the back row.'

The tension eased sharply, but there was no applause. Just the shuffling of feet and the rustling of papers. Naomi had got the disc. She must have a customer who'd pay a healthy premium, I thought. Someone who wasn't willing to risk attending the auction.

'Before you go,' Julia was saying, 'I'm happy for anyone who bid over seventeen million to stay behind. Just in case there are problems with the winning bid. Everyone else, thank you for coming. I'm sorry you weren't successful.'

People started to file out. Naomi and her minder came forward. She smiled at me.

'No hard feelings. I'm still well ahead on this. Haven't made as much as I'd hoped, but it's enough to keep me in business.'

Nothing about having tortured me and threatening to kill me. She turned to Fred.

'As for you. I'd planned to have you killed. But now I've got the disc, I'm in a better mood. I may just mutilate you. Now, let's fix the cash. I don't need to check the disc, you wouldn't be stupid enough to double-cross me twice. Just hand it to me, and I'll authorise the funds.'

I looked round. Twelve registrants were still in the room. The main bidders were among them. I knew the group had to include Special Branch and MI5, but I couldn't pick them out. I gestured the two security guards towards me.

'We're going to do the transfer now,' I said. Don't allow anyone to leave without permission.'

I noticed that Naomi's minder had retreated to the rear door. I felt uneasy, but Fred, Naomi and Julia clustered round Barb and her laptop, and Julia reached out to draw me in. I didn't see how Naomi could possibly get away without paying, so I handed the disc to her.

'Thank you, George.' She smiled at me again. 'Here are the account details, all you need to do is verify the money's there and transfer it to your own account.' She handed a sheet of paper to Barb, who began tapping keys rapidly. Fred peered over her shoulder.

'I'm having trouble getting through to the bank,' said Barb.

'Let me see,' said Naomi, moving forward. Suddenly she threw herself to the ground.

There was a deafening bang and I was knocked over by a blast of air. I bounced on the floor and then something hit my head. A flash of red and gold. Then nothing.

TWELVE

The first thing I saw when I opened my eyes was Julia's face. Close, staring down at me. For an instant I thought it was some kind of flashback.

'George, George, are you all right?'

I reached up and felt my head. There was a tender lump just above my right temple, but it didn't feel sticky. I looked at my fingers. No blood. I looked up at Julia again, now aware of the noise and bustle around me.

'I think so. What happened?'

'There was an explosion. You were knocked out for a couple of minutes. Can you sit up? Let me help you.'

Julia took hold of my nearest arm and pulled gently. Hit by a wave of dizziness and nausea, I instinctively lowered my head to my knees. After it passed, I looked up and gazed around me.

'My God, what a mess.'

'Yes,' said Julia. 'Don't know if anyone was killed, haven't had a chance to find out. But by the look of things there've been some nasty injuries.'

'I'll try standing up. Give me a hand.'

A second wave of dizziness and nausea lasted only a minute. I held onto Julia's arm. Then I let go, risking a step or two.

'Thanks Julia, I'm OK now.'

I saw Fred and Barb sitting in chairs by the wall. Their faces were blank with shock, and their clothes covered in debris. But I could see no sign of injuries. Six or seven people lay on the floor. Pieces of plasterboard and masonry were scattered everywhere, and chairs lay at random throughout the room. The portable lectern had been blown over. I looked up. A large part of the ceiling had collapsed. Then I saw a face I knew well. Superintendent Brock had arrived.

'Julia, look who's arrived. It's Brock.'

'I know,' she replied. 'And he's seen us. Should we go and talk to him? Or go over to Fred and Barb?'

Without replying I walked to where Barb and Fred sat. Barb looked up at me, forcing a smile.

'Is that you, George? You're just a blur, I've lost my glasses. I think they were blown off. But it could have been much worse. Apart from ringing in my ears and feeling dazed and numb, I think I'm OK.'

'What about you, Fred?' asked Julia.

'Just a few bruises and scratches. I'm still trying to figure out what happened.'

'I saw nearly all of it,' said Julia. 'Somehow I escaped the worst of the blast.'

She stopped when she saw Superintendent Brock approaching.

'I was just saying,' she continued, 'that I escaped most of the blast, although it did knock me over. Or something did. But I saw almost everything. Naomi Freeman threw herself to the floor just before the explosion. Then she got up and ran out the rear door, her bodyguard close behind her.'

'So she placed the bomb,' I said, 'and set it off so she could get out with the disc. Without paying for it, the damned woman.

I remember now, I saw her bodyguard at the rear door, it worried me, but I didn't say anything, I wish I had.'

'Good thing you didn't,' said Brock. 'He'd have set it off earlier, injured more people. It was in a brief case, on a chair in the back row. That's how the four of you escaped serious injury, you were all at the front.

'Has anyone been killed?' asked Barb.

'No, but five people were badly injured including one of your security guards. And three ... customers, shall we call them? All sitting or standing close to the bomb. Blast injuries mainly. The bomb wasn't very powerful, thank God. And most of the blast went straight up. That's why the ceiling caved in.'

'I think that's what knocked me out,' I said. 'A piece of the ceiling.'

'And Naomi Freeman,' asked Fred. 'Any sign of her?'

'None. She got clean away, even though we had people everywhere.'

'People everywhere?' asked Julia.

'Yes, it was a big operation. Combined Special Branch, MI5 and Metropolitan Police. We'd planned a lot of arrests, expected a spot of bother, but nothing like this, not even from Naomi Freeman. She must have been utterly desperate to get her hands on the disc. We ended up arresting no-one, dammit.'

I remembered that we had told Brock everything about the auction. But we hadn't mentioned that Fred had created a spare copy of the disc. Now didn't seem the time to do so.

'I suggest you leave now,' said Brock 'or you'll be taken in for questioning. I'll lose my authority here shortly, when MI5 take over. If there's anything else, you know where to get hold of me.'

We decided to go back to Hammersmith to debrief.

'Fred, are you OK to drive?' asked Barb.

'No, I'm still very dazed. What about you?'

'I feel a bit better. Amazingly, I've found my glasses. If we drive slowly I'll cope. As long as George and Julia drive behind me. George, you're obviously in no state.'

I didn't argue. We got back to the Hammersmith flat just as it was getting dark. No-one refused Fred's offer of a drink, and within twenty minutes we were all tipsy.

'As the resident shrink,' I said, 'I think we need to do some debriefing before we go to bed. I'll go first. Talk about how it felt to be blown up, how it feels now.'

The next time I checked my watch it was half past nine. Our session was winding down. The last nine hours had been an amazing experience. We'd all wept, sobbed even. And we'd all laughed, sometimes with a touch of hysteria. Although we tried to focus on the bombing, memories of other trauma kept surfacing. No-one held anything back. It reminded me of the encounter groups so fashionable in the seventies, except there were no performances. We all spoke from the heart.

'I'm about ready for bed, 'said Julia.

'Me too,' I added.

As Julia and I said our good nights, I wondered about the relationship between Barb and Fred. Neither had spoken about it. I'd assumed it was purely business. But tonight there was a closeness between them I hadn't picked up before.

'Should we offer them our bedroom? 'I asked Julia. 'It's not really fair we should have it exclusively.'

'George dear, we've been through a hell of a lot more than they have. And they're younger. If they want to make love, they'll do it. So don't worry. And talking of making love ...'

I fell asleep soon after reaching a climax that had me crying out even louder than usual. I stayed awake long enough to worry about offending Fred and Barb with my noisy ejaculation. I'd always been a screamer. Now that word's for women, I thought. Why isn't there one for me? I'll have to invent it ...'

No-one surfaced till nine-thirty. But by ten all four of us were squeezed round the table in the kitchen eating toast and drinking strong freshly brewed coffee.

'How did you sleep?'

Barbara's eyes were on me.

'Surprisingly well. No nightmares. Not even a bad dream. I think being knocked unconscious must have protected me from any psychological after-effects. What about you?'

'I had this dream I used to have as a child. A giant flash, being blown high into the air, then floating, gliding over fields, hedges, trees. I thought they meant I'd be struck by lightning one day. Maybe they really were premonitory dreams. About the explosion.'

There was silence as we took in the meaning of Barb's words.

'And you Julia?' asked Fred.

'I'm surprised I didn't disturb George. I was awake half the night. All sorts of disturbing dream images kept popping up. Some from yesterday, some from childhood. But they faded, and for the last couple of hours I lay there suspended between sleep and wakefulness, relaxed and peaceful.'

'Like George, I slept surprisingly well,' said Fred. 'Considering the sleeping arrangements. Not a trace of PTSD! And I never dream.'

'Everyone dreams,' I countered. 'Some of us remember them, some of us don't. Freud described dreams as the royal road to the unconscious. Maybe you're missing out.'

'Compared with cyberspace, the unconscious is old hat,' he replied. 'I can't download dreams on my computer! But enough of this waffle. Let's get back to reality. Like how the hell we get out of our financial mess.'

'Just how serious is it?' asked Julia.

'Bloody serious. Tell you what, let's move into the work room, I'll lay it all out for you. We can discuss it, maybe come up with some ideas.'

'There are other things we have to talk about,' added Julia. Like is it safe for George and me to go back to our flats. Barb as well. Is she in any danger after yesterday?'

We assembled just as we had when planning the auction. Fred stood at the white board, writing the heading 'Assets' on the left, 'Liabilities' on the right.

'Assets are simple,' he said. 'They're this building, less mortgage, and the equipment in this room. Debts are more complicated. There's the mortgage on this place, a couple of business loans, and a bank overdraft. Which is over the limit. I've no assets of my own, the place where I live is rented. I've put everything into the business. So has Barb. She's in the same mess as I am, except she owns only five or six per cent of our worthless company. Ray and Tony have about eight per cent each. I've got the rest.'

'Is it a limited company?' Asked Julia.

'It is now. Since we nearly went under. So we're not talking personal bankruptcy. Just losing everything we've worked for. But I don't have any personal assets, anyway. Except a CD player and some sticks of furniture I couldn't give away.'

'Same with me,' said Barb.

'What about Ray and Tony?' I asked.

'They're a bit better off. But when the business folds they'll be out of a job. I'll ring them this morning, suggest they start looking for other work. If they haven't already.'

'So what's the total excess of liabilities over assets?' asked Julia.

'About ninety thousand, give or take a couple.'

'Supposing you get hold of the money. Would you pay off your debts, continue in business? Or have you had enough?'

'We'd carry on,' said Fred and Barb in unison. 'We've got lots of good ideas, enough talent and know-how to develop and market them. It's what we like doing, what we're good at. We could get jobs with other software companies. Perhaps that's the sensible thing to do. But we'd be selling not just our skills, but our souls.'

'If I sold the rest of my shares,' continued Julia. 'I could raise about a hundred thousand pounds. But I'd end up owning the company.'

'I'm sure you'd be a great boss,' said Fred. 'But I'd still be working for someone else. And we'd need at least another fifty thousand in working capital.'

'That's beyond my resources.' She looked at me. 'And you've got your own financial problems, haven't you, George?'

'Sure have. In fact, one of the things I have to do, might make a few calls this morning, is put my flat on the market. The mortgage repayments are draining me dry. I might get a million and a half for it. When all my debts are paid off, I'll be lucky to have two hundred and fifty thousand. Maybe enough for a tiny flat some-where like ... like Croydon or Purley. Not what I'm used to. Where I'll live on the dole. Unemployable. Unless ... unless,' I said with mock drama, 'we can get Paul Kirk's funds out of his Swiss bank account. That would solve all our problems.'

'Before we discuss this further,' said Fred 'there's a crucial decision to be made. Immediately. The data I downloaded from Sulaiman's files. I propose sending it all to Superintendent Brock. This means he'll know more about Sulaiman's operation than Naomi. Working with special branch, MI5 and MI6, he might find a way to trap Naomi and get the disc back. Before she sells it on. Whoever she sells it to, it will be disastrous. We must do our best to stop it.'

After a moment's silence, there was a chorus of agreement. 'OK,' said Fred. 'I'll do that now.'

When Fred had finished, we resumed our previous topic. 'He never told me how much was in the account. But he implied millions.'

'That money,' said Barb. 'Who does it really belong to? Has anyone else got a claim on it? Legitimate or not.'

'According to Paul Kirk, the funds came from Iran. He implied government, but I suppose it could have been Hezbollah.'

'Hezbollah?' asked Barb.

'It's an extremist Muslim organisation founded by a faction of the Iranian revolutionary guard in 1979. Most of its operations are in Lebanon, but it has bases in Iran, and it's supported by the Islamic government there. It also has close links with other terrorist groups, especially one called Islamic Jihad. Now there's increasing polarisation in Iran between the Islamic fundamentalists, who still run the country, and the emerging moderates. This could drive the fundamentalists into an even stronger alliance with Hezbollah. So even if Hezbollah don't get the disc from Naomi, they'd end up sharing the fruits of Iran's nuclear efforts. The last I heard, Iran will have an intercontinental ballistic missile, range about two thousand miles, within a year. Obtaining the accurate disc means they can stick an A-bomb on the end of one within two years or so. If they do finally get hold of the disc, look out Israel, look out Europe.'

'And we're partly responsible,' said Julia, looking at me.

'Don't let's get into all that again,' I said sharply. 'Remember, Naomi Freeman was planning to sell the disc to a right-wing group in America. I don't remember Hezbollah being on her list. Though God knows what's she's planning now. Anyway, it's not our problem any more. Leave it to the experts. They might even catch her.'

'Don't make me laugh,' said Barb. 'That lot couldn't catch a cold.'

'We haven't answered Barb's original question,' Fred reminded us. 'Who else has a claim on the money? Or thinks they do?'

'If it was me who bought the fake disc,' said Barb,' I'd be very keen to get my money back. I'd start off with Paul Kirk, but he's no longer with us, rest his soul. Next I'd go for anyone else trying to make a buck out of the disc. Which means Naomi Freeman.'

'You've got a point,' I said. 'Naomi must now be the target of, let us assume, the Iranians. Unless she obtained the disc on their behalf.'

'Which means they'll leave us alone,' said Julia. 'No-one else knows about my stepfather giving you access to his Swiss bank account. Or about the spare disc.'

'All this is pure speculation,' interrupted Fred. 'Let's try and stick to the facts rather than scaring ourselves shitless. Assuming there really is money in the account, how do we get it out, and what can we do with it? Two separate questions, both equally important. It's one thing getting the money out, it's another thing keeping it, using it.'

'I've lost you,' said Barb.

'I'll try and explain. I learned all about it while I was working for Sulaiman. George, I know you don't have the account number with you, or the access code. They're in your safe deposit box. But can you remember the name of the bank?'

'No, but it was just one word.'

'Gutzailler? Baer? Vontobel?'

'None of those ring a bell. I think it was only one syllable.'

'Hecht?'

'That's it, I'm sure.'

'Makes sense. Hecht is one of the biggest private banks in Switzerland. Based in Geneva. Very choosy about their clients. You need a personal introduction before they'll let you open an account.'

'That's not our problem,' I said. 'We want to get money out, in case you've forgotten. How do we go about that?'

'Depends on what Kirk gave you. Most holders of numbered accounts have extra security arrangements, often a code built into the account numbers.'

'I recall three numbers. Along with other details. And he'd signed his name at the bottom of the page.'

'Three numbers implies two security codes. Unusual. But understandable in the circumstances. And good news for us. With both codes and his signature, they won't be able to keep you out. Does he name you on the access document?'

'I don't recall. Maybe just in the covering letter.'

'You'll have to go to Hecht in person, anyway. Take everything remotely relevant just in case they're difficult. And you'll need absolute proof of your identity, a passport won't be enough. It's just possible they will have notified the authorities about the account, but it's very unlikely, given that it was set up by a senior member of the British government.'

'In spite of all that's happened since?'

'Oh yes. They'll be able to argue that when the account was opened they had absolute guarantees of its legitimacy. And don't forget, the Swiss banks still do everything they can to protect their client's privacy. Much of their business depends on it. But let's move on. I can't be of any more help unless I see exactly what Kirk gave you. As I was saying, holding on to the money could be more of a problem than getting it out of the bank. Blame the United States for that. I'll tell you why.'

'You've all heard of General Manuel Noriega and the Medillin drug cartel. Well, their bankers were forced to admit that two of its subsidiaries had been laundering money for Noriega. There were forty-two branches of the bank in Britain, but the authorities didn't crack down on it until the Americans made a huge fuss. Actually, the Noriega affair was just one of many that had frustrated the Drug Enforcement Agency and the United States treasury for years. Out of all this came the American Anti-Drug Abuse Act. This requires other nations to make their banks notify the regulatory authorities about any suspicious activity. And to release account details of suspected money launderers. If they refuse, they can incur heavy financial penalties, including exclusion from the United States payments system.'

'So what does all this mean for us?' asked Barb.

'It means that if we transfer millions of dollars or pounds from Geneva to any bank within the G10 countries it'll be assumed we're part of a money laundering scheme, acting on behalf of international drug or arms dealers. Almost nothing else generates such huge amounts of cash outside of well documented, legitimate business transactions.'

'Can we create a legitimate business transaction?' asked Julia. 'Or a convincing illusion of one?'

'We could. But it would take weeks, months probably. And money we haven't got. We'd have to get the accounts audited, pay company tax, lose some of our privacy in the process. It could become a nightmare. And if they traced the true source of the funds, we'd end up in jail.'

'So what do you suggest?' persisted Julia.

'It really depends on what you want to do with the money,' Fred replied. 'That means each of us making big decisions, maybe irrevocable ones. About where we want to live, what we want to do with our lives. Take Panama. Its free zone at the end of the Panama Canal makes it a bit special, and they've managed to restore high levels of bank privacy. We could transfer the funds there, invest them safely, and get a good return. But we'd have to set up a legitimate business, perhaps apply for residency, have to live there for much of the year. Now Panama's a pleasant enough place to live if you're wealthy. But it's a bit light on Western culture. So if you like opera, art galleries, art-house movies, think again.'

'And other South American countries? 'asked Barb.

'The problem there is American aid, most of them get it. In return they have to comply with American financial disclosure requirements. The same is true of the Caribbean. Which has made tax havens there much less popular recently. Hot money is shifting from places like the Bahamas, Bermuda, even the Cayman Islands, mainly to Switzerland. Although the British Virgin Islands are resisting the trend. They'd be worth thinking about if you wanted to spend the rest of your life on a tiny speck in the middle of the Atlantic. That's where I set up the account for the auction proceeds. Actually I already had one there, in the company name. I just had to activate it, add a code.'

'Supposing,' I said, 'we collected the money in high denomination notes, say a mixture of dollars, sterling, Swiss francs. Brought it home in a suitcase. Perhaps not all at once, make several trips.'

'Problem is customs, of course. If they found it, the whole lot'd be confiscated. And they'd try and fine you as well. If you got through, you'd still have to find a way of using this mountain of cash, getting some kind of return on it. Unless you kept it under the bed, paid for everything in cash for the rest of your life. Or until inflation wiped you out. I wouldn't risk it. Be better off buying diamonds. You'll find dealers in Zurich, though you'd get better value in Amsterdam. But you'd have to drive there with the cash. Smuggle them back to England, sell them when you need to. Most banks won't ask awkward questions about cheques from a reputable London diamond dealer.'

'Hearing all this,' said Julia, 'you can keep the money. George. I don't really need it. I just want my old life back, be a good lawyer. But I'm going to make some changes. A bit less work. See what it's like to have a social life, interests outside the law. And you know I dearly want you to be part of it.'

'Goes without saying,' I replied. 'But I'm in a very different position. I can't resume my old life. I'm barred from my trade, I've no other skills. I'm facing poverty. A few hundred grand would transform my life.'

'Would it really, George?' asked Julia, her voice rising. 'You're so dumb. There's no way you'd be happy doing nothing. In Croydon, Regent's Park, the fucking Bahamas, wherever.'

I was astonished at her rage. 'What's this about, Julia?'

'I'll tell you what it's about. I'm absolutely fucking fed up with your attitude. Every time you talk about the future it's the same. You come over all hopeless and pathetic. Doomed to poverty my arse. What a load of crap. You're a highly intelligent, creative and talented man. If you can't go back to psychiatry, you'll find something else. You have to. You can't just rot, what a fucking waste. Not if we're going to be together, I won't let you. I won't spend time around a ... a fucking vegetable.'

There was a stunned silence. I couldn't look at the others. So I sat there with my head down, trying to come up with something to restore my dignity. But Julia hadn't finished.

'And in case you try psychologising, tell me it's just projection, transference, well it's not. I've thought about this a lot. Up till now I've bottled up my anger. Now it's all coming out. Don't expect me to apologise.'

'For Christ's sake, Julia, give me a break. I've been through a hell of a lot, don't forget. Struck off, lost everything, been tortured, blown up. To say nothing of being shot. Most people would be asking themselves what's next on the list. They'd be starting to think of themselves as just a bit unlucky. I reckon I'm allowed a bit of pessimism.'

Julia's gaze softened. 'Maybe I have been a bit hard on you. Perhaps I am putting some of my own shit on to you. So I will apologise.' She offered me a shy smile. I didn't respond. I was still angry.

Fred gave up on the white board and sat down. 'What I want is to get back into the software business. Make a real success of it. A second chance, if you like.'

'Me too,' said Barb. 'Preferably with Fred. But in equal partnership. Seventy thousand pounds would do that nicely, thank you.'

'I don't know if you remember, George,' continued Fred, 'but I told you about this idea of doing some good with Sulaiman's data.'

'Of course. You, Ray and Tony. Soon after you started working for Sulainman.'

'So you left me out,' said Barb with a touch of petulance.

'It wasn't that. The three of us go back a long way, remember. We used to talk for hours about what was wrong with society, how we'd change it. And this stuff had nothing to do with the business. But if it came up now, I'd want you in.'

'Sounds like it is coming up now,' said Barb, her perkiness returning.

'The original idea,' Fred went on, 'was to build on Sulaiman's data, all the stuff I was smuggling out, use it to set up our own intelligence network. Then we'd expose corruption, hypocrisy, double-dealing in governments and industry. That was incredibly naïve, I see that now. We didn't have the resources to gather useful amounts of secret or sensitive material, and certainly not to protect ourselves from the people we planned to target. But with some real money, it might just work.'

'Sounds like you want to be the Noam Chomski of the Internet,' I said with a grin.

'Chomski as in psycholinguist turned philosopher?' asked Barb.

'He's much more than that,' I replied. 'He's one of my heroes. Have any of you read *The Manufacture of Consent*?'

No-one had. I hadn't either. But I'd seen a documentary on it, and then rushed out to buy it. Along with most of the other books I'd bought, it was still waiting for my serious attention.

'It's an amazing book. Chomski shows how democracies create consensus, keep people under control. How they manipulate minds with subtle and not-so-subtle propaganda, distortions of the truth, convenient omissions. The media play an active part in the process, but it's not a true conspiracy. It just sort of happens, mainly through the influence of powerful men, like Rupert Murdoch. Chomski exposes all this.'

'How do you think he got his information?' asked Fred.

'He had a small team of people who actively searched the media for inconsistencies. They traced particular issues and stories, the classic case was East Timor, looking at what happened there, what people were told or not told. He's 92, but still active. He hates Donald Trump, of course. Let me give you some recent quotes that I memorized. "Donald Trump is the worst criminal in human history" and "we have a sociopathic maniac in the White House".'

'This is all very interesting,' said Julia. 'But let's get back to business.'

'It sounds,' said Fred, 'as if we're all planning to stay at home. None of us want to live in the Caribbean or South America. If we're all certain of that we can start some detailed planning.'

Finally, we decided to take Fred's advice about buying diamonds, but hadn't decided whether to get them in Zurich or Amsterdam. Smuggling them back to London was risky, but it seemed our best chance of ending up with money that was fully laundered. Julia had insisted on coming with me, so I'd rung a travel agent and booked two seats on a flight to Geneva. It would leave Heathrow at twelve forty on Monday, which left us plenty of time to go to the bank and get the account details out of my deposit box. Julia would ring her office and let them know she wouldn't be in for another week.

Next morning, we all ate bacon and eggs with tomatoes and plenty of toast. After my third cup of freshly brewed coffee, I felt brave enough to talk about what was on my mind.

'Julia and I will have to go back to our flats today. We need passports for tomorrow's trip, and I need my birth certificate, driver's licence, a few bank statements, that sort of thing, to prove my identity. And some decent clothes.'

'Let's go to your place first,' said Julia. 'Sort things out, then go to my place, do the same.'

I kept a spare set of keys with an elderly couple who lived on the ground floor. They rarely went out, and were there to open the street level door when I announced myself through the intercom. As usual, they loved to chat and it was difficult to get away. Then Julia and I were standing outside my flat door. It was only two weeks since I had been there, but it seemed much longer. I opened the door anxiously. A cautious look around showed no signs of fresh disturbance.

'That's a relief,' I said. 'No more break-ins.'

It took nearly an hour to find what I needed and pack a suitcase. Before we left I listened to the answering machine. There were no messages.

We were less anxious about what we would find in Julia's flat because everything had been fine when she'd gone there the Saturday before last. The flat looked exactly as she'd left it. She took longer to pack than I had, and it was close to five when she'd finished.

'You want to stick to the plan and go back to Hammersmith?'

'Yes. I know there's no reason to fear Naomi Freeman any more, but I still feel uncomfortable about staying overnight here or at your place.'

We got a cab to Hammersmith and spent a quiet evening with Fred and Barb. Mostly we went over our plans. Trying to find flaws, talking through the details.

'I assume you've both got European driving licences,' said Fred.

We did, so hiring a car in Switzerland wouldn't be a problem. We'd need one if we decided to go to Amsterdam.

Next morning, Fred and I were at the bank when it opened. He came down to the vault with me and together we lifted the lid of the safe deposit box. Fred studied the back of Paul Kirk's letter.

'Basically he's named you as having full authority over the account. Just as you thought, it's the Hecht bank in Geneva, and there are two security codes. So all you'll need to do is take this along with your passport, birth certificate, and European driving licence. That should be enough to satisfy them, but they might ask for some bank and tax statements. I know you anticipated that.'

Julia and I got the Heathrow barely twenty minutes before the flight was due to leave. As we were walking to the terminal access point, I had a moment of panic. I glimpsed from behind a woman who looked like Naomi Freeman.

'Julia, quick, look over th-'

But the figure had disappeared.

'I'm seeing things. I thought I saw Naomi. It must have been a figment, she'll be out of the country by now. It was just someone who looked like her, I'm sure.'

THIRTEEN

'd visited Geneva over twenty years ago, but I hadn't flown in. I'd heard that Lake Geneva was bluer than the other Swiss lakes, but today it was many shades of grey, matching the overcast sky. The number of foam-topped waves suggested a high wind.

As we hailed a taxi to take us into the city, a light rain began to fall. The wind whipped it into our faces. Julia had never been to Geneva, and she peered out of the cab windows with interest. I didn't see any familiar landmarks until we neared the main railway station, Gare de Cornavin. That's where I'd arrived last time. I recognised Place des Cantons and then, as we drove west along it, the stately old buildings of Rue de Chantepoulet. The bank was on Rue du Mont-Blanc, not far from the bridge of the same name which crossed the Rhone at the point where it ran into the lake.

'What a beautiful city,' exclaimed Julia. 'I had no idea its history went back so far. Some of those buildings look fourteenth century.'

'The cathedral's twelfth century. I gather Geneva was of some importance as far back as Roman times. Oh, here we are.'

The bank occupied a dignified eighteenth-century house set back slightly from the road. The doorman must have heard us talking because he asked in English if we had an appointment.

He looked faintly distressed when we said no, but Julia gave him a smile and he risked taking us through the glass door into the reception area. I spoke in English to a young woman sitting behind an impressive teak desk.

'We don't have an appointment, but I'm sure the manager will see us when you tell him it concerns the account of Mr Paul Kirk. Er, deceased.'

'Diseased?'

'No. Deceased. No longer with us. Passed away. *Il est mort.*'

'But this is a bank, not an ... an *ordonnateur.*'

I looked pleadingly at Julia, who was trying not to laugh. 'What the hell's she talking about?'

'She says this a bank, not an undertaker's. She's being awkward because you spoke in English, rather than trying French. Let me have a go.'

Julia's French was much better than mine. The receptionist smiled and spoke rapidly into a phone. 'The manager will see you in ten minutes. His office is over there. If you want to sit, *voila.*' She pointed to an elegant leather chaise longue on the far side of the foyer. 'You can leave your suitcases with me.' We walked over and sat down.

'Shit, this place stinks of money,' said Julia.

'Let's hope some of it's sticking to us when we walk out,' I retorted.

We spent the next few minutes in repartee, at which Julia could be brilliant. There'd never been any such banter between Celia and me. In fact, spontaneity of any kind had been rare. We'd been too much on guard with each other. It would take me a while before I relaxed fully around Julia, learned to accept her occasional outbursts and not sulk after one, as I had with Celia.

Most of all I wanted to learn how to have simple, spontaneous fun around her. Perhaps that was the truest intimacy.

The manager came out of his office and walked towards us.

'Doctor Milton and Ms Richmond? I'm Henri Couture, the manager. Please come into my office.' His English was almost without accent. He didn't offer to shake hands. We followed him and sat down in two matching wood and leather armchairs facing his desk.

'The receptionist mentioned Paul Kirk's account. Please explain your connection.' His manner was aloof to the point of rudeness.

'How much,' I asked, 'do you know about the circumstances of his death?'

'After the news broke I made some inquiries. I found out that the coroner's verdict was suicide. But how does this bear upon your visit?'

'Paul Kirk was one of my patients. Before he died he entrusted me with certain information. Then he gave me this.' I stood up and handed over Paul's last letter to me. He studied it intently for several minutes, his face expressionless.

'This seems entirely in order, subject to confirmation of your identity.' He carefully studied all the documentation I provided, and was satisfied.

'There is a problem, I'm afraid. It concerns our privacy laws. Or rather the exceptions to them.'

'Not the Basel Statement?'

Couture allowed a flicker of surprise to cross his face. 'You're very well informed. It's exactly that. With some later modifications. So you understand our dilemma.'

I went straight to the point. 'Have you reported this account to the authorities?'

'Ah. The heart of the matter. Unusually direct for an Englishman. I've been under pressure to do so, and was about to yield. So your visit is timely. If you can assure me the money in this account is the result of a legitimate business transaction, I need take matters no further.'

'What evidence do you require?' I asked.

'Let me put it this way. As a manager, I have to make the final decision. If you can persuade me, I will allow you full access to the account, with a guarantee that the authorities will not discover your involvement. But this decision is not without risk to me. It's possible I could be reprimanded for not reporting it, perhaps fined, demoted, even sacked. By then of course the money will be safe with you, and all traces of the transaction will have mysteriously disappeared. What do you think is a reasonable, uh … fee for the service that I'm offering you?'

Julia understood what the manager was after before I did. 'You're asking for a bribe, aren't you? Let's be straight about it.'

I looked at Julia with alarm. Why the hell was she being so provocative?

The manager had lost some of his composure. 'Ah, Mademoiselle, you misunderstand me. There is no question of a bribe. It's a matter of insurance. I'm taking a big risk for you, one that could cost me a great deal of money, even my career. Normal business practice requires a transaction fee in such circumstances. Usually a very large one.'

'In percentage terms?' asked Julia, apparently oblivious to my warning glare.

'Oh, shall we say … thirty per cent?'

'That's outrageous,' Julia exclaimed. 'Daylight robbery.'

'Please, Julia. Let me handle this. It's my money.' I smiled at the manager. 'Er, we don't know exactly how much is in the account. Once we do, it'll be easier to discuss your fee.'

Couture punched keys and studied the screen of his computer. 'With interest to date, exactly 9,103,148 pounds sterling. At the current exchange rate.'

I gasped. Julia looked disappointed.

'That's a bit less than we'd hoped,' she lied. 'Kirk implied at least ten million.'

The manager looked incredulous. 'Mademoiselle. This is pounds sterling, not dollars. It is not enough?'

'It'll just have to do, I suppose. But it means thirty per cent is out of the question. We can't go above ten.'

'Julia!' I finally lost patience with her. 'I asked you to leave this to me. If there's any haggling to be done, I'm more than capable.' I directed what I hoped was a forceful gaze at Couture. 'My partner has a point. Ten per cent is nearly a million pounds. You could retire on that. We won't go above it.'

'I have a large family to support. Fifteen per cent is my absolute minimum. If you won't accept that, forget the whole thing. I'll report matters to the authorities, and you'll never see a franc of the money.'

'Fifteen per cent then. But on one condition. We withdraw the entire balance. In high denomination notes, a mix of currencies. Close the account.'

'Let me see. Fifteen percent is … 1,365,471 pounds. So the balance is … 7,737,680. Hold on.' Couture spoke into his phone. 'I can do it. A mixture of dollars, sterling, Euros, Swiss francs.'

'Will it all fit into a small case?' asked Julia.

'Easily. Do you have one?'

'No, we have only our travelling cases. We came straight from the airport.'

'I can provide one.' He smiled for the first time. 'All part of the service.'

The bank had closed by the time Julia and I walked out into the waiting taxi. At our request, Couture had booked us into a hotel. The taxi took us there in less than ten minutes. I blanched at the five-star tariff, but Julia laughed at me.

'Darling, we could probably buy the damn place. Anyway, what's wrong with a little luxury for once, a little pampering?'

The first thing we did when we got to our room was put the chain on the door. Then we opened the black leather case Couture had provided.

'What a beautiful sight,' breathed Julia.

'Wait till you see the diamonds,' I said.

'The diamonds. We must get onto them first thing in the morning. Shouldn't we put the case in the hotel safe?'

'Only if we're going out. Who knows we're here?'

'Apart from Couture, his secretary, and half the bank staff, you mean?'

'You're not suggesting a double cross?'

'It's entered my mind that we're very vulnerable here. Couture could make a call to the police. Imagine us trying to explain this lot.'

'But we'd implicate him. And he'd get nothing out of it. Unless the local police take bribes.'

'Well of course they do, 'Julia responded. 'Same as everywhere else. I think we should move hotels. It's not foolproof, but at least we won't be sitting ducks.'

I groaned. 'I suppose you're right. As long as it's got a spa bath like this one. I need a long soak.'

The reception staff politely accepted our excuse about deciding to travel overnight. We ordered a cab to the Gare de Cornavin. When we got there we took another to a four-star hotel on Rue de la Confederation. There was a fuss when we insisted on paying cash, but smiles appeared when we brandished a large bundle of Swiss francs. We registered as a married couple under a false name. No-one asked for our passports. We ordered room service and went to bed early. There was no spa bath, so I settled for a long shower.

At nine the next morning we started ringing jewellers. None had unset stones larger than half a carat. We knew the resale value of set diamonds would be barely half of unset gems, so we avoided them. There were only two diamond traders listed. Both were unhelpful to the point of paranoia on the phone, but we were able to arrange visits that morning.

We checked out of the hotel, leaving our suitcases in the storage room. The first trader had no high grade stones larger than a carat, and the other had only one, a fine stone of one point four carats. He assured us there was no significant local trade in unset stones. This meant we couldn't avoid a trip to Amsterdam.

We hired a Peugot 605, picked up our luggage from the hotel, and were on our way by one-thirty. The customs at the French border waved us through when they saw we were British. The black leather case was on the floor behind the front passenger seat. We'd made no attempt to hide it. The chances of being stopped and searched were very low, but if it happened, they'd find the case wherever we put it.

We reached Trier in Germany at nine-fifteen. It wasn't quite half-way, but when we spotted a good hotel we decided to stop. The next morning we were on our way again by seven, staying in Germany till we got to Aachen. Then we crossed into the Netherlands. As at every border so far, we were waved through when they saw our passports.

We entered the outskirts of Amsterdam about seven-thirty. Even though we'd shared the driving evenly, we were exhausted.

'See that white Mercedes,' said Julia, 'two cars behind us. I'm sure I've seen it before. Or one just like it.'

'White Mercs are ten a penny. What makes that one special?'

'It's got a roof rack. Unusual out of the ski season. You'll say I'm imagining things, but I have this strange feeling we're being followed.'

'If they're still behind us when we get into town, let's try and lose them. But who the hell could have picked us up? And why?'

The white Merc turned off after a couple of miles and we relaxed a bit. The darkness made it difficult to see if it'd been replaced by another vehicle, but I assumed it hadn't.

'Let's choose a five-star hotel,' I suggested as we approached the city centre. 'It's probably safer.'

'You don't need to justify it. Let's spend it while we've got it.'

We found a five-star hotel in Nieuwe Dolenstraat, close to the heart of the diamond district. It had its own parking, a rare luxury in Amsterdam. Or so they told us in reception. The tariff was mind boggling. This time we waved a bundle of American dollars before saying we'd pay cash. There were no problems. Our room was huge, and we soon succumbed to its fin-de-siecle charm. Even though there was no spa bath.

'Let's order room service,' said Julia, 'and then ask reception to send up everything they've got on diamonds. Look, they've got lobster thermidor. I know you love lobster as much as I do. Which means a vintage champagne. And look at those desserts!'

Although I'd been comfortably off in recent years, I'd never shaken the frugal habits I'd learned from my parents. 'Jesus, Julia. We're talking about over two hundred pounds all up. That's criminally extravagant.'

'Damn it, George, we're lucky to be here. Maybe tomorrow Naomi or another maniac will pop up and shoot us dead. I've never been good at seizing the day, and you're even worse. We're too controlled, too obsessive. But we've got to try and change. Why not start now? Let's splurge!'

'Before we do, I'll ring Fred and get him up to speed.' Then I discovered that the battery in my phone was flat. I used Julia's mobile to ring Fred on one of his secure land lines. He answered at once. 'Thank God, you rang,' he said. 'I've been trying desperately to contact you. Superintendent Brock told me that Special Branch, MI5, MI6, Mossad and the CIA all worked together to set up an incredibly clever sting. And it worked brilliantly. They got the disc, which was destined for Iran. Somehow, Naomi escaped yet again. But she's lost everything. The security services have dismantled her operation, and made sure she can't access any funds she might still have. Even if she knows about Paul Kirk's swiss bank account, or suspects its existence, she lacks the resources to do anything that might affect you.'

Julia had overheard the conversation and was ecstatic. To celebrate, we ordered a second bottle of vintage champagne and then dined on our hugely expensive room-service meal.

We got to the nearest diamond dealer, at nine-twenty the next morning. We explained what we wanted and said we'd pay cash. I waved the black leather case, and they politely asked to verify its contents. When they saw the neat rows of bank notes, they became much friendlier, bringing out a good selection of gems. We picked out stones to the value of about nine hundred thousand pounds.

'We can't make the final selection until we've seen how your prices compare,' said Julia, I thought rather too bluntly.

'You're the first place we've visited,' I added. 'We need to get the feel of things. But we're serious buyers, I can assure you.'

Next we visited a dealer on Amstelstraat, and then a well-known one on Niewe Uilenburgerstraat. By the time we got down to Albert Cuypstraat, we thought we'd learned enough to start buying. We'd spent two million pounds by late afternoon. This had bought us a total of eleven diamonds, all between seven and ten carats. The largest was nine point nine carats, a bargain at three hundred and eighty thousand pounds. The smallest was exactly seven carats, at one hundred and forty-five thousand pounds.

As soon as we got back to the hotel, we put the diamonds in the hotel safe, a reassuringly large object in its own small room, bolted securely to floor and wall.

The stress of buying diamonds and the physical demands of walking all day had left us exhausted. We showered and lay on the bed. I dozed off, not waking til past seven. Julia was still asleep beside me. She woke when I got off the bed.

'Any thoughts about this evening?' I asked when she was fully awake.

'I'm easy,' she replied. 'But I wouldn't mind going out to eat. Somewhere nice.'

We dressed and went down to reception, where we got advice on local restaurants. We chose one within walking distance, booked, and left straight away. The night was cold, but there was little wind. I managed to subdue my deeply ingrained frugality, ordering regardless of expense. Julia did the same. We started with a bottle of vintage champagne and then had a bottle of sauvignon blanc, with a half bottle of sauternes to complement our rich chocolate desserts. We lingered over cognacs, and it was well past eleven before we started back, slightly unsteadily, to the hotel. In spite of my late afternoon nap, sleep came almost at once.

The next day, Thursday, started like the day before. By nine o'çlock, we were walking towards the first diamond dealer on our list. We'd left fifty thousand pounds in the hotel safe, together with yesterday's booty. The balance was in the black leather case.

'I didn't mention it yesterday,' said Julia, 'but it's still with me today. The feeling of being followed. See that fashion shop. Let's stop and look.'

We gazed through the plate glass window. Although it was early November, the mannequins were clothed in winter fashions. Julia looked casually sideways, scanning the street behind us. I concentrated on looking nonchalant.

'See anything?' I whispered, feeling slightly foolish.

'Nothing unusual. It goes back to this feeling, it's just a feeling. You think I'm being paranoid?'

'Good heavens, no. I'm not going to dismiss any of your hunches, strange feelings, instincts, premonitions. I get them myself occasionally, but they don't fit with my scientific background. So I tend to dismiss them. I should pay more attention.'

We started walking again. Just before we got to the first dealer, Julia stopped once more, staring into the window of a book shop. A surprising number of the titles were in English.

'Another strange feeling?'

'It's there all the time.' She looked sideways again, saw nothing. 'Don't let's go into the dealers right away. I'm a bit uncomfortable about yesterday, wondering if we got value for money. Perhaps we bought too many diamonds too soon.'

'There's a coffee shop over the street,' I said, pointing. 'Want to go and sit down, talk it through?'

'Why not? It'll only take a few minutes, could save us a bundle.'

I sipped at my coffee, looking at Julia expectantly.

'We've relied totally on Fred's advice,' she began. 'I'm wondering if we shouldn't have done some more research, got a second opinion. A third. We're talking about over seven million pounds.'

'It's just that Fred's advice made so much sense, I replied. And it was based on working for Sulaiman. Stick to white diamonds, standard cuts like round brilliant. Only flawless stones, or near flawless if the price is right. Don't go above ten carats, selling bigger can be difficult, dealers might expect a certificate of provenance, tracing where and when we bought it. And don't bother with anything below seven carats. As a basic strategy it still makes sense to me. We know we can sell stones like that without anyone asking awkward questions. If you've got a better idea, spit it out.'

'I haven't, George. It's just so much money so quickly. On diamonds, which we know nothing about. Why do we still believe in their value?'

'Brilliant marketing. And tight control of supply by central selling organisations. Don't worry, Julia. The value of our investment might fluctuate a bit, but in the long term it'll be up. If only because there'll always be people like us. Needing a safe, portable alternative to cash that's protected against inflation.'

I wasn't sure I knew what I was talking about, but I wanted to sound convincing. The last thing I needed was a vacillating Julia. So far we'd worked together remarkably well, even when it came to deciding which diamonds to buy and how much to pay. Several times Julia had squeezed lower prices out of dealers when I thought we'd made the best possible deal.

'Thanks for being so patient with me, George. I feel clearer about it now. You ready to go?'

Julia's ambivalence resolved, I'd found myself more willing to let her take the lead in our negotiations. In the end it came down to haggling, and it seemed to be in her genes. We did rather better than the day before. By the time the last diamond house closed its doors behind us well past five, we'd spent all the money bar about thirty thousand pounds in assorted currencies. Our black leather case contained several cloth pouches. Inside them was a total of twenty-three diamonds, all between seven and ten carats.

'Now we've finished buying,' said Julia, 'we should leave town as soon as possible. It's too late to fly out tonight, but I'd like to get seats for tomorrow morning. Say, around ten. If we go straight back to the hotel, we'll make it before the booking agency closes.'

We got seats on a flight leaving at twenty-five past ten.

'The hire car,' I said as we walked towards the hotel safe. 'I'd forgotten about it. We should take it back to the rental agency.'

'Why don't we drive it to the airport? We can leave it there. That's what people do these days.'

When the safe had been opened for us, Julia reached in and took out the packet of diamonds we'd bought yesterday.

'I know what I'm doing George.'

Her smile dissolved my impulse to challenge her. I said nothing till we were back in our room. 'Please explain. I thought we were putting diamonds in, not taking them out.'

'George, we haven't discussed getting them through customs. That's what this is about. Unless someone tips them off, and there's no reason to expect that, the worst that will happen in customs is a thorough search of our luggage. I don't know how they choose who to pick on, but I've had totally innocent friends whose luggage was searched with a fine-toothed comb. Perhaps it's done on a random basis, one in twenty, one in fifty. Or if they see something suspicious. We'd be unlucky if they chose us, but we can't ignore the risk. So I suggest we keep the diamonds on us.'

'If they go to the trouble of combing through our luggage, surely they'll check our pockets, your handbag. Maybe pat us down. Everything short of a full body search. For that they need reasonable grounds, don't they?'

'Reasonable grounds,' responded Julia, 'can be anything from a tip off to not liking the way you look. But basically you're right. The chances of a body search are miniscule. You know what that means, don't you?'

'Of course. Tiny. Very small indeed.' I grinned.

'You idiot.' She grinned back. 'It means-'

'Oh no, Julia,' I broke in. 'I'm not ready for this.'

'Got a better idea?'

'Stuffed in your bra and panties?'

'George, you're pathetic. They'll spot that the moment I take my coat off.'

'Now I get it. You took the stones out of the safe ... to practice. Didn't you?'

'Well done, Sherlock.'

'Make sure the chain's on the door. Then we'll put all the stones together. Work out exactly what to put where.'

'Before we do that,' said Julia, let's order room service. I'm starving.'

After we'd ordered, I was suddenly seized with a fear of losing some of the diamonds. So I insisted we keep them inside the leather case. I carefully emptied them out of their cloth pouches. Then I counted them. Thirty-four. I moved a few of the diamonds so that the overhead light shone directly on to them.

'Look at the way they sparkle.'

'Yes, they really do,' Julia responded. 'They really are sparklers.'

The diameter of the diamonds ranged from eleven to fifteen millimetres. Their total volume was about ninety cubic centimetres. 'They should all fit comfortably into your ... front passage,' I said rather tactlessly.

'Christ, George,' Julia snapped. 'I know there's plenty of room for you in it, but I'm sorry to tell you, size isn't your strong suit.'

I didn't rise to the bait. After all, I'd asked for it. Given Julia's background, insensitive remarks about her sexual apparatus invited trouble. 'There's no need to get personal. Anyway, I'm beyond jokes about penis size. I know I'm at least average.'

I just caught her mumbled response. 'For a prepubertal pygmy perhaps.'

I glared at Julia, then realised she was struggling to keep a straight face. We dissolved into laughter.

'What I think's fair,' said Julia when we'd recovered, is that I take two-thirds and you take one-third. They should fit up your bottom with room to spare. So let's divide them.'

We separated the diamonds into two separate piles, the larger one comprising twenty-four.

'What will you wrap them in?' I asked.

'French letters, of course. Strong, elastic, lubricated.'

'You have some?'

'No. But it's just a matter of going downstairs to the chemist. There's one in the hotel arcade.'

'What about a shower cap?' I suggested. 'Just for practice. You can lubricate it with lanoline cream. I've got some in my sponge bag.'

Julia put the larger pile of diamonds carefully in one of the transparent shower caps provided by the hotel. I found a rubber band and used it to tighten the wrapping round its precious contents. Then Julia smeared it with lanoline cream.

'Need any help?' I asked hopefully.

'Don't be revolting. I'll do it in the bathroom.'

While Julia was performing the delicate task I closed the lid of the black leather case and placed it carefully on a chair. She came out of the bathroom stark naked, with a broad grin on her face.

'I think I've invented the world's most expensive sex toy.'

'And Amsterdam's the perfect place to market it,' I quipped.

Julia paraded round the room.

'Can you tell?' she asked.

By now I had a huge erection but tactfully kept it out of sight. 'A stranger wouldn't notice anything unusual, but I can tell you're holding your legs together. Just a fraction. It's safe to relax. They won't fall out.'

There was a knock on the door.

'Yes,' I called out.

'Room service.'

'Great. That'll be our meal,' said Julia. 'I'll just slip on a bath robe.'

I opened the door, leaving the chain on. A young woman in room attendant's uniform stood behind a trolley laden with food. I undid the chain.

'Come in. Put it over there, please. You don't have to stay, we'll open the champagne ourselves.'

The room attendant wheeled the trolley through the door. Suddenly, a small woman pushed in behind her. Then two men. The door slammed shut. I retreated quickly, bumping into Julia, now in a bath robe.

'Surprised to see me, George?' asked Naomi Freeman. 'I think you've met my colleagues.'

I recognised her bodyguard from the auction and the man who'd searched me at Naomi's flat in Regent's Park. Both had taken out guns.

'Sit down on the bed. All of you.' She looked at the room attendant. 'How long before they'll wonder what's keeping you?'

'We're not that busy, it's early for room service. They'll think I'm chatting with a guest. Maybe fifteen minutes.'

Naomi shifted her gaze to me. 'Where are the diamonds?'

'In the black leather case,' I croaked, pointing at the chair.

She opened the lid and looked closely at the diamonds.'

'Is this all?'

'Yes,' I lied. 'Three million pounds worth.'

'Then you've been ripped off. Unless you're lying. Now, where would you hide them?'

'Why would we do that? I replied. 'We weren't exactly expecting you.'

'We'll search, anyway.' She turned to her henchmen. 'We've got fifteen minutes to turn this place upside down. Start with their pockets.'

Our pockets were searched and we were carefully patted down. Then they began a systematic search of the room. Starting with our luggage. Naomi talked while she searched.

'You probably don't remember everything you said, George, when Travis was playing dentist with you. You mentioned something about a Swiss bank account. I didn't pay much attention at the time. But things have changed. I became public enemy number one after the bomb went off. Everyone started looking for me. There was unheard of cooperation between intelligence agencies. The CIA, MI5, MI6 and Mossad all hand in glove. And they found me. Just as I was handing over the disc. Yes, I bid on behalf of others. Well, there was some shooting and general chaos, during which I managed to escape. But MI6 got the disc. The only copy, I didn't have time to duplicate it. Fred made it far too difficult. How is he, by the way?'

'He misses you dreadfully,' I said. 'Apart from that, he's fine.'

Naomi gave a low chuckle. 'So there I was. Almost destitute. I knew I was finished in the arms trade, that it was time to get out. I put my London flat on the market, through an intermediary, of course. But I had no cash. Then I remembered the Swiss bank account. Suddenly it made sense. If Kirk gave you the disc, why shouldn't he give you any money he made from it as well? So I started looking for you. Had no luck until you and Ms Richmond here went back to your flat last Saturday. Since then, I've had you tailed. These two men are the only ones who've stuck with me. They'll be well rewarded.'

'I'll never doubt any of your hunches or strange feelings again,' I said to Julia.

'We followed you all around the diamond district,' continued Naomi. 'Today and yesterday. I could have picked you up any-where between Geneva and Amsterdam and taken the cash. But what would I do with it? I'd have exactly the same problem as you. I knew it was too risky for me to buy diamonds myself. So I let you do all the hard work for me. And here I am to reap the benefits. Capitalism at its best.'

'There's nothing else here, Naomi,' said the bodyguard.

'Let's go then.' She looked at me gravely. 'Well, George, this really is goodbye. I'm not as well off as I'd hoped, but I can afford to retire. Somewhere warm and sunny and very far away. You won't see me again.'

As soon as Naomi and her men had left, the room attendant burst into tears. Julia comforted her while I rang reception.

'There's been a robbery. No-one's hurt. Please don't call the police. I'd like hotel security to deal with it.'

The head of security arrived almost at once. He was as keen as we were to keep the matter in house. To help him, I lied about the value of the diamonds, telling him the thieves had stolen worthless imitation gems. Because we'd been worried about just such a robbery, I explained, the real gems were safe elsewhere. He accepted this, but insisted we write a statement and leave a contact number. His main concern was the room attendant, and the possibility she might make a claim against the hotel for psychological trauma.

Our meal was cold by the time everything had been sorted out. The hotel management sent up a free replacement by way of apology. When it arrived we realised we'd got over our shock enough to be interested in food.

'I still can't believe it,' said Julia as she buttered a piece of bread roll.

'Nor me. Specially the timing. A few minutes earlier or later and Naomi would've got away with the lot. We were incredibly lucky. We still have most of the diamonds, and Naomi's finally off our backs.'

'And with the disc off the market for good, no-one else will be looking for us. There's just one problem left. Getting the diamonds through customs.'

We got to the airport at twenty to ten the next morning. Julia went to the ladies toilet and inserted the diamonds just before we went through the terminal access point. To my horror, she triggered the alarm as she walked through the scanning frame. The uniformed guard passed his mobile scanner over Julia's body. It buzzed when it approached her groin.

'The bracelet on your wrist,' said the guard in passable English. 'You forgot to take it off.'

Julia handed it to him and went through the frame again, this time silently.

'Your left wrist was dangling close to your groin,' I said as we walked towards the departure lounge. 'I thought it was the diamonds triggering the buzzer. I nearly fainted with fright.'

We had no trouble with the customs at Heathrow, but it was pouring with rain outside, so getting a cab was a nightmare. We went straight back to my flat. It was exactly as I'd left it.

'How about a celebratory drink?' I asked Julia as she came out of the bathroom brandishing the diamonds.

'Whisky and soda. Light on the soda.'

As I fixed it, I felt safe for the first time since Paul Kirk had confessed to me in my consulting room. It seemed a long time ago.

FOURTEEN

After a couple of homecoming drinks, I rang Sarah.

'Sarah. It's George. I'm ringing to say we're back in circulation. And to see how you are. We're both safe and well.'

'George! We've been waiting to hear from you. I'm so relieved you're OK. Got so much to tell you. Can you come over?'

'You'd sacrifice a Saturday night for us?'

'For you, George, I'd sacrifice a month of Saturdays.'

'Then we'll come down about seven if that suits.'

'Let me check with Sid. He'll want a word with you, anyway.'

There was brief pause before Sid picked up the phone.

'I was beginning to think you'd forgotten us, George. It's been over two weeks.'

'We've been busy. Tell you everything when we see you. Seven OK?'

'Seven's fine. I'll ring Sylvia and Charlie. They've split up, but I know they'll both want to see you.'

When I put the phone down I remembered I hadn't checked my answering machine.

There was only one message.

'Brock here. It's er, ten Saturday morning. Just letting you know that we've got hold of the disc. Naomi Freeman was about to hand it over to the people who paid for it in the first place. The Iranians. It's been destroyed, so you can stop worrying. Freeman got away somehow. We've no idea where she is, but I can't think of any reason for her to bother you again.'

Julia had come to listen. 'It's reassuring,' she said, 'to have Brock confirm what both Fred and Naomi told us.'

'It's obvious he doesn't know about the Swiss bank account. That's reassuring, too.'

Now, we should ring Frank and Barb.'

Julia rang her mother and arranged to meet her late on Saturday afternoon. I couldn't face ringing my father.

Sid and Sarah greeted us at the door of their flat together, obviously delighted to see us.

'We've just ordered a Chinese takeaway,' Sarah said. 'We know what you like by now. Sylvia and Charlie said they'd be here about half past eight. They've already eaten.'

The food arrived just after we'd sat down with our drinks. We moved to the table.

'We want to hear everything,' said Sid. 'But we can wait until Sylvia and Charlie get here. Save you telling it all twice.'

'While we're waiting,' I said, 'tell us what you've been up to.'

'Well,' said Sarah, 'the biggest news is about Sid. He's packed in his job.'

'What?' exclaimed Julia and I together.

'It's true,' confirmed Sid. 'I took a voluntary separation package. Part of what used to be called down-sizing, now it's right-sizing. They hadn't targeted me for redundancy, but I had a word with the union, some pressure was bought to bear, I was put on the list. I'm getting a lump sum, over three hundred grand, it includes all my pension benefits. Mind you, I was with them more than twenty years.'

'I thought you were happy there,' said Julia.

'So did I. It's complicated. The main reason, to be honest, was Sarah. The changes in her. You know what I was like, lugging about this old-fashioned picture of the world. I had to be the bread winner, and in return for my hard work and protection, Sarah had to keep a clean and tidy home and look after me.'

'Wait on you hand and foot more like it,' interjected Sarah.

Sid nodded and grinned with embarrassment. 'And I didn't allow her a life of her own, I tried to control everything she did. Well, you know, of course. My morbid jealousy. Anyway, when she went back to work it all changed.'

'It had to,' Sarah added. 'Or we'd have split up.'

'She's right. And I couldn't face losing her. So you could say I didn't have much choice. At first I hated Sarah working. Then there was the kidnapping, and that, as I've explained, made me feel differently about Sarah. After that, my morbid jealousy just sort of faded away. I'm not saying it's gone completely, but it's more normal now, just normal jealousy. It's no longer a problem we can't handle. Though I still have to work at it.'

'Its true,' said Sarah. 'It's really not a problem anymore. Nor's my agoraphobia. I won't say it just faded away. It took lots of hard work. And I'm still not keen on crowded places, especially buses and trains. But I don't avoid them anymore. In fact, I don't avoid anything that's important for me to do. That's because I've got much more self- confidence. I gradually realised I was capable, valued. Oh, I haven't told you. I got promoted. Now I'm a manager.'

'She was earning more than I did,' said Sid ruefully. 'That really made me think. She didn't need me as a bread winner, so why was I working? In fact, what bloody use was I at all? Once I started asking questions like that, I couldn't stop. I realised I didn't like my job, anymore. It wasn't compulsory, so why not leave?'

'What will you do next?' asked Julia.

'Well, Sarah gave me this book on the mid-life crisis. Which really made me depressed, because it showed how most of the things I'd planned were typical mid-life ... er ... fantasies, that's the word. Except I wasn't thinking of running off with a younger woman! So I'm not rushing into anything. I'm going to do a lot more reading. And I've started seeing a counsellor. Not a psychiatrist. She's got a background in social work.'

There was silence. I brought out a small package. 'There's something I want to give you before Sylvia and Charlie arrive, I've got something for them, too.'

Sylvia took the package from me and opened carefully under Sid's gaze. She gasped.

'We can't accept this. It's far too much.'

Inside the package were two diamonds. I'd chosen them carefully. Their combined resale value was about three hundred thousand pounds.

'Then give them to your favourite charity,' I said. 'I won't take them back. I can't find any more words to say how grateful I feel. This gift speaks for me.'

'And for me,' Julia added softly.

Sid's eyes glistened, and we waited for him to say something.

'Your timing is perfect. This will come in very handy. Now I really can take my time, find a new direction, not worry about money.'

The doorbell rang. When Sylvia and Charlie were seated with their drinks, Julia and I told our story. Once we'd all discussed it enough, I handed one small package to Sylvia, another to Charlie.

In each was a diamond worth about a hundred and fifty thousand pounds. I made a very short speech thanking them for the risks they had taken for Julia and me. After initial protests they accepted their gifts.

'So what have you been up to since we last saw you?' said Julia, addressing the space between Charlie and Sylvia.

'Well, you know we've split up, of course,' responded Charlie. 'But we're still friends.'

'And you, personally, Sylvia?'

'Well the big news is I got a job. First in nearly eight years. It's nothing much. I work for a cleaning agency, mainly offices. But there's as many hours as I want. You won't believe how nervous I was at first, but I knew I could do it. I've only been there a week, but already I'm getting more confident. What's really amazing, my OCD symptoms have almost gone. Social phobia's still a bit of a problem, but I don't avoid situations so much. I've got the confidence to do things on my own, I don't depend on Charlie. Or anyone else. At last I'm facing up to my fears.'

'And I've made some changes, too,' said Charlie, 'at least in my attitudes. Sylvia's the first woman who's stood up to me without it ending in a serious fight. I now know it's possible, it's better, to have a more equal relationship.'

'I just decided I wasn't going to do things I didn't like anymore,' said Sylvia. 'Then I chose the right time to discuss it. Charlie was really pissed off, but he didn't get violent or storm out. We managed to talk it through. He admitted he wasn't ready for that kind of relationship. So we agreed to split up. Then we found ourselves chatting on the phone. And now, well, somehow we've become friends. Who knows where this might lead. We could end up together again.'

I remembered how Sylvia couldn't go anywhere without thick layers of make-up and huge false eyelashes. This evening she was wearing only lipstick and a little eyeliner.

It was nearly one when Julia and I got back to my place. When I'd suggested going back to hers, she surprised me by saying she liked my flat much more.

'Now that you can afford it,' she said, 'I assume you'll keep this place.'

'Definitely. Money's no longer a problem. It's a matter of what I'm going to do, how I'm going to stop myself going crazy.'

'I could move in with you.'

This was totally unexpected. To give myself breathing space I tried levity. 'I could look after you. Save me having to find meaning and purpose in life.'

Julia was hurt. 'I just thought –'

'I'm sorry. I didn't mean to upset you. But last time we talked about this you said living together was out of the question. That we had to keep our independence.'

'Well, now I'm not so sure. We're both workaholics, or near as dammit. Which is just a transfer of dependency, and a way of protecting ourselves from loneliness. And from asking questions like what the fuck are we here for. Your flat's more than big enough for two. Mine's poky in comparison. Don't worry. I wont sell it. If living together's a catastrophe, I can move out with minimum fuss.'

'We'd have to draw up a proper cohabitation agreement.'

'Oh shit! George, you're an uptight controlling anal-retentive prick. I don't know what possessed me. To even think about moving in with you. After what we've been through together all you can think about is a fucking cohabitation agreement.'

'Julia, it's one o'clock in the morning. Not the best time to decide our future together. And frankly I'm amazed. As a lawyer I assumed you'd think a cohabitation agree-'

'Oh, shut up, George. We'll discuss it tomorrow.'

Julia got up in a huff. But I found her in my bed when I went to get undressed. And when I slipped in beside her she turned and pressed her warm body against mine.

We rose late on Sunday morning, leaving barely enough time to get to Fred's place by eleven, as we'd arranged. We didn't continue last night's argument. Fred and Barb had organised brunch. Bacon, eggs, tomato, champagne, the works. We didn't start talking until we were seated round the kitchen table.

Julia and I told our story for the second time that weekend.

'When Naomi asked about me,' inquired Fred, 'did she seem hostile?'

'Positively homicidal,' I replied, keeping a straight face. Fred looked so alarmed that I relented. 'Just kidding. You've nothing to worry about. She's put all that behind her. By now she'll be in South America somewhere, or the Caribbean, with a new identity. It'll take a few months for her to get bored, start planning a come-back. But none of us will figure in that. We've nothing more that she wants.'

'I hope you're right,' Fred responded. 'But if she decides to get back into the arms business, she may want to pick my brains. Literally, if she hires that sadistic maniac Travis.'

For the first time, I didn't react to that name with a surge of anxiety. 'She won't have to hire him. He'll do it for nothing. But stop catastrophising. I've got something for you. And you, Barb.'

Once again we went through the ritual. I'd chosen two diamonds worth a total of about four-hundred-thousand pounds for Fred, and one for Barb, worth about a hundred and sixty thousand. After protests had turned into silent gratitude, I asked them about their plans.

'We've already come up with a brilliant new idea,' said Barb. 'I won't bore you with the details, but it will help new players compete with the internet giants like Facebook, Microsoft and Google'

'If it works as well as we hope,' said Fred, 'there'll be enough money to start the Chomsky thing. Which is what I really want to do. Ray and Tony have decided to get out, by the way. The Naomi Freeman thing scared them off.'

We went on talking until it was time to visit Julia's mother. I dropped her off. She'd get a cab back to my place.

It was a quarter to eleven before she returned. Her face showed a mixture of fatigue and excitement.

'I've had the most incredible evening,' she began. 'We talked and talked. About everything. I'm beginning to understand her. To see her as a person.'

'Do you want to talk about it now? Or wait till tomorrow?' I remember how the late hour had contributed to last night's argument.

'I won't sleep. I'm too wound up. You want a rum and Coke?'

Julia talked fast, sitting upright in her chair. It was classical stuff, fairly predictable, though of course I didn't say so. Julia already understood why she'd hated her mother, refused to see her for years. But now she no longer blamed her for the rapes by her stepfather.

'I know she tried to talk to me after the rape, but I just closed my ears. Today, we made up for twenty years. I learned so much about her, how she coped with my stepfather, what he was really like. What she wants from life now. I discovered she's a likeable, warm, caring person. We might even become friends.'

I knew how important all of this was for Julia, how crucial it was in the task she had before her. The task of integrating all the warring elements of her psyche, welding them into something like a true sense of self.

A little after twelve-thirty she began to slow down. "All of a sudden I'm exhausted. I think I'll go to bed.'

'I'll join you later.'

Julia's words had started me thinking about my own parents, especially my father. I knew him about as well as Julia had known her mother. I resolved to go and talk to him. To sit down and insist, as far as I could, that he talks about himself. Maybe that would help me make some decisions about my own life. I knew now that my problems were much the same as Julia's. But I was starting to grapple with them nearly ten years further down the track.

Julia went back to work on Monday morning. I put the bulk of the diamonds in my safe deposit box. Then I began the task of contacting the people Paul had named in his last letter to me. There were four of them. One had died less than a month ago. His widow was defensive on the phone. When I explained that Paul had wanted to give her husband some money, she hung up.

The other three all lived in London, and I arranged to meet them over the next two days. Paul had indicated an amount for each, and the total was covered by the sale of a nine-carat diamond.

Julia got back from work at nine fifteen, tired but happy. 'George, it was so good to be back at work. I told them I was fully recovered, and my boss commented on how well I looked. You know how worried I was that work would be boring, seem trivial. Well, it's been just the opposite. I'm falling in love with law again. Maybe I needed a break.'

I was pleased for Julia, but her happiness and certainty reminded me how much these elements were missing from my own life. Should I make a belated appeal to the general medical council, allowing Julia to give extenuating evidence? There was a chance that I'd be restored to the medical register. But did I really want that?

The answer came with surprising force and clarity. I saw myself sitting in a consulting room with a difficult, aggressive, dependent patient. I was hit by a wave of anxiety, which by its strength forced me to further explore my feelings. After only a few minutes, I knew with absolute certainty that I could never go back to psychiatry. Too much had changed, both within and around me. Julia got back about seven. I wanted to tell her what had happened to me, but she had an agenda of her own.

'I had the most amazing day in court. My cross-examinations were unbelievably good. It's like I'm a new person, George. I've lost that crippling anxiety I used to get before standing up in court. Instead I have this energy, this excitement. There's still a tinge of anxiety, but I'm glad of it, it gives me an edge.'

I tried to respond with enthusiasm, but Julia sensed my underlying despair.

'George, are you OK?'

'It's just... I've realised I don't want to be a therapist, anymore. But I can't see an alternative. I feel lost, scared.'

Julia was very supportive. We went out for a meal, spending most of the time discussing my dilemma. Only towards the end did Julia get a chance to talk about her own plans.

'So I've decided to become a barrister. Which will cost money. Until I get a bit of a reputation, some well-heeled clients.'

'You will never have to worry about money once we've agreed on how to share the diamonds.'

Over the next three days, I coped by keeping busy. I had the remaining diamonds valued. This took time because I didn't want anyone to see the whole collection. I divided it into four and had each quarter valued separately. By Friday afternoon I knew I could sell the whole lot for close to five million pounds. I decided to give Julia half. I told her that evening, soon after she got back from work.

'George, it's far too much.'

'Not the way I see it. I've ended up as your stepfather's executor. Nothing will change the hideous things he did to you, I know that. But I want him to compensate you for them. On Monday I'd like you to come with me to the bank, open your own safe deposit box, put half the diamonds inside it. I'll be left with more than enough.'

After a few more protests, Julia capitulated. She even found a gap in her diary for Monday morning, and that settled things.

When she left for work on Saturday morning, Julia told me she wouldn't be back till after five. Tactfully I didn't remind her of her resolution to work less hard. I faced the gloomy prospect of another day spent in solitary agonising. The phone rang mid-morning. It was Fred.

'George. I've got something really important to discuss. Are you free?'

I drove to Hammersmith at once. Fred was there alone.

'I want to offer you a job,' he said the moment I arrived. 'I've had another idea. A new way of breaking security codes. It's so simple I'm amazed no-one's thought of it before. I can use it for my original plans to expose arms dealers. And it dovetails both with the Chomsky set-up and my last idea: to help create real competition with the internet giants. I know this sounds absurdly ambitious, but I have to give it a try. Barb has agreed to join me, but we'll both be exclusively focussed on-line.' He paused.

'Your role will be in real time, not cyberspace. Checking out leads, interviewing people, using your psychological and interviewing skills. Confronting people we've proven to be corrupt, deciding whether to expose them publicly or have them make recompense in private. That sort of stuff. We can work out details later.'

I knew it was perfect for me. 'I'm yours. I'll even put my own money into it.'

'Wonderful. Though I believe that the project will become self-funding, very profitable in fact. When can you start?'

'What about Monday? I'll need to discuss it with Julia, but I can't see any problems there.'

I left about an hour later. So Fred wanted me to help him be the Robin Hood of cyberspace. It might be dangerous, but psychiatry hadn't been exactly safe. Not since I met Paul Kirk. If I met others like him in the future, it would be on more equal terms. As I turned into Baker Street, I remembered its most famous resident, Sherlock Holmes.

'The Sherlock Holmes of Cyberspace' was a better nickname for Fred. I knew I'd make a good Doctor Watson.

THE END